BIKER BABY

I WAS ABOUT TO MAKE A MISTAKE. ABOUT TEN INCHES' WORTH.

PENNY DEE

Biker Baby
Kings of Mayhem MC Series Book 3

Penny Dee

This book is a work of fiction. Any references to real events, real people, and real places are used fictitiously. Other names, characters, places and incidents are products of the Author's imagination and any resemblance to persons, living or dead, actual events, organisations or places is entirely coincidental.

All rights are reserved. This book is intended for the purchaser of this book ONLY. No part of this book may be reproduced or transmitted in any form or by any means, graphic, electronic, or mechanical, including photocopying, recording, taping, or by any information storage retrieval system, without the express written permission of the Author. All songs, song titles and lyrics contained in this book are the property of the respective songwriters and copyright holders.

Disclaimer: The material in this book contains graphic language and sexual content and is intended for mature audiences, ages 18 and older.

ISBN: 978-1096744931

Proofreading by Elaine at Allusion Graphics
Formatting by Swish Design & Editing
Cover design by Marisa at Cover Me Darling
Cover image Copyright 2019

First Edition
Copyright © 2019 Penny Dee
All Rights Reserved

DEDICATION

To all those dreamers out there,
Sometimes you just gotta go for it!

PATH OF FAMILY

The Calley Family
Hutch Calley (deceased) married Sybil Stone
Griffin Calley
Garrett Calley (deceased)

Griffin Calley married Peggy Russell
Isaac Calley (deceased)
Abby Calley

Garrett Calley married Veronica Western
Chance Calley
Cade Calley
Caleb Calley
Chastity Calley

The Parrish Family
Jude Parrish married Connie Walker
Jackson Parrish
Samuel Parrish (deceased)

Jackie Parrish married Lady Winter
Bolt Parrish
Indigo Parrish

The Western Family
Michael 'Bull' Western
Veronica 'Ronnie' Western

KINGS OF MAYHEM MC

Bull (President)
Cade (VP)
Caleb
Grunt (SIA)
Davey
Vader
Joker
Cool Hand
Griffin
Matlock
Maverick
Tully
Nitro
Hawke
Ari
Picasso
Caveman
Chance (on tour)
Reuben (honorary member)

Employees of the Kings
Red (Chef, clubhouse housekeeper)
Mrs Stephens (Bookkeeper, administration)

I WAS ABOUT TO MAKE A MISTAKE. ABOUT TEN INCHES' WORTH.

PENNY DEE

PROLOGUE

HONEY

I was about to make a huge mistake.

And when I say huge, I mean, approximately ten inches' worth of mistake.

But after the week I'd had, it was just what I needed. A night of big bad mistakes with a big bad cock.

I focused on the mouth moving sensually over mine. The way this guy kissed had me pulsing in places I hadn't pulsed in months.

"What's your name again?" The guy with the tattoos and all those muscles asked between kisses.

"Let's just keep that to ourselves," I said, drawing his mouth to mine again and kissing him hard. "It adds to the mystery, don't you think?"

We tumbled through the door to the motel room we had just paid for. The guy behind the counter had hardly batted an eye at us when he took down our details. And I shouldn't be surprised. This place probably rented rooms by the hour.

We fell into the room, and the man who was kissing me into nirvana kicked the door closed behind us and pressed me up against the wall.

He pulled away briefly and his eyes rolled over me, they were full of heat. "You're so fucking hot."

I grinned and tugged at his belt buckle. "You're not so bad yourself."

When my hand brushed over the hardness punching against his zipper, I gasped. My hand went in for a second look. *Holy hell.* This guy was packing a giant erection.

An unfamiliar thrill ran through me.

This guy was something else. He had muscles for miles and the type of height that commanded everyone's attention.

I dropped to my knees and peeled his jeans down to reveal the biggest cock I'd ever seen in my life. I looked up at him, unsure how I was going to fit all of him in my mouth. He grinned down at me, but it faded into a look of pure molten heat as I took him in my hand and ran my tongue along the length of him and across the shiny, throbbing head. My mouth closed over him and my tongue tortured the wide crest, licking at it, sucking it, curling and swirling around the sensitive skin at the base of the head. He groaned and it was primal. Virile. *Pure man.* His hands tangled in my hair and his knees weakened. As his arousal started to peak, his cock began to dip and lift against my lips.

One big arm guided me to my feet and he cupped my face in his hands. "When I come, I'm going to come inside you."

He pulled my face to his, and with a groan, kissed me hard. He moved me across to the bed where he peeled every item of clothing from my body, savoring the experience by removing them slowly and kissing every area of exposed flesh. My head spun and my body clenched with every purposeful lick and touch of his lips against my skin. He lay me down and crawled over me, his hard body covering me in heat and rock-hard muscle. I'm not sure when he took his jeans off, I was too lost in sensation, too lost in the feel of his tongue on my skin and the deep moans of appreciation escaping him as he slowly worked my body into a fever.

I was drowning in desire when he reached for the condom in his wallet. And I could barely breathe as he ripped the foil package open and rolled the sheath of latex over his very hard, very big cock.

He crawled back over me, and the heat on his face and the vibrant need in his eyes made me forget to breathe. With one long, hard push he was inside me, and the sudden intrusion sent fireworks zip-zapping through me. His size opened me, stretched me, and he thrust into me with a physical prowess I'd never known, hitting every delicious spot inside of me. He was a lot of man to take. He was big, with broad shoulders and huge biceps, and just the sensation of all that muscle on top of me was enough to send pleasure soaring throughout my body. What he did with his mouth, his tongue, his body, it made me crazy.

My orgasm was swift, its ferocity overwhelming me completely. My eyes closed and I clutched his massive shoulders as I cried out again and again, utterly lost in ecstasy. He thrust my arms above my head, grinding hard into me to draw out the pleasure spiraling out from where our bodies connected.

"That was amazing," I gasped, floating on the dizzying heights of my afterglow.

He smiled against my lips as I panted against him. "You think that was amazing? Baby, I've only just started."

With a deep thrust of his hips, he made me cry out again and again as he drove my body toward more delicious orgasms. He was relentless. Powerful. He knew how to use his cock, and he wasn't afraid to show me.

Hours later, we fell into an exhausted sleep. Our bodies spent, the muscles between my legs swollen and deliciously tender from the most incredible night of sin.

Sometime before dawn, I slipped from the bed, careful not to wake him. As soon as my feet hit the floor they felt the empty condom wrappers we had discarded throughout our evening of debauchery. One. Two. Three. Four.

Yep. Four condoms and numerous, mind-blowing orgasms. Even now my body clenched and pulsed at the memory.

But this was where our story ended. It was time to hit the road.

I slipped into the bathroom and turned on the light. I splashed water on my face and then stared at my reflection in the mirror. I had gotten what I had come here for. I had successfully fucked Charlie out of my mind, and there was no point hanging around to complicate things further.

Again, my body pulsed and throbbed with the memory of that ten-inch cock and what it had done to me.

I dressed quickly, trying to be as quiet as possible so I didn't wake my one-night stand.

Before I turned off the light, I stared at the sexy bulk sprawled on the bed. He was on his stomach, his muscular back and perfect ass on display, and I paused to take him in one last time.

"Goodnight, handsome," I whispered into the shadowy room.

Then, turning off the light, I slipped through the door and into the early morning.

CHAPTER 1

CALEB

The gorgeous blonde squirmed on the bed.

"You okay, sweetheart?" I asked.

"It hurts," she moaned.

No shit, it hurt. No one ever said getting inked was a day in the park.

"You want me to stop, give you a break?"

She shook her head. "No," she moaned. "I like it."

I returned my attention to the heart tattoo I was adding just south of her belly button.

"Ooh, that's sensitive." The way she said it with that whimpering moan, it went straight to my balls.

"You just tell me if you need me to stop, darlin'."

She gripped the edge of the tattoo bed and gasped again. "Keep going, Caleb."

Christ, the way she was moaning, anyone would think I was fucking her.

And so it went on for the next half an hour. Every few minutes she would moan or whimper, or a strange sound would strangle in her throat and she would bite down on her lip. Then she would move restlessly—that in itself is annoying for any tattoo artist—and moan again like she was about to come.

Finally finishing up, I wiped the new artwork clean and dressed it.

I straightened and gave her a wink. "We're done."

She parted her legs so I could see she wasn't wearing panties and looked up at me with serious come-fuck-me eyes. "Are you sure about that, Caleb?"

Her invitation was unmistakable. And fuck it, after all that moaning, I was in the mood.

"What are you offering, sweetheart?"

She sat up and her long blonde curls tumbled over her shoulders. She parted her legs wider so I got a good look at her smooth pussy, and goddamn, I needed to get in there. She pulled me to her by my belt buckle and brushed her fingers over the growing hardness behind the zipper.

"I've heard about you," she batted her lashes up at me. "Heard about how big you are."

She undid my belt buckle and lowered my zipper. When she saw the size of me, she licked her lips and slid her hand between me and my Calvins, her fingers curling around the width of me and squeezing. Holding on tight, she lay down and guided me toward her parted pussy.

"Whoa, there, baby, let me get a condom," I said, pulling back.

She grabbed my hand to stop me.

"We don't need one, I'm clean." She tried to look innocent, but it was hard to pull off given she was lying half-naked on a tattoo bed with her legs spread and her shaven pussy on show. "I don't want anything coming between me and that big cock of yours."

I began to second-guess fucking her, and my arousal began to fade. I was a wrap-before-you-tap kind of guy. No pussy was worth any kind of cock rot, or worse, a life sentence. And the fact that she was offering it to me, made me wonder how many other guys received the same offer.

But I hadn't fucked anyone since that hot brunette a few weeks earlier.

The one who wouldn't tell me her name.

The one with the smokin' body.

The one with the lush mouth and unforgettable pussy.

The one I hadn't been able to get out of my head for weeks.

Remembering her juicy body and the way it milked my cock made me hard again. A sweet anticipation began to coil in the base of my belly. I reached for the condom, ripped it open and rolled it on. Yeah, that brunette was something else. The way she rode me. The way she got up on her knees and offered me her perfect pussy. The way she opened up for me and sucked me in, milking me with that tight, little pussy of hers, making me come over and over again.

I rolled the head of my cock through the folds of slippery flesh on offer. The blonde moaned and whimpered. I didn't know if she thought it was a turn on or not, but it wasn't, and I had to fight the urge to tell her to stop.

Instead, I thrust hard into her, right to the hilt, and straight away, she started to whimper and moan . . . and perform.

"Yeah baby, fuck me good."

But as soon as we started, I realized it was a mistake.

"You're such a big boy, Caleb. Fuck me hard with your big cock."

It didn't take long and I was praying she would stop. And when it didn't, I closed my eyes to drown her out.

"You're going to make me come, baby. Fuck me, fuck me hard."

But it was no use. Her annoying voice kept dragging me back to the present.

"Fuck me, fuck me now!" she demanded.

So I pumped into her. Hard. Just like she was begging me to.
Shut. The. Fuck. Up.

I flipped her over and rammed into her again, my pelvis slapping against the flesh of her peachy ass. With every thrust, she cried out like she was a freaking porn star. My cock started to lose interest. To block her out, I let my mind rewind back to the brunette with the killer body and sassy mouth, and bingo, instant steel. I know what you're thinking. What a douche. Focus on the one you're with. Not about the one you've already had and who disappeared on you before you woke up the next morning. And that's all well and good, except the one I was with wasn't doing this because she was interested in me. She didn't want anything from me other than the ten inches I was thrusting into her. Later she would brag to her friends about fucking Caleb Calley and his ten-inch cock, and how the rumors were true. He really was that big. Now that Cade was a one-woman man and they knew they had no chance with him, the interest in me from the MC groupies had intensified. So yeah, the fact that I was thinking about the stunning brunette with the creamy skin and a body that made me come four times in one night, while I fucked another woman, didn't make me feel one ounce of guilt. This was a mutual exchange. She wanted bragging rights because she got a King's cock, while I simply wanted to come.

So I grabbed her by the hips and drove into her from behind. And when I closed my eyes I let my mind roll back to the beautiful brunette.

The sweetest sensation began to swell in the base of my belly as it all came back to me. Her tight little body. Her big boobs. Those big, blue eyes warm with lust. The way she gripped the bedsheet when I made her come, time and time again. Oh yeah. That girl was something alright. And don't get me started on how good it felt to watch her wrap those plump lips around the head of my cock. The memory swirled in me and pleasure surged through me, exploding from me and making me come. I gripped onto the blonde's ass and pumped hard into her until there was nothing left to give her.

The regret was immediate. She whimpered when I pulled out and gave me a pout over her shoulder. "I want more," she purred.

But I was already pulling up my jeans. I removed the condom, wrapped it in a paper towel and disposed of it, while she stayed on the bed.

"Ohhh," she moaned as she sat up. "I can still feel how big you were."

Ice ran through my veins. I felt numb. But I wasn't a total dick, so I gave her a wink and a forced smile. "Pleased I could satisfy, sweetheart."

But my attention only inspired her to ask what I couldn't give her.

"Can I have a kiss?" she asked, starting to realize our time was up. "Even if it is a kiss goodbye."

"I don't kiss, baby."

Which was normally true. Except, I had kissed that dark-haired beauty with no name. In fact, I had spent the entire night kissing her and losing myself in the magical sensation of those lips against mine.

I don't remember why I kissed her, only that I really wanted to.

And if we ever crossed paths, I'd do it all over again.

CHAPTER 2

HONEY

Fuck.

Two pink lines.

How the fucking hell had this happened? When I had sex, I had sex with a condom, so how the hell did I end up in my mid-twenties, knocked up by a guy whose name I didn't know.

I held up the pregnancy test and checked it again. Yep. Still pregnant.

I threw the test into the sink next to the other two tests.

A knock on the bathroom door made me jump.

"Are you in there?" It was my best friend Autumn. After peeing on a stick, I had texted her and asked her to come over. "Or have you been kidnapped?"

I cracked the door open so she could only see an inch worth of my face.

"You're hiding. Why are you hiding?" she asked.

"Is Amy home?"

Amy was my roommate.

"No?" Autumn frowned. "What's going on? Why are you hiding from your roomie?"

I opened the door wider and stepped out.

"Because I don't want her to witness the emotional meltdown I'm about to have."

Selfish and self-centered, Amy wasn't the supportive type. Somehow my positive pregnancy tests would be all about her.

"You're about to have an emotional meltdown?" Autumn looked even more confused. She folded her arms across her huge boobs and gave me her teacher scowl, like I was one of her fifth graders. "Aright, Honey Bee Scott, what the hell is going on? When you messaged me and asked me to drop by on my lunch break, I thought you must be sick. And just as well, I have a key, Honey, because I was knocking on the door for a full five minutes! Now, for the love of God, what the fucking hell is going on?"

I steadied myself against the door. "I'm pregnant."

All the oxygen seemed to leave the room. Vanquished by the P word.

Autumn cocked an eyebrow. "That stopped being funny when we turned twenty-one. What's really going on?"

I didn't argue. I took the three pregnancy tests out of the sink and showed her. She avoided touching them by leaning in and looking at the little window on the top of each test. Two pink lines.

She looked up at me. "You're pregnant!"

"Yes, and I have six pink lines to prove it."

My best friend exhaled deeply. "Fucking hell."

"I know, right?"

I threw the tests back into the sink and stomped out to the family room where I flopped down onto the couch. I grabbed hold of my DO WHAT YOU LOVE EVERY DAY pillow and hugged it to me.

Autumn sat next to me. "It's going to be okay."

I looked at her. "I'm pregnant, Autumn. How on Earth is that ever going to be okay?"

"Is it Charlie's?"

"No. We didn't have sex after my last period, which was only a few days before I caught Charlie getting his dick sucked by his Amazonian girlfriend." I huffed out a deep breath of the disappointment I always felt when I thought about him having another girlfriend. "I mean, maybe it's a possibility, I don't know. But I don't think so."

"So Mr. No Name is the daddy?"

"When you put it like that, it sounds even worse."

But she was right. I didn't even know the name of my one-night stand.

All I knew was that he was a member of the Kings of Mayhem motorcycle club, and that he had the bluest eyes I'd ever seen.

And the biggest cock I'd ever fucked.

"What are you going to do?"

"I'll make an appointment to see Doctor Perry this afternoon. Find out how far along I am. My night of debauchery was just over nine weeks ago. The last time I had sex with Charlie was almost twelve weeks ago."

"If it's Charlie's?"

"I'll tell him."

"And if it's ol' blue eyes?"

I sighed and hugged my pillow tighter. "I don't know."

"Either way, you're keeping it?"

I looked at her over my pillow. "Yes."

She exhaled deeply, but then smiled. "Well, then. Let's go find out who your baby daddy is."

Biker Baby

"Are you ready?" Autumn asked.

I was about to find out if my baby was going to have Charlie's brown eyes, or the blue eyes of my one-night stand. I was on the bed, waiting for the doctor as she prepared the ultrasound, and drew in a deep breath. My heart was a drum in my chest. I was at a crossroad. A big fucking crossroad. And the outcome of this sonogram was going to decide what road I was going to go down. I glanced nervously at Autumn. She squeezed my hand and gave me one of her comforting smiles.

"Right, here we go," Dr. Perry said as he squirted a cold lube on my flat belly and began rubbing it around with a transducer. Within seconds, the boom-boom of a heartbeat filled the small treatment room.

"Is that my baby?"

It was a totally lame question.

But Dr. Perry smiled. "It sure is. And it sounds like a strong heartbeat." Totally unexpectedly, tears stung at my eyes. I looked at Autumn, who grinned back at me. That was my baby's heartbeat. All of a sudden it was all very real. I had a tiny little human growing in my belly.

"Can you tell how far along I am?" I asked.

"Absolutely." Dr. Perry leaned over to press a key on the ultrasound. "You are exactly nine weeks and two days along."

My heart launched itself into my throat.

Mr. Blue Eyes was the father.

My baby wasn't going to have brown eyes after all.

Sorry, Charlie.

I wasn't really sorry. Truth be known, I felt relieved. Charlie and his lying, douchey ways were now firmly rooted in my past.

Having a child by him would tie me to his cheating ass for the rest of my life, but I didn't have to worry about that now. I exhaled as the weight of anxiety left my body. I was free of him forever.

"So, what's the game plan?" Autumn asked later as we sat in a booth at our local Starbucks afterwards.

I shrugged. "I grow a baby and work it out as I go along."

"What about the baby's father? Mr. No Name?"

"Do I have to tell him?"

"Um, yes."

"Why?"

"Because, he is going to be a father."

"Now there's an awkward conversation," I said, staring into my double-shot skinny chai latte.

"He has a right to know. But at the end of the day, it's your choice. You don't have to make all these decisions today."

"Yeah, but we don't know each other. I don't know if he wants kids. Hell, I don't even know his name."

"Then we find out his name."

"How?"

"We go down to the clubhouse and find him."

"Just like that?"

Autumn leaned forward and grinned. "Just. Like. That."

CHAPTER 3

HONEY

"Remind me again, why are we here?" Autumn asked.

"I'm about to go and tell some biker that I am pregnant with his child," I replied.

"Oh, that's right. But remind me why we are still sitting in my car, parked on the curb outside of the Kings of Mayhem clubhouse."

"These things take time," I said, my throat as rough as sandpaper. I sucked down the rest of the contents in my water bottle and stared out the window at the clubhouse down the street.

"Can we speed it up a little? We've already been sitting here for twenty minutes."

"I'm waiting for the right moment."

"Well, if the right moment doesn't show up in the next five minutes, I'm going in there myself."

"You can't just go in there. They don't let just anyone through that hallowed threshold." I nodded toward the six-foot gate that was being rolled open by a guy in a Kings of Mayhem cut. A catering truck pulled up and drove in, followed by two guys on Harleys. For a moment, I thought one of them was my one-night stand, and without thinking, I ducked down.

Autumn looked at me like I was crazy. "What are you *doing*?"

"I think that's him."

"How can you tell? He's like ten yards away." Autumn took a bite of the red licorice she had been sucking on for the last ten minutes. "Plus, isn't that a good thing? Now we can go in and get this over and done with."

"I don't think that is a good idea," I whispered.

"Why the hell are you whispering?" She turned to me and raised a perfectly shaped eyebrow at me. "Being pregnant is making you a Class-A psycho, did you know that?"

"Yes," I whispered loudly. "I do know that."

She dropped the eyebrow, but gave me a pointed look. "That's it, I'm going in there."

She undid her seatbelt but I grabbed her wrist. "You can't."

"That's where you're wrong." She shook me off and opened the car door. "And if you don't want me asking a room full of bikers who has the ten-inch cock, then you'd better come with me."

She wasn't kidding. Autumn wasn't the shy type. She'd stand on a table and ask the entire clubhouse who was packing that much manhood in their jeans, and not bat an eyelid doing it.

"Please, let's just go home and forget about it," I pleaded.

"No."

"I'll bake you treats for a month."

"No."

"I'll make you those mini cakes with the marshmallow frosting and jam centers that you like. Or those lava cakes with the chocolate ganache."

"No and no." She climbed out of the car and closed the car door, flipping her long, auburn hair over her shoulders as she started to walk away.

Hell.

I had to stop her from going in there and doing something stupid. *Like asking a room full of bikers who had the ten-inch cock.* I climbed out of the car and jogged to catch up with her.

"Glad you decided to join me," she said with a smug little smirk.

"I hate you right now."

"Ouch. That really hurt. You're right, we should go home."

"Really?"

"No."

I huffed out a deep breath of air and resigned myself that this was about to happen whether I wanted it to or not.

We got to the huge gate just as a guy in a Kings of Mayhem cut was closing it.

"Wait!" Autumn called out to him.

The guy stopped and looked over. He gave us both the once over and grinned. He reminded me of the lead singer of the band who sang that 90's hit, *Epic*. He had dark hair, dark eyes, cheekbones most women would kill for, and a jawline that belonged on *Vogue*. When he moved, I could see he was wearing a *Star Wars* shirt under his cut.

"Well, hey there, ladies, what can I do for you?"

"Is this the Kings of Mayhem clubhouse?" Autumn asked, even though it was quite obvious it was. She gave him her best fuck-me eyes, which he fully appreciated.

"Sure is, sweetheart. Someone expecting you?"

"Well..."

"Because you can't come in here without an invite, darlin', not tonight. We're having a welcome home party for one of the guys. So it's invite only."

Autumn licked her lips and batted her long lashes at him. "Of course we're invited. We're part of the entertainment."

My eyes widened.

We're part of the what?

The biker gave us another appraising look. His eyes swept up and down the length of me, and inwardly, I groaned. There was no way I could pass for any kind of *entertainment*. Autumn, yes. Especially in those capri pants and tight, tailored shirt. But me, no. I had on my high-support panties under my skirt, the ones I usually saved for when I had my period and felt bloated and angry.

"If you're the entertainment, where are your costumes?" the biker asked.

"Costumes?" Autumn asked, confused.

"You know, the ones you wear on stage?"

"Ah, yes . . . our . . . costumes. We're already wearing them. They're real small, if you know what I mean."

He grinned. And again, his eyes did a full sweep of Autumn's body. "Well, goddamn!"

"Wait til you see us . . . *entertain*."

I watched his Adam's apple bob up and down as he swallowed thickly. His eyes glittered over to me.

"You two ladies do a double act?" he asked.

Autumn winked at him. "Tonight, just might be your lucky night, baby. We might do that just for you." She was convincing. While I, on the other hand, just stood there like a deer in headlights. There was no way I could pass as the *entertainment*.

But apparently, the biker felt differently because he grinned and opened the gate wider. "Welcome to hell, ladies."

We entered the compound and when he was out of earshot, I stopped my best friend. "Have you lost your fucking mind?"

"Again with the whispering. Who are you, a special agent?"

"No, I'm the *entertainment*, apparently!"

Biker Baby

She waved me off. "It got us in here, didn't it?"

Before I could answer, another biker approached us. He looked like James Hetfield, circa "Enter Sandman." His hair was long and his handlebar mustache and goatee were epic.

"Vader said you were the entertainment," Fake James Hetfield said. "Rang through and told me to show you inside. Said to tell the hot redhead to make sure she saves him that last dance."

Autumn grinned at him. "Sure thing, baby."

He smiled, revealing a mouthful of pearly whites.

From where I was standing, I could catch a glimpse inside the room. There was a long bar with all the trimmings, and leaning up against it were five bikers, all in Kings of Mayhem cuts. Over the sound of Eric Clapton's "Cocaine," I could hear the sounds of a game of pool.

Two women in very tight jeans, boots, and tight t-shirts walked past us, barely glancing in our direction. They exuded authority. Biker-chick authority. I glanced down at my modest skirt and pink Chucks. I didn't belong here. This was my baby daddy's world, and it couldn't feel more foreign to me.

"Come on, Honey," Autumn smiled, taking my hand.

Fake James Hetfield looked me up and down, and gave me an appreciative wink. "Hey, baby."

I just shook my head at him and let Autumn lead me into the clubhouse.

Inside, the smell of cigarette smoke, weed, and alcohol hit me in the face. Normally, I had a real good sense of smell, but being pregnant amplified it. I had to exhale deeply to steady my nerves and try not to throw up.

Autumn stopped walking and scanned the room.

"Right, where is Mr. Blue Eyes?"

I looked around the large room. Besides the long, polished-timber bar, there were red leather booths, pool tables, and two stripper poles. On one of the poles, a girl with long purple hair and tattoos up both arms, twirled solemnly along to the last few seconds of Eric Clapton. When "Cocaine" switched to Inglorious' "Where Are You Now," another girl joined her. This one had short blonde hair and not a tattoo in sight. I watched, slightly intrigued by their talent as they twirled and slid up and down the pole. It was a definite skill. They were strong women. Sexy. Their core strength was phenomenal. I placed my hand over my flat belly. Today I was twelve weeks pregnant. My core strength had been invaded by a stranger's baby.

"Hey there," came a smooth, manly voice behind us. Autumn and I swung around and had to tilt our heads back to look up at the origin of the voice. Standing in front of us was a tall, godlike man who made Jason Momoa look small. With long, messy hair, and muscles for miles, he was as formidable as he was good looking. He wore a Kings of Mayhem cut over a plain black t-shirt that strained against his broad chest, and had arms the size of my thighs. Autumn's eyes lit up, and her tongue slid along her already glossy lips as she took him in.

And there was a lot to take in.

"Well, hey there, yourself," she said, offering him her most flirtatious grin.

"I haven't seen you ladies here before. Can I offer you a drink?" he asked, his attention firmly fixed on my best friend.

I shook my head, but by the look on Autumn's face, she was going to accept the drink and whatever else he was offering.

"Name's Maverick," he said, offering her his hand. She took it and their eyes remained glued to each other as he slowly raised it to his lips. Lust sparkled in the space around us.

Great. In the space of two minutes, I'd become the third wheel.

I glanced around the room looking for a familiar set of blue eyes and a head of dark hair. Across the room, a woman who looked like Cher in her "Turn Back Time" days was doing shots with an older man in a wheelchair and a tall bald man who looked like he'd stepped straight out of the Israeli army. He towered above them and had muscles. Muscles for miles.

Farther along in another booth, a formidable looking biker in dark sunglasses smoked a cigarette while talking to another biker who looked as out of place as I felt. Clean cut and with Coke-bottle glasses, he looked more like a singer from an 80's boy band, although he did look cool and relaxed, his geeky image slightly tarnished by the Kings of Mayhem cut. In the booth over, two blonde girls laughed and flicked their hair, trying to get their attention.

Autumn and I followed Maverick to the bar. He and Autumn did a shot of tequila followed by a beer chaser, while I nursed a Coke.

"You want whisky in that?" Maverick asked.

I shook my head. "No, thanks. I'm good with just Coke."

"You driving or somethin'?"

Again I shook my head. "Nope."

He gave me a strange look, like me not drinking a beer was the weirdest thing in the world. But then he shrugged. "S'pose you're not the only babe in here not drinking." He nodded to a beautiful blonde girl who was heavily pregnant, standing across the room. She was with another biker in a Kings of Mayhem cut, and for a moment my heart stalled because he looked just like my one-night stand. Tall. Big. With mesmerizing blue eyes and tattoos down his arms. But it wasn't him.

"Indy's full of arms and legs," Maverick said, taking a sip from his beer bottle.

"Who is that guy she's with?" I asked.

"That's Cade. He's our VP. You know him?"

I shook my head. "No, he just reminds me of someone."

"A King?"

"Yeah, I believe he is. I don't know his name. But he looks like your VP."

"Cade's got two brothers, Chance and Caleb," he said, glancing around the bar. "Chance is still deployed overseas, but Caleb is around here somewhere."

Caleb.

The name played over in my head, and anticipation tingled in my stomach.

That was *him*. I was sure of it.

Caleb.

"Hey, Mav." A girl wearing the smallest pair of Daisy Dukes leaned across the bar and tapped Maverick on the shoulder. "Can you give me a hand? I need one of the beer kegs from out of the back? We're running low."

"Sure, babe." He put down his bottle of beer and looked at Autumn. "Don't you run off, darlin'. I'll be right back."

We watched the big sexy biker walk off to help the girl from behind the bar, and Autumn nudged my shoulder. "I'll be honest with you, Honey. I'm going to get me some of that tonight."

That was my best friend. Straight to the point.

"Is that such a good idea?"

She gave me a very pointed look. "I haven't had sex in months. Not since that loser from the PE department at school."

"The one with the little dick?"

"No. That was Roger from the AV department. No, the PE guy was Joey. He was the one who wanted me to call him Daddy when he was fucking me from behind."

Autumn didn't have much luck with men. She also struggled with commitment. So the two together meant she had never had a long-term boyfriend.

"Don't you worry about me," she said, bringing her bottle of beer to her lips. "I'm a big girl. I'm going to get me some action tonight. And I'm getting it with him."

Maverick walked back into the bar carrying a keg of beer. Massive biceps bulged and flexed as they worked hard, his rugged face barely showing any effort as he carried the keg and put it down behind the bar. Autumn gobbled him up with her eyes and licked her lips like she could hardly wait to put her mouth on him. Judging by the attraction crackling between them, they would be naked within the hour.

"But first, we've got to find your baby daddy," she said. "You want to circulate the room?"

No.

I wanted to go home.

Because coming here was a crazy mistake.

I looked around suddenly nervous. Exactly what was I going to do when I finally came face to face with my one-night stand?

Hey, you'll never guess what.

It's the funniest story…

I took a sip of my Coke. I wasn't ready to face him.

"I need to pee," I said getting up from my stool. "Are you okay if I leave you for a bit?"

"If we get separated, you make sure you text me before you go anywhere," she said as I began to walk away.

Before disappearing down a hallway toward the restrooms, I glanced over at Maverick. The bar girl had rewarded his help with another two shots of tequila and he slid one across the bar to Autumn. After they downed them, he pulled her into his chest and mashed his lips to hers. In return, she melted into him and kissed him hungrily.

I turned away and continued down a long hallway. The restroom was at the end. I pushed the door open and immediately stopped because leaning up against the wall was a beast of a man, his head dropped back in pleasure, his mouth slack, and his eyes squeezed together. On her knees in front of him was a girl with yellow hair. She had her hands on his thighs and her mouth full of his cock. It took me a moment to register what I was seeing. Unfortunately, my realization coincided with his orgasm, and I got to see him grab himself, give his cock a couple of frenzied pumps, and ejaculate all over her lips. Rooted to the spot, there was no time to make an escape before the girl rose to her feet and stormed over to where I stood in the doorway. She gave me a filthy look.

"There's another restroom down the hallway," she snapped, and then slammed the door in my face.

Right.

So that just happened.

If I didn't feel like fleeing before, I definitely did now.

But before I could make my escape, I really needed to find another restroom first.

I glanced down the hallway to my right where the yellow-haired girl said there was a second restroom. It was a longer hallway than the first one, dimly lit with doorways leading off into what I assumed were bedrooms.

Thankfully—because my eyes were already bleeding—the bathroom was vacant. I turned on the light and quickly locked the door, taking the time to catch my thoughts and calm my nerves as I peed.

Okay. New plan. I would go find Caleb and I would just come out and say it. Hey. I'm pregnant. It's yours. Thought you should know. Oh, and hey, my name is Honey.

And then we would work it all out like the grown adults we were.

I didn't want anything from him. I was here only because I thought he deserved to know. It would be awkward. It would be a shock. But after tonight, it would be done and I could move forward and focus on the baby and how it was going to impact my life. I didn't need a boyfriend, or to start anything with a man who was only ever meant to be a one-night stand, because now wasn't the time to complicate an already unexpected situation.

Feeling more confident, I finished up and left the bathroom and started back down the hallway, but was stopped by a warm, familiar voice.

"Well, I'll be goddamned, it *is* you," it said. I swung around and there he was, Mr. One-Night Stand. *Caleb.* He was leaning against the door, his big arms folded across his wide chest, and his bright blue eyes glittering in the dim light. He was just as damn beautiful as he had been the night we met. My insides did a double flip, and every female part of me clenched and pulsed, and as if they had a mind of their own, my eyes drifted down the length of that hard body and stopped at the decorative belt buckle. Behind that belt buckle . . . ten inches of trouble.

My hand went to my belly.

"It's you," I breathed, momentarily caught in the blueness of his vibrant eyes.

He didn't move from the door, but he smiled, and boy, something wild unfurled inside of me.

"I woke up and I was alone," he said, pushing off the door and walking toward me. "Thought you were a dream. Thought I had imagined you."

He stopped in front of me and my skin rippled with goosebumps. He was tall and broad, and all kinds of handsome. My body began to buzz as soon as he was close.

"No. I'm real," I said. Christ, how was I going to tell him I was knocked up when I could barely talk. "Right here, in the flesh."

Something close to raw desire shimmered across his face, and my nipples turned so hard they could cut diamonds. I shifted uneasily on my feet. And suddenly, every part of me—every single cell, wanted him inside me.

He must've felt the same, because one minute we were standing there staring at one another, and the next we were attacking each other's mouths and tearing at our clothes.

I couldn't explain it. But I had never felt so aroused in my life. I was wet and throbbing, and all common sense left me the moment his lips touched mine.

Kissing me fiercely, he backed me against the wall and lifted me up in his arms. I wrapped my legs around him, and blindly reached for his zipper. He broke away and looked at me, those glittering baby blues searching my face for something. A sign. A pause. A yes. A no.

I gave him a yes when I drew his mouth back to mine and kissed him hard. He growled and pulled me off the wall, somehow opening the door behind us and walking us into a bedroom. While we continued to kiss ferociously, he kicked the door closed behind us and walked me over to the bed.

Tell him. Tell him now, before this insanity goes any further.

But then he pulled his shirt over his head, and holy hell, all I could see, think, and know, was the wall of abs in front of me.

Just for tonight. Let me enjoy him just for one more night.

I reached for his jeans, and a minute later, the man-god in front of me was rolling a condom over those magical ten inches and I was naked and throbbing on the bed. He walked toward me, his impressive erection tapping his belly as he approached. When he got to the end of the bed, I reached for him and pushed him down. I wasn't sure what had come over me. I was all kinds of turned on, and it made me assertive and selfish. I straddled him, and without waiting, sank down on his cock with a long, drawn-out moan.

"That's the girl I remember," he growled in my ear as I rode him.

Lost in the grinding of my pelvis against his, I kissed him and he moaned against my lips, drawing my tongue into his mouth with his, kissing me hard.

I slowed my grinding. I was close. Only a few more rolls of my hips and I would fall apart on top of him. But I wanted to savor this for a moment longer. One last time.

Our orgasms hit at the same time. He grabbed my hip with one hand, holding me tight against him as he bucked into me, while his other hand held my face to his as he continued to kiss me hard.

He pressed his forehead to mine as he came. "Goddamn, you're something..."

As my climax receded, I smiled. "You're not so bad yourself."

When I went to climb off, he stopped me. "Wait. Are you going to tell me your name?"

I couldn't help but laugh. I'd forgotten we hadn't exchanged them yet.

"Honey." I smiled at him, and his cock pulsed inside me. "My name is Honey. What's yours?"

"Caleb," he replied. "*Honey*. Is that your real name?"

"No, it's my stripper name."

He cocked an eyebrow. "You're a stripper?"

I chuckled. "No, I was joking. My *real* name is Honey. It's on my birth certificate. But thank you for thinking I could pass as a stripper."

Again, I moved to climb off him, but again he stopped me.

"You're not running away again, are you?"

"No."

"Good. Because the night is still young and I've got a lot more in store for you."

CHAPTER 4

HONEY

In the small bathroom off the bedroom I stared at my reflection in the mirror, slightly stunned at what I'd just done.

"What the hell is wrong with you?" I whispered to myself.

I pressed my palm to my flat belly. I had to tell him that I was pregnant with his baby. I raised my chin. I would go out there and just say it. Just tell him that the condom had been faulty, and *surprise, we made a baby together.*

I checked my phone. There was a missed call and a couple of messages from Autumn.

> **Autumn:** *I'm taking Mav back to my place. Want a ride home?*
> **Autumn:** *I take it you found your baby daddy. Or are you lost? Do I need to send for help?*
> **Autumn:** *It's been half an hour girlfriend. Where are you?*

I quickly fired off a message to her.

Me: *Ran into Caleb. Might be a while. You go.*

She replied straight away.

Autumn: *I'm taking Mav home to ravage his body.*
Me: *Of course you are. Don't drive.*
Autumn: *I'm calling an Uber.*
Autumn: *Have you told him yet?*
Me: *I'm working up the nerve.*
Autumn: *For the last half an hour?*
Me: *Not exactly.*
Autumn: *Stop playing with his giant penis and go tell him.*

I flicked off the light and walked back into the room. Caleb looked up from the pillows and smiled, his white teeth gleaming in the dim light. Outside the room, Avenged Sevenfold's "Save Me" filled the clubhouse, and laughter floated in through the walls.

I sat down on the bed next to him and leaned down to find my skirt.

"Hey," he said, his voice deep and raspy. "Where are you going?"

I couldn't look at him because I would probably have sex with him again if I did, judging by my recent behavior. What I needed to do was get my clothes on so I wasn't so naked and exposed when I told him about the baby.

"I need to get dressed," I said.

"I beg to differ. I much prefer you naked."

I shook my head as I smiled and reached for my skirt on the floor.

"I thought you said you weren't running away."

"I know but . . . it's just . . . I should go."

"Brutal," he said with a hint of amusement in his gloriously raspy voice.

I finally looked at him over my shoulder "What do you mean?"

He sat up and his stomach rippled with the deep grooves of his abdominals. "I get the feeling that you like to fuck and run," he said, moving behind me and dragging my hair over one shoulder. Pleasure tingled across my skin. "But I'm the type of guy who likes to take his time."

He bent down and kissed the back of my neck and my eyes closed at the touch of his lips against my skin. I trembled, the core of me melting at his touch. A delicious pulse took up between my thighs, and my nipples hardened. I shivered and turned around, and captured his mouth with mine. We both moaned as the air around us crackled with sexual excitement. This was going to happen again. His lips slanted against mine and he tugged me to him, gently guiding me down to the pillows and climbing onto me. Slowly, he began to make love to me again. This time taking his time to enjoy my body. He flooded my skin with kisses, gave me an orgasm with his tongue, and then another one by driving slowly and purposely into me with deep, hard strokes.

Much later, as our breathing stilled and our bodies sank spent into the mattress, he pulled me to his chest. Lulled by the rhythmic beat of his heart, my eyes felt heavy and I closed them, just for a moment.

When I opened my eyes, sunlight was peeping in through a break in the curtains and a stillness had settled throughout the clubhouse. I looked at the alarm clock on the bedside table.

Oh hell.

It was 7:25 AM. And I had spent the whole night.

I tried to move but Caleb had me secured to his chest with one big arm. As soon as I tried to shift it off me, he stirred.

"Always trying to run away," he murmured sleepily into my ear. He tilted his hips toward me so I felt his naked erection against my ass cheek. His breath left him in a soft whisper as he began to rock his cock against me.

"I didn't mean to stay," I whispered.

He pressed his lips to my jaw, leading a small trail of kisses to my ear while his hand slid across my belly. "I'm pleased that you did."

I felt him pull away for a moment. Heard the rustle of foil. Felt the mattress move as he moved. Smelled latex.

Not waiting for my response, he flipped me on my back and slid into me with one lazy, sleepy stroke. I was still sore from all the lovemaking, but his size and the fullness of him was the perfect elixir. I was slick and he groaned deeply in my ear as he sank farther into me. He kept his face buried in the crook of my neck and my head caged between two big biceps. His breath was hot against my cheek, his moans heavy and desperate as he ground farther and farther into me.

When we came, we came together in a sleepy, hazy moment that left our bodies warm and slick, and our pulse beating rapidly in song with one another.

As he waited for his breathing to calm, I took a moment to marvel in the bulk of the man lying on top of me. My fingers slid across golden skin colored with a collage of intricate pictures, symbols, and words. My palm curved around strong deltoid muscles that were well-rounded and powerful. He was big. Strong. Lethal. *And probably not interested in being the father of my baby.*

The thought made me shift uneasily beneath him. I had to get out of there. I needed to be alone to collect my thoughts and find my senses. I wiggled, and Caleb rolled off me. I thought he would let me go, but he didn't. Instead, he turned my face toward him and kissed me hard on the mouth.

But I was leaving.

I sat up and began looking for my panties on the floor. Finding them wedged under the corner of the bed, I slipped them on and began hunting for my skirt…again.

"Where are you going?" he asked.

"I have to go."

"Why are you always running away from me?" he questioned, an amused sparkle in his eyes. "Will I see you again?"

I paused and looked at him over my shoulder. "Do you want to?"

He grinned and I was momentarily taken back by how beautiful his smile was.

How beautiful *he* was.

"Hell, darlin', I don't want you to leave."

I resumed looking for my skirt. "I have to leave. I have things to do."

I found my skirt in a tangle with my shirt at the foot of the bed.

"At least let me give you a ride home." He sat up.

"It's fine. I can call a cab." I stood up and slipped my shirt on.

"I'm not letting you take a cab."

"Really, it's fine."

He climbed off the bed, unfazed by his nakedness, and began looking for his boxer shorts. I paused to drink in the fine display of his muscular body and his still-swollen manhood swinging between his powerful thighs. It was obvious he took very good care of his body.

He slipped on his jeans, and by the time I had buttoned my blouse and found my phone and shoes, he was fully dressed and securing his wallet chain to his jeans.

"Ready?" he asked.

There was no point arguing.

As he opened the bedroom door, I mentally braced myself. I wasn't looking forward to the walk of shame through the clubhouse. But the hallway was quiet and the clubhouse was still. Sometime during the night the music had stopped and the party had wound down.

As soon as I entered the bar, the stench of last night's partying hit me like a bat to the face, and I had to hold my breath. The bar was littered with snoring bikers and the odd club girl asleep where they had passed out. Bottles lay scattered and spilled everywhere. Stale booze and body odor were ripe in the air, and it was enough that I had to hold my breath to keep from vomiting. Caleb took my hand and led me through the mess, stepping over discarded bottles and sleeping bodies. Musty smoke glittered in the dusty rays of sunlight bursting into the room from a window above the jukebox.

Across the room, an older biker was quietly having sex with a large, partially dressed woman up against the pool table. His jeans were down around his ankles and his eyes were closed as he lazily rocked into her. The slap, slap of her large, wobbly boobs against the pool table broke the stillness of the morning.

Farther away, a naked woman lay slumped at the base of a stripper pole with everything open and on display. She hugged a half-spilled bourbon bottle and snored loudly. As we passed by her, Caleb shook his head and grabbed a discarded shirt from a nearby chair to cover her.

"Is she alright?" I whispered.

"Yeah, that's Candy. It's not the first time she's passed out there, and it won't be the last."

I glanced around me. This place. These people. This was Caleb's world. And it reeked of bad choices. Nausea roiled in the pit of my belly, and I barely made it outside in time before losing the contents of my stomach.

"Jesus, are you okay?" Caleb asked, coming up behind me.

I gestured for him to give me a moment as another wave of nausea washed over me, and I vomited again.

"You drink too much?" he asked when I finally straightened and walked over to him. "I don't remember you being drunk."

I shook my head. "I didn't drink a thing."

He handed me a helmet. "Are you okay to ride? Or do you need a minute?"

"I'll be okay."

He led me over to a row of motorcycles parked alongside the clubhouse. His was a big black beast with lots of chrome gleaming in the early morning light.

Before he climbed on, he touched my hand. "Are you sure you're okay?"

I smiled brightly but it was fake because I felt weird. Out of place. I didn't belong there.

"Yes. I'm fine," I said, very aware that I needed to get out of there. I secured my helmet and climbed onto the back of his bike. "Let's ride."

CHAPTER 5

HONEY

The moment we pulled up outside my apartment, I knew something was wrong. I looked up at my bedroom window that overlooked the street and realized the curtains were missing.

Caleb sensed something was wrong, too, and insisted on following me inside.

When the door swung open, my heart sank. The place was completely empty.

Everything was gone.

Even the window furnishings.

"What the fuck?" Caleb stood right behind me. "Who did this?"

My head shot up.

Amy.

She had stolen everything. Apart from a discarded candy wrapper in the middle of the floor, my apartment was completely empty. My comfortable couch. *Gone*. The table and drawers I'd found at a secondhand store and had lovingly restored. *Gone*. Even the giant picture of James Dean walking through a rainy New York City ... *gone*.

Penny Dee

I ran to my room, but came to a halt in the doorway. The room was bare. My bed. My furniture. The pictures off the wall. Hell, even my clothes—all gone.

I raced to the loose floorboard near where my bed used to be and pried it open.

"No!" I cried, dropping to my knees.

My money roll was missing.

$670 of savings... *stolen.*

I sat back and put my head in my hands. I needed that money. Caleb crouched down in front of me.

"She's taken everything," I sobbed.

He pulled my hands from my face. His eyes were gentle, but the rigid tick in his jaw let me know he wasn't happy about this.

"We will get your stuff back," he said darkly.

I looked away, but he turned my chin to face him.

"I promise you, Honey. I will make this right."

I didn't believe him, but I appreciated his attempt to make me feel better. I went to thank him, but the sudden onset of nausea sent me straight to the bathroom where I threw up again.

"Are you sure you didn't drink last night?" he asked when I came back to the bedroom.

I leaned a hip against the doorjamb. I felt dizzy. "I'm sure."

Tell him. Tell him now.

"Maybe you have a stomach bug."

I wanted to tell him about the baby, but not while this disaster was unfolding.

I pulled my phone out of my jacket pocket.

"What are you doing?" he asked.

"I'm calling the police."

He crossed the room briskly and closed his hand over mine so I couldn't finish making the call.

"Let me handle this," he said, his blue eyes gleaming with a formidable glint.

"You don't have to do anything. I can handle this."

But even as I said the words I knew my stuff was gone forever. I would fill out a police report but hear nothing, while Amy got to enjoy all of my belongings. Unfortunately, this wasn't my first rodeo.

"I can assure you, I can get your stuff back a lot quicker than the police," he said.

"You can?"

When he nodded, my face crumpled and he drew me into his arms and held me against his broad chest, pressing a kiss to my hair before releasing me. He was warm and big, and so comforting that it made me want to cry harder.

"What's her name?" he asked.

"Amy," I replied, bewildered. "Amy Russell."

"Do you know where she works?"

I hesitated. I didn't know Caleb. And while his fierce masculinity was a turn on, it was also a reminder that I had no idea what he was capable of. He was a big guy, both in size and presence. And despite his easy-going nature, there was something formidable about him. I didn't know what he would do to Amy once he found her. Would he threaten her? Hurt her? Hurt the person she was with?

Hell, was this guy a killer?

"Look, no one is going to hurt her," he said as if he could read my mind. "Usually the cut is enough."

I relaxed a little. "She lost her job at the supermarket last week. But I know she hangs out at Skylar's."

"The bar over on Juniper Street?"

"Yeah, she goes there a lot. Last time we spoke she said she might be able to pick up a few shifts."

"Let me handle it," he said and I could see on his face that he would. "In the meantime, can I drop you somewhere?"

My head shot up.

My car.

I ran to the window overlooking the parking lot, my heart pounding at the chance Amy might have stolen that, too. It was the last thing of value I owned. I was up to my eyeballs in debt with the bakery I'd just started, and until I started making money on my new business venture, I couldn't afford another car.

Thankfully, Amy hadn't added grand theft auto to her list of crimes and my little Fiat sat untouched in its parking space. I breathed a sigh of relief. It was a small blessing.

Caleb crossed the room and stood behind me. "Your car?"

I turned around and nodded. "It's still there."

I couldn't look at him. I didn't want him to see me cry. And as reality began to sink in, I could feel a decent ugly cry coming on.

"Hey," he said, stepping closer and gently lifting my chin. "I'm going to take care of this."

The darkness in his usually vibrant blue eyes told me he meant what he said. And I had no doubt he was capable of doing so. What I couldn't understand was why he would. "You don't have to do anything."

But he ignored me. "Have you got somewhere to stay tonight?"

When I nodded, he leaned closer and took my phone out of my hand. Feeling dazed, I watched as he added his number into my contacts list and mine to his.

"You need anything, you call me." He handed me back my phone. "I'll call you when I've dealt with this, okay?"

Still dazed, I nodded. "Sure."

He leaned forward and pressed a warm kiss to my forehead before heading out the door. Still feeling a little overwhelmed, I watched the six-foot-four wall of muscle climb on his bike and take off into the early morning with a flick of his wrist and a loud roar down the road.

That man. He was something. He was strong and capable. And oh so irresistible.

He was also the father of my baby.

The baby he still knew nothing about.

CHAPTER 6

CALEB

I rode back to the clubhouse with Honey on my mind. I wanted to help her. The Kings had a lot of friends, and there wasn't a hell of a lot that went down in this town that we didn't know about. Outside of the club, we had a network of alliances and people who stood firmly in our camp. People who would do what we wanted. People who would tell us what we needed to know. From hookers and business owners, to town councilors, members of criminal syndicates, government employees, even a mayor. It's what helped to keep the Kings of Mayhem the biggest and most powerful club in the south.

Finding Honey's dick roommate—sorry, *ex-roommate*—wasn't going to be a problem. What would be difficult would be holding myself back from knocking her lights out. I didn't touch women. But I hated thieves. Scumbag low-lifes who took from others because they couldn't be fucked working for it. And this Amy sounded like a real low-life flea. But for me, like my brothers, violence against women was never an option. I would never raise my hand to one. I was raised to treat women with

Biker Baby

respect, and as equals. In my home and in my club, if you hit a woman, you should expect her to hit you back. The Kings of Mayhem married queens. Strong, independent women who fought back. And as men, we lived the philosophies of my grandfather, Hutch Calley, the man who started it all back in the sixties. You didn't hit women. And we didn't tolerate men who did.

I remembered an incident when I was just a kid, when our neighbor, Jackie Parrish, laid a fist into his wife's cheek at a club barbecue. The fallout afterwards had been massive. Sure, not much happened on the surface. But behind the scenes things were put in place, eyes were set on Jackie, and I overheard my dad telling Jackie to cool it, to get some help or lose his patch. He went easy on him because Jackie's son had just died of leukemia, but if his wife showed up with any more bruises, he told him he was out. And when you got thrown out of the club, it hurt. A lot.

My daddy, Garrett Calley, had been a mean sonofabitch. He'd done bad things. *Bad* things. Lied to people. Hurt people. But he never once raised his hand to my mom—which was good for a lot of reasons, but mainly because I know my mom would've shot him if he did.

When I pulled into the clubhouse parking lot, I parked my bike next to the barbecue tables and shoved my sunglasses into my t-shirt. Walking toward the entrance, a gorgeous blonde in a tight pink top and a barely there denim skirt came toward me, her glossy lips giving me a bad-girl smile as she walked past in her high-heels and legs that went on forever.

"Hey, baby," she cooed.

Her name was Tiffani. She was a club girl. She liked MC cock. And for the last few months she had been chasing mine. But I hadn't been down that well-traveled road.

"Hey, Tiff. How you doing, darlin'? You ain't misbehaving now, are you, sweetheart?"

She paused to give me a wicked look. "If you're offering, baby, you know I'm keen to misbehave with you."

I grinned and shook my head. "Thanks for the offer, but I'm already late for official club business."

That was a lie. The *official club business* I was talking about was a warm shower and a cup of coffee so strong it could restart the heart of a dead man.

"Well, I could always come back later, if you like," she offered.

But I kept walking.

"You know where to find me!" she called out.

Inside the clubhouse, the cleanup was already underway. Red, our resident cook, was walking around with a garbage bag picking up beer bottles, ashtrays, and other litter, while a couple of our club girls were wiping down tables and mopping the polished concrete floor. When I saw Tiffani, she didn't look like she'd been helping with the cleanup so I assumed she had been leaving someone's bedroom. And when Hawke walked in eating cereal out of the box, and with a trail of hickeys up his neck, I was pretty sure whose bedroom it was.

"Hey, Caleb." Behind the bar, Randy our one-armed barman, was pouring Candy, the naked girl who'd passed out at the end of the stripper pole, a cup of coffee. "You want one of these?"

When I nodded he poured me a cup and I grabbed it on my way to my room. My hangover was non-existent thanks to a night spent in bed with a fine woman versus a night spent drinking hard liquor with my brothers. But damn, that first mouthful of coffee was euphoric.

In my room I drained my cup and stripped out of my clothes. I had a big day today. Things to do. People to see. Some bad memories to douse in bourbon.

Stepping into the shower, my thoughts wound back to Honey. I didn't know why I couldn't shake her out of my mind. I wasn't the relationship type. I enjoyed being free and not having to

Biker Baby

answer to anyone. And since breaking up with Brandi, my crazy ex-girlfriend, I was convinced I was meant for the single life.

But there was something about Honey. I couldn't deny it. I wanted to see her again.

Only, I got the feeling she wasn't interested in anything more than my dick.

The first night, she didn't even want to know my name.

Or my number.

And then she'd skipped out on me while I slept off our wild night in that cheap motel room.

Next thing, she appeared at the clubhouse looking so damn fine I wasn't able to keep my fucking hands off her.

Yet despite the fucking amazing sex, and the numerous orgasms, she still wanted to run away from me.

If I hadn't given her a ride home, chances are she would have disappeared from my life forever.

So I was going to help her get her belongings back because she needed my help.

But also because it gave me an excuse to see her again.

CHAPTER 7

HONEY

"That bitch!" Autumn seethed, taking a sip of her hot chocolate. We were sitting on her couch, the one I would be sleeping on until I got my bed and furniture back. "I always knew you couldn't trust the little thief."

"Caleb seems to think he can get my things from her," I said, leaning forward and taking my peppermint tea from the coffee table. I took a sip of the minty water and savored the sweetness on my tongue. It was the only thing I could keep down, and thankfully, it also calmed my nausea.

"I don't doubt it, he seems very . . . *capable*." She looked at me over her mug and I could see the twinkle in her eyes. "Did you tell him about the baby?"

I glanced away. "No."

She gaped at me. "Honey!"

"I know. I should've told him but—"

"But—?"

"I got distracted!"

She gave me an unimpressed look. "That is the worst excuse ever. You got distracted? By what, his big cock?" When I glanced away again she *tsk-tsk'd* and shook her head. "You ho."

I gave her a pointed look. "Speaking of hoes, how was *your* night?"

She shrugged it off as if it was nothing. "It was . . . you know . . . it was okay."

She tried to sound nonchalant, but her voice raised an octave, so I knew she was lying.

"Just okay?" I eyed her suspiciously because she wouldn't look me in the eye. "Oh my God, you like him!"

Again, she tried to downplay it. "Of course I like him, I let him inside my vagina. Three times, to be precise."

"But you *like* like him! I can tell."

She avoided making eye contact with me and busied herself picking at the cushion on her lap.

"Don't try to deny it. I've been your best friend for too long. I know when you like someone."

She sighed. "Okay, so I like him."

"But?"

"I don't know. I guess I just didn't expect to like him."

Autumn had trouble with commitment.

"So are you going to see him again?"

"Don't try to change the subject," she said, cocking an eyebrow. "We're talking about you telling Caleb about the baby you're growing in your womb."

I bit my bottom lip.

"You know, maybe I don't need to tell him," I said.

Autumn looked at me like I was crazy. "You're joking, right?"

"Why do I need to tell him? I don't need some guy to help me with this. I'm quite capable of raising this baby on my own."

"He's not just *some guy*, he's the baby's father. And don't you think he deserves to know?" Seeing the pained look on my face, she gave me an empathetic look. "Look, you of all people know how hard raising a kid by yourself can be."

She wasn't wrong. My childhood had been a disaster thanks to my hair-brained, selfish mother. It was the kind of childhood that made you not want to have children. I saw firsthand how easy it was to crush someone's self-worth and confidence. My childhood was lonely. I grew up in a one-bedroom apartment in Vegas with a mom who was always out cruising the casinos and bars for her next meal ticket.

I spent most nights home alone, and on one of these nights, after watching a Martha Stewart show about cupcakes, I decided to learn how to bake. Mom wasn't home to supervise or to tell me how to do things, and one time my eight-year-old self almost burnt down our tiny kitchen. But thanks to some fast thinking I was able to stop a disaster from unfolding. Although, the stench of burnt cake and wax paper was hard to get rid of. Not that Mom noticed when she got home hours later, reeking of booze and too drunk to care.

By the age of nine, I was an enthusiastic cupcake baker who knew her way around the kitchen. Money was tight. So I would use the walks home from school to wander through parking lots of the casinos looking for spare change so I could buy ingredients for my next baking adventure.

I was also really good at English, so at school I started my own essay writing service, selling five-hundred words for five bucks. Some weeks I made up to twenty-five dollars, which meant I could afford to buy some baking books and experiment with different recipes and ideas.

My mom made my childhood lonely and sad, but her abandonment gave me the love of baking, and as a result, a rewarding career.

And probably the best mothering skills in the world.

Because I wasn't going to be anything like her.

Biker Baby

I took another sip of my tea. "I want to tell him. I do. But I just don't know how to do it."

"Stop having sex with him would be a start."

"I'm serious, Autumn. I don't know how to bring it up."

"So am I." She gave me a stern look. "You need to go over there right now and tell him you're having his baby."

Autumn was right. I needed to tell Caleb. So when she left for her college night class where she was studying business, I tried calling Caleb but there was no answer.

So I took a shower, put on fresh clothes, and tried to steady my nerves with a cup of ginger tea. When I rang his phone a second time again, it went straight to voicemail. He was busy. It was only five o'clock so he was probably out and about, or doing club stuff. I didn't really know anything about him, so it was hard to guess, and it did little to help my nerves. Because now that I'd made up my mind I was telling him today, I wanted to get it over with.

I splayed my fingers across my stomach. So far I only had a slight bump, but it wouldn't be long and I wouldn't be able to pass it off as a food baby or too many egg rolls. My body was changing and I would have to start telling people sooner rather than later.

To hell with it.

I stood up quickly.

I needed to stop by the grocery store anyway, and the clubhouse wasn't that far away from it. I could stop by on my way, tell Caleb he was going to be a father, pick up milk, and still be home before Autumn got home from her night class. I picked up my bag from the kitchen counter, and with a stomach full of butterflies and my head full of all the words I was going to say to Caleb, I left for the clubhouse.

I arrived just at sunset and was walking into the clubhouse when I ran into Maverick.

"Hey, Teetotaler." He flashed his big white smile at me. "Where's that hot patootie girlfriend of yours. She hasn't called me."

"Didn't you just see her this morning?"

Autumn said he didn't leave her place until she'd fed him breakfast and given him a blowjob in the shower.

"That was hours ago. Said she was going to call me. Tell her I'm beginning to feel used." He made a heart-shape with his fingers and held it up to his chest. Then the six-foot-seven biker attempted a sad face as he broke his finger heart like it'd been blown up. I had to admit he did look kind of adorable. Then he grinned, a deliciously perfect smile and squinty eyes as he turned and disappeared out the door.

Shaking my head, I headed for Caleb's room, but as I approached it, a sudden tingle of anxiety washed over me.

What if he wasn't happy to see me?

What if he was annoyed because I'd shown up without any notice?

Why hadn't he answered his phone?

Suddenly hating my decision to show up unannounced, I stood there for a moment, weighing whether it was a good idea to knock or flee. Maybe he was busy. Maybe he already had plans and I was interrupting them.

I turned to leave, but then swung back. Indecision washed over me and prickled at the back of my neck. With a frustrated huff, I turned to walk away again, but in a second of maddening confidence I strode right up to his bedroom door and knocked.

Biker Baby

I heard a murmur behind the door, and then it opened, and Caleb's face appeared in the crack. He looked disheveled, his eyes hooded and heavy, his hair messy like he'd been in bed all afternoon.

"Honey, hey," he said, obviously not expecting me. He didn't open the door any wider, and something about him seemed off.

"Hey," I said, trying to ignore the bad feeling tingling in the base of my stomach. "I hope I'm not interrupting."

He frowned, just slightly, and shook his head. "Is everything alright?"

"Yes. Well, I guess. I don't know actually. I tried ringing. Shit. I'm sorry." I started to ramble. "Can I come in?"

He paused. Closed his eyes and swallowed deeply before opening them again.

Was that a hesitation to let me in?

Wait. Was he … drunk?

"Caleb…?"

When he opened the door wider, the reason for his hesitation sat on his bed.

A very sexy brunette.

A very sexy brunette who appeared to be hugging his pillow to her chest.

Nausea rolled through me.

Fuck.

"I'm so sorry," I said again, feeling like a fucking fool for turning up unannounced. I made eye contact with the woman, and heat flared in my cheeks.

Off course he was with a woman.

Earlier, he hadn't asked to see me tonight and this was the reason why.

I was so naïve.

Caleb was a gorgeous guy. He probably had a girl for every night of the week.

This is a huge mistake.
All of it.

"Should I come back later?" I didn't wait for a response. Because even after I'd said it, I knew I wouldn't be stepping into that clubhouse ever again. "You know, don't worry about it. Call me when you're free."

I needed to get out of there. My cheeks burned with humiliation. My spine tingled with embarrassment. And for some stupid reason, tears pricked at my eyes.

I felt like a giant fool.

I turned to leave, but Caleb's voice stopped me.

"Wait, don't leave," he said, stepping after me. When I turned back to him, he was swaying slightly in the doorway. "I think I know what you're thinking and you're wrong."

I was?

"I am?"

Over his shoulder, I watched the brunette get up off the bed, her long dark hair swirling around her like a dark halo as she walked toward us. She stood next to Caleb and gave me a smile. Her lips were plump, her smile warm.

"Hi there, I'm Chastity." She had the same bright blue eyes as Caleb. And dimples. "Caleb's sister."

His sister.

I breathed a deep sigh of relief.

"Chassy, this is Honey," Caleb explained.

He looked tired. His eyes were heavy. As I watched him soften against the door, I realized I was right. He was drunk.

"I didn't mean to interrupt you," I said, noticing how he was gripping the door handle so he wouldn't sway. "I should've tried calling you again."

Chastity smiled again and shrugged. "I was just leaving. I had to make sure his drunk ass got home, is all."

On her tiptoes, she gave her brother a kiss on the cheek.

"Thanks for the lift to the cemetery," he said to her.

She winked. "Only one more year and I'll be twenty-one. Then I won't be the designated driver anymore and you won't be the only one who can get drunk on this day." She smiled warmly at me. "He's all yours. It was lovely to meet you."

"You, too," I replied.

When she left, Caleb invited me into his room and closed the door behind us.

"Cemetery?" I asked, worried I had encroached on some kind of family time.

I watched Caleb move unsteadily across the room to a tall chest of drawers up against the window. He lifted his t-shirt over his head and discarded it, revealing that same chiseled chest and flexing abs I'd had my hands all over last night. Every female instinct in me lit up like a firecracker. Smooth skin. Muscles. Tattoos. The deep grooves and shadows of a flexing six-pack. He was hard to ignore.

Pulling a clean t-shirt from a drawer in the dresser, he pushed his head through it and pulled it down over his thick torso.

"My father died thirteen years ago today." He threw a flannel shirt over his white t-shirt. "A few of us visit his grave each year."

"I'm sorry," I said, taken by surprise.

"We do some shots while we're there," he explained as he unclipped his wallet chain to his black jeans and threw it on his dresser. "It's kind of a tradition."

"I'm sorry about your dad."

He gave me a fleeting smile. "Don't be." He leaned over as he walked past me to the bathroom and planted a kiss on my forehead. It was an unexpected, warm gesture and happiness lit up inside me.

"What are you doing here?" he asked from the bathroom.

I let out a huff of air. Caleb had just come home from visiting his father's grave at the cemetery. And he was clearly intoxicated. Now wasn't the time to spring this on him.

"I was in the neighborhood," I said lamely. "Thought you might like the company."

Tomorrow. When he was sober I would tell him.

CHAPTER 8

CALEB

I went to the bathroom and splashed water on my face in an attempt to wake myself up. The bourbon I'd drank at the cemetery, and then some more on the ride home, was making me tired. *Depressed.* I had consumed more than I usually did. Probably because this year the cemetery was more crowded than it usually was. Last year, we'd been under attack, the focus of a personal vendetta from one of our own club members. A few of my club brothers were murdered, including my cousin, as well as an old lady, and it had rocked the club to its very core. The man responsible had also kidnapped Indy and she'd suffered at his murderous hands. But she had fought hard enough to keep him from raping and murdering her, before Cade had shown up and put two bullets in him.

Today, it was hard visiting my father's grave knowing my cousin was only a few plots away. He'd left behind a son and a pregnant wife, and the pain of it still lingered in my bones.

I splashed more water on my face.

I was feeling morose.

I closed my eyes against the pain. Unfortunately, it was a pain I was all too familiar with. Growing up in the MC, I'd been surrounded by it my whole life. But I had never shared my grief with anyone. Never spoken about how it felt living with the threat of death tingling in my bones on a daily basis.

I leaned against the sink and dropped my head, feeling the fucking weight of the world on my shoulders.

I felt her move behind me.

Felt the gentle touch of her hand on my shoulder.

Felt the warmth of her presence and the calmness it brought me.

"Are you okay?" Honey asked gently.

No, I wasn't. But I never was on this day.

"It's been a rough day. I'm beat, is all."

She turned me to face her, and the moment I saw those big blue eyes I had a sudden urge to spill my story to her. I don't know why. Probably because I was drunk and sick of this day tearing at my guts every time it rolled around. But instead, I stumbled past her, back into my room, and went straight for the bourbon bottle sitting on my dresser.

"Should I go?" she asked. "I can come back another time."

"No," I said over my shoulder. I didn't want her to go. "Please."

I watched as she sat down on my bed, and then I turned back to the bottle of bourbon and unscrewed the lid.

"So you go every year to visit your dad?" she asked.

"It's MC tradition. We pay our respects every year to every fallen brother or sister." I raised the bottle to my lips. "This year we'll be visiting the cemetery a lot."

I drank back a strong mouthful.

"Why is that? Did something happen?"

I thought about the last year and closed my eyes against the pain. *Yeah. Hell happened.* Opening them again, I carried the bourbon bottle over to the bed and sat down next to her. "It's

Biker Baby

been a rough twelve months. And when I'm sober, remind me to tell you about it."

I looked at her. I mean, I really looked at her. In five minutes, I would be seeing two of her. But for now, the one image of her was beautiful. Big blue eyes. Smooth skin. Full, plump lips I could lose hours to kissing.

Without realizing it, I started to fall toward her. Like I was going to kiss her. I was too drunk to make a move, but according to my body, that wasn't the case. It slowly leaned in, pulled by the lure of those perfect, pink lips.

Seeing me focused on her lips, Honey shifted on the bed and tucked one leg under her.

"Did the whole club go to the cemetery today?" she asked, breaking the spell.

Realizing I was too damn hammered to kiss her anyway, I straightened. "No, it was just immediate family today. My sister, my brother and his wife, my mom and my uncle."

"Maverick said you have another brother?"

"Chance is deployed overseas at the moment." I took another swig from the bottle and felt it coat my lips in sugar. "But even if he was here, he wouldn't come to anything to do with our father. Ever. Chance never forgave him for the things he saw as a kid. They had a rocky relationship."

She nodded slowly, her beautiful blue eyes gentle and empathetic as they absorbed what I was saying without judgment or bias. "What about you, were you close to him?"

I took a moment to think. "He died before he could fuck with me like he did with Cade and Chance."

The weight of my words hung between us.

My father never got to fuck me up like my older brothers. It was the moment of his death that lingered over me, weighing me down.

"Maybe talking about it will help." Honey's voice was gentle.

I frowned. It wasn't like me to open up about this stuff. About my dad and the shit he did to us kids. What he exposed us to. How he manipulated everyone around him for his own benefit. But this girl, this beauty curled up on my bed, she made me feel comfortable. Good. *At home.* Like I could tell her anything.

And I'd had enough bourbon to do exactly that.

"My old man was a mean sonofabitch," I started. "He was the president of the biggest motorcycle club in the South. And it wasn't because he was the son of the original founder, Hutch Calley. It was because he'd taken his title. That's what he did. He took things. Manipulated people. He did what he wanted, when he wanted. And if anyone stood in his way, then he would just mow them down."

I resisted the urge to swig back some more bourbon because I was starting to feel really hammered. And I was probably slurring my words, but fuck it.

"He wasn't a good man. He was a self-absorbed asshole who put himself before anyone else. He did what he wanted. Fucked whom he wanted. Hurt whoever stood in his way." Fuck it. Another mouthful wasn't going to hurt, and it sure beat the dark feelings swirling through me when I recalled what happened on this day thirteen years ago. I tilted the bottle to my lips and drank. Swallowing it down, I savored the burn as it seared the back of my throat and spread through my chest.

And then for reasons my drunk ass couldn't even fathom, I started to tell Honey everything. "I saw him die," I said.

She gasped softly and placed a slender hand across her mouth. "Caleb, I'm so sorry."

I looked away and shook my head, not at her, but at the memory of that night.

"We were coming back from Humphrey," I continued and absentmindedly fingered the St. Christopher medallion around my neck. "As a kid, I had a lot of ear infections, and on that day

Biker Baby

we had traveled to see a specialist about another procedure I needed. On our way home, my dad said he needed to stop at this bar real quick. Said he had to pick up something for chapel at the clubhouse later. Said he'd only be a couple of minutes, so Mom, Chastity, and I sat in the car and waited for him. Chastity was young and impatient and she started complaining, so my mom got her out and took her across the road to the park while we waited. I sat in the car. I was a moody fourteen-year-old. It was getting dark. The stars were out. And I remember looking out the window, up at the stars, when the door to the bar burst open and a man tumbled through it and onto the path outside. My dad appeared in that doorway, looming over him, and it was obvious he had thrown him through those doors. There was a lot of yelling. And I can still see it today, thirteen years later, my dad's big booted foot as it laid into the man on the ground. I remember thinking how mean and vivacious my dad looked. How big and terrifying. He was yelling at the man on the ground. Then there was a bang. And my dad stopped yelling, and the anger on his face turned to surprise. He looked down at his chest and stared stunned at the blood stain spreading across the fabric of his shirt. When he fell to his knees, I hurried out of the car and went to him, calling out to him, reaching for him." My breath left me in a tortured huff, and I ran my hand through my hair before raising the bottle of bourbon to my lips again. I slung back another mouthful, the searing pain in my throat and chest barely registering in my alcohol-soaked brain. "His eyes were glazed. And he had this weirdly resigned look on his face like he always knew that this was how it would end. He fell to his knees and into my arms. I was terrified and I didn't know what to do, what to say. And then he was gone. I looked down at him and I saw his eyes go vacant as he died. He went limp, soft. So heavy in my arms. He was a big man and I couldn't hold him. I had to let him roll onto the concrete because I was fourteen and no match for the weight of a two-hundred-pound, six-foot-five man."

My hearted thundered in my chest. I'd never told anybody that story. Other than the detectives immediately after the murder. And even then I'd kept to the facts.

But in a strange way it felt good sharing the burden of what I had carried around with me every day for thirteen years. Watching my father die and not knowing what to say to him in those last moments of his life. I was the last person he saw. The last person he heard. Felt. Touched. And I'd always felt I'd let him down in those final moments of his life.

Now with bourbon cascading through my veins, I felt the heavy weight of it on my shoulders.

Honey rose up on her knees, moved across the bed closer to me, and placed her cool hand in mine.

"I'm sorry that happened to you," she said gently and her words were like music to my ears.

I turned to her, unable to keep the tears from my eyes. When I struggled to swallow she pulled me into her arms and wrapped them around me, and I settled with my head in her lap, engulfed in the softness of her.

My eyes felt heavy. And Honey's warmth was comforting.

Lying in her arms, I was lulled into peace by the gentle caresses of her fingertips against my skin, so I relaxed into her body and let sleep and peacefulness carry me away.

CHAPTER 9

CALEB

"How on Earth did you manage this?" she asked in disbelief.

Honey and I stood on the front lawn of her apartment, watching two Prospects unload her belongings from a truck parked at the curb.

It'd been two days since I'd seen her at the clubhouse.

"It's what I do. I get things done." I gave her a wink. "Oh, but I left your bed behind. Amy sold it to some douche roommate with greasy hair and rather questionable personal hygiene. I didn't think you'd want it back. You know, all those flaked-off skin cells and . . . DNA."

"DNA?"

"By the looks of him, there would have been a lot of DNA. All over it."

She wrinkled her nose, and damn, it was the cutest thing. "Thank you."

The Prospects and I carried the bulky items inside, while Honey followed behind with the lighter things. Twenty minutes later, it was done. As the Prospects drove away in the *Shadow Choppers'* truck, I handed her a roll of money.

"It's not all there. Your ex-roomie went on a shopping spree. Apparently, she likes shoes."

She looked at the roll of money. "I don't know what to say. Thank you."

"You're welcome."

I loved her smile.

The air crackled with an electrical charge between us, and the urge in me to kiss her was fierce. But I had to get to chapel.

"Listen, I have something I need to talk to you about," she said, her body language suddenly becoming awkward.

"Yeah? I hate doing this, but I have chapel in twenty minutes. It sounds serious, is everything okay?"

"Yeah, of course. I was just . . . I mean . . . I was going to ask if you wanted to do dinner sometime this week." She smiled awkwardly. "I have to warn you though, I suck at cooking but if you're willing to risk it . . ."

I grinned. "I would fucking love to do dinner this week. Is it okay if I call you later to organize something?"

"Sure."

I pressed a quick kiss onto her cheek before slipping on my sunglasses. "I'll call you tonight."

Twenty minutes later, I sat in chapel, listening to our president, Bull, discuss club business, but I was so distracted, I barely heard a word. Despite being surrounded by my brothers, I couldn't keep my focus and found my mind drifting back to Honey. I couldn't explain it. As a rule I didn't do girlfriends. Aside from Brandi, I really hadn't dated at all. And let's face it, Brandi only lasted because she was forward and demanding, and I'm not ashamed to admit, she was a hot babe who liked sex—sex she always wanted with me.

And it worked when it was just that.

Biker Baby

Unfortunately, at some point Brandi decided the hot sex wasn't enough and she wanted more from me. But I wasn't into the idea. Brandi was great in bed, but outside of that we didn't have a lot in common. I shouldn't have let it get as far as it did, but it was hard to think straight when a good-looking woman consistently turned up on your doorstep wearing barely there outfits and fuck-me boots.

I'm a guy. Sometimes my cock takes charge. So shoot me.

But Honey. She was something *different*. Sure, she was beautiful and sexy, and from what I could tell, she liked fucking me. But there was something else about her that had me thinking about her all the time.

Had me wanting to see her.

Had me thinking I was really into her.

Had me thinking I could do more than a *friends with benefits* thing.

But was I ready for something like that?

If you weren't used to it, club life could be hell to live with. Old ladies came and went. The turnover was high because some women got tired of being left alone to raise the kids and take care of the home while her old man took care of club business. Or they got fed up with their man hanging out with their club brothers at a place where there were a lot of women who were only too happy to suck club cock. Sometimes the close-knit family wasn't enough. Sometimes having the support of the other old ladies just wasn't a good enough substitute for their old man. I looked across the table at Davey. His old lady went crazy on him because she was jealous of the club. He was unable to take her wild mood swings and acts of lunacy, so he'd left her. But her craziness peaked and she'd shot up Indy's car in the clubhouse parking lot in a fit of madness.

I'd seen a lot of heartache rip marriages apart.

Although, there were a few *happy ever afters.*

Cade and Indy were happily married with a baby on the way.

And if my cousin hadn't been murdered, he and Cherry would still be happily married and living a good family life with their children.

Same with Mirabella and Jacob. I'd never seen two people more in love. But Mirabella was also murdered by the same man who had killed Isaac, and unable to cope with life without his wife, Jacob had laid his bike down in front of a truck.

Given a chance, their lives would have been rich with love and happiness.

They were proof that love in an MC *was* possible.

My brother's fingers snapped in front of my eyes and broke my daydream. "Dude, what the fuck? You high?"

I gave Cade an up-close look at my middle finger and turned back to face Bull. He'd just asked me a question. "Sorry, man, what did you say?"

Bull took off his glasses and fixed his bright, piercing blue eyes on me. He suffered from acute color blindness and it affected his ability to tolerate light, so he usually wore dark sunglasses, even at night. When he took them off, the vibrant blue of his eyes was almost other worldly. It made him look formidable. That and the fact that he was six foot something and radiated a powerful ruthlessness you didn't want to fuck with.

He was my mother's younger brother and he had taken the reins of our club following my father's murder.

"Everything sorted for Tully's bucks night?" he asked me.

Somehow I was in charge of arranging Tully's bucks night. He was marrying one of the actresses from Head Quarters, the adult entertainment studio we were invested in. The studio produced adult movies, and more recently, capitalized on its reputation with a line of sex toys. The wedding was due to take place on the grounds of the new studio. A few months ago, someone had burned down the original warehouse, but we'd just finished rebuilding it, and it was bigger and better than before.

Thankfully, I had Mrs. Stephens to help me with Tully's bucks night. She was our conservatively dressed, modest personal assistant with the horn-rimmed glasses and knee-length tweed skirts. She arranged and supplied everything for the club, from toilet paper and condom supplies, to strippers, weddings, funerals, and birthday celebrations at the clubhouse. She was methodical. Unassuming. But I would bet my balls she had a gimp stashed in her closet. So far she hadn't batted an eyelid at anything we'd requested for Tully's bucks night, which was only days away.

"It's all sorted." I nodded at our President.

"Any other business to bring to the table?" he asked the room.

"What's the word on the two overdoses in Humphrey last week?" Hawke asked. "My kid sister is a senior in high school, she said one of them was from West Destiny High and was a football player. Said there is talk about a bad batch of E. Think we need to visit the Knights and see what shit they're letting loose into our town?"

"The weed drought in this town has extended across the southern belt," Cade said. "Indy says they've had a lot more drug overdoses lately and they think it's because people can't get their hands on any weed, so they're turning to liquor or blow, while some are dabbling in meth, horse, special K, all kinds of shit. Not to mention the oxy and other prescribed meds."

"People are used to getting a high. If they can't get it one way, they're going to get it another," Bull said.

"Hawke's right, we need to reach out to the Knights and find out what the fuck they're up to," Maverick said.

"Agreed. I'll reach out to Saber. Find out what shit they're letting into our goddamn town." He looked directly at me, Cade, and Maverick. "Make yourselves available this evening. The four of us are going to pay him a visit tonight."

And with that, Bull brought down his gavel and brought an end to chapel.

CHAPTER 10

CALEB

The next day, I saw it on my desk as soon as I walked into my office at Sinister Ink.

It was a bright pink box with a clear window on the lid. Splashed across the cardboard in a quirky font was the name *Honey Bee Cupcakes.*

"Ooh, a present!" Pandora said, walking in and putting a box of latex gloves onto the stainless-steel equipment station in the corner of the room. "Is it from *her?*"

Her being a secret admirer I had somehow acquired over the last couple of months. It had started out innocently enough. At first, she sent me small stuff to the studio—a hip flask of Jack Daniel's, movie tickets, and a limited edition *Easy Rider* movie poster that now hung in my workstation. But lately it had gotten weird. A few days ago, it was a lacy thong attached to a Polaroid of a shaved pussy, legs spread and all.

And the thong had obviously been worn.

I didn't know what to make of it. I'd be lying if I said it wasn't a fine looking pussy. But all the creepiness surrounding the gifts and the stalking meant my dick was asleep in my pants. If she was so interested in me, why didn't she approach me like a normal person? You know, come up to me and speak to me instead of all this crazy shit.

I picked up the box. But these weren't from her, they were from Honey. She had attached a note.

Thanks for being that guy who gets shit done xx

I glanced at Pandora who was staring at me. "No, these are from someone else."

"You got a new girl?" she asked, surprised. Her perfectly made-up eyebrows disappeared behind her straight, blonde bangs.

I couldn't keep the smile from my face at Honey's gesture.

I'd hoped to see her last night, but when Bull organized a sit down with the President of the Knights, I messaged her and told her I would call her today sometime.

"She's a friend," I said, opening the lid of the box.

There were six cupcakes in total, all with different toppings and decorations. I picked one with a heap of chocolate frosting and sank my teeth into it.

"Goddamn!" I mumbled with a mouthful. They were out of this world. I offered one to Pandora, but she waved it away.

"I'm not sure if you've noticed this killer dress I'm wearing, Caleb. But if you take a good look, you'll see there is nowhere for me to hide a fucking cupcake on my hips!"

Pandora had always been a bitch; in a way, it was a necessity to work at the tattoo shop. But since she'd gotten engaged to her boyfriend a few months ago, her moods had been crazy.

"Relax, you'll work it off in time for the wedding." I winked at her, but she scowled at me and folded her arms across her impressive rack.

Before she could reply, the front door to the studio opened and Cade walked in. He looked a little tired. Indy was due to give

Biker Baby

birth soon, and my older brother was so pussy whipped, I imagined he was doing everything he could to satisfy his queen's pregnant whims.

He nodded toward the cupcakes. "Are they from *her*?"

Cade also knew all about my mysterious stalker.

When I shook my head, he picked out a cupcake with a generous marshmallow frosting and took a mouthful.

"Goddamn, that's incredible." He moaned dramatically and then looked at the box. "*Honey Bee Cupcakes*. Man, I'm going to have to take some of these home to Indy. They'll get me brownie points for days."

Ari walked in from his office down the hallway. He nodded toward the bright pink box in my hand. "Are they from *her*?"

When I shook my head he picked out one with pink icing and devoured it, nodding his head in approval. Ari wasn't one for showing too much excitement, so this tiny display of enjoyment said something.

Pandora rolled her eyes at all the moans of appreciation.

"You guys sound like a bunch of teenage boys in a fucking whorehouse," she said, walking off.

My phone buzzed. It was a message from Honey, and I couldn't help but smile.

> **HONEY:** *You like your cupcakes?*
> **ME:** *Hell yeah, lady. Might need to swing by and get some more. Cade wants some for Indy.*
> **HONEY:** *I'm not at work. But I can arrange to have some sent over.*
> **ME:** *Why aren't you at work??*
> **HONEY:** *I just bought a bed :)*

I couldn't help myself.

ME: *I can be there in ten*

My phone buzzed almost straight away.

HONEY: *Make it five*

I didn't need any more encouragement.

"I gotta go," I said grabbing my keys. "I'll be back in a couple of hours." I paused in the doorway and looked back at Cade and Ari. "And you fuckers better keep your hands off my cupcakes."

CHAPTER 11

HONEY

My orgasm was quick. We didn't make it to my brand new bed at all. When Caleb turned up, he was so turned on he took me on the kitchen counter.

Followed by the couch.

Then the recliner chair.

Now he stood in front of me doing up his belt buckle while I sat on the kitchen counter feeling well and truly satisfied.

"What are you doing later?" he asked.

"I have to run a few errands this afternoon. Then I'm going to spend the afternoon reading a book on my new bed."

He stepped between my legs and kissed me. "How about I come and join you when I'm finished."

The kiss deepened.

"I don't think I'll get any reading done if you do."

He grinned and teased me more with his delicious lips. "I promise you, you won't."

His mouth and tongue kissed me into all kinds of crazy, lighting up my body and making me want more.

"How about I cook you that dinner?" I asked.

Tonight I would tell him about the baby.

"Dinner sounds fucking great." He moved away and grabbed his cut off the recliner and his wallet from the coffee table. "I should be done by about six o'clock."

"Okay, then, I guess I will see you sometime after sex," I said. Then realizing what I'd said, quickly added, "Six! I mean I will see you sometime after six!"

Caleb grinned and leaned in to kiss me again. "Sure you did."

I grinned against his lips. "I really did mean six o'clock."

"Six, sex. They both work for me." He winked as he clipped his wallet to the silver chain attached to his jeans, and shoved it into his back pocket. Throwing his cut on, he gave me another delicious grin as he disappeared out the door.

After he left, I showered and dressed. In the bathroom, I noticed the bottle of pregnancy vitamins on the counter. I picked them up and looked at them in the palm of my hands.

Tonight.

I had no idea how he was going to take the news. I'd seen him four times since our one-night stand but the timing had been wrong every time.

But tonight was different. Tonight his world was going to change.

We would sit down and work out how this was going to work. The baby was going to change everything, and it would be better to establish clear lines in the sand before things went any further.

First, the sex would have to stop. Because sex would only complicate an already complicated situation. Sometimes sex wasn't *just* sex. No matter how many times you told yourself that. No matter how many times you dressed it up with labels like *friends with benefits* or *fuck buddies*. Sometimes real feelings crept in unnoticed, hidden behind all those delicious orgasms you were having without commitment, or so you thought. Then suddenly he was off with someone else and you were hurt.

And if I was really honest, I already liked hanging out with Caleb more than I should.

So, the sex was out.

Secondly, I didn't expect anything from him. I was ready to be a single mother. I could do this on my own; but he had a right to know about his kid.

That settled, I visited the market and picked up some ground beef, sun-ripened tomatoes, fresh thyme for homemade meatloaf, as well as a fresh Vienna loaf to make garlic bread. Ironically, I wasn't much of a cook, and meatloaf was about my limit.

I also grabbed some fresh produce for a green salad and a bottle of red wine for Caleb because I had a feeling he was going to need it.

I got home just after five and set about making the meatloaf while fighting off a wave of nausea. These days I was lucky to keep anything down besides peppermint or ginger tea, black coffee, and crackers. And I'd developed a weird craving for chopped up cucumber doused in vinegar. But today my upset stomach was more about nerves than morning sickness.

When the doorbell rang, I drew in a deep breath and then slowly exhaled. I was about to send Caleb's life tumbling on its axis.

But when I opened the door, it wasn't Caleb on the other side. It was Charlie.

Immediately, he started yelling at me. "What the hell, Honey. When were you going to tell me?"

He pushed past me to get into my apartment.

"What?" Was all I could manage to say.

"The baby! When the fuck were you going to tell me about it?" He put his hands on his hips and stared at me, waiting for an answer.

This couldn't be happening. Not now. Not when Caleb was on his way over.

"Who told you?"

"I got a call from the doctor's office this afternoon confirming your sonogram. You had me down as your emergency contact, and when they couldn't get hold of you, they called me." I briefly closed my eyes. Dammit. I'd forgotten to update my details. "But that's besides the point. Is it true?"

I felt sick.

"Well, is it?" He pressed impatiently.

Standing there, watching him lose his temper and his usually cool demeanor, I wondered what I had ever seen in the cheating, impatient loser.

"Yes, it's true," I said.

"Goddammit!" He ran a frustrated hand through his perfect hair. "When the fuck were you going to tell me? Or were you planning to wait until it was born and then hit me up for money?"

I glared at him. "I don't want anything from you."

But he just looked at me like I was ridiculous.

"Of course you do." His eyes narrowed. "Why else would you have it? We're not together anymore. I don't love you."

It was crazy, but even after everything that had happened, his words still stung. Even though I hated him. They were a reminder of just how little I had meant to him over the past two years.

He pulled some money from his billfold and threw it onto the breakfast counter. "There's my half of the abortion."

I stared at him, my mouth agape.

"An abortion?" I said in disbelief.

"I'm not having you and some bastard child fuck things up for Samira and me."

Apparently, his six-foot Amazonian girlfriend had forgiven him.

I glanced at the money and my blood boiled. I stomped over to where he had thrown it down, and scooping it up, I threw it at him. "How dare you come here and try to tell me what to do. Who the fuck do you think you are?"

"You're pregnant and I don't want it."

"Good, because it's not yours!" I yelled at him.

Something drew my attention away from my loser ex-boyfriend. I looked up, and to my horror saw Caleb standing in the doorway.

For a moment, he looked at me, a look of confusion on his face. But when he realized there was a guy standing in my apartment acting like an asshole, he charged in.

"Everything okay, Honey?" he asked, and even though it was me he was talking to, his bright eyes were sharp and firmly fixed on Charlie.

"Who the fuck are you?" Charlie barked.

Caleb glared at him darkly. "I'm the guy who's going to throw you on your ass if you don't back away from her."

Charlie scoffed and turned back to me. "I don't want this baby."

I stood very still. My cheeks burned. I didn't want it to come out this way but I wanted Charlie gone and this was a surefire way to make that happen.

"Like I said, it's not your baby."

But of course Charlie was too arrogant to think it wasn't his baby. He balked. "I don't believe you."

I glared at him. "That's your problem, not mine. But I assure you, Charlie, the baby isn't yours."

A weird look crossed his face. Like he could hardly believe I had been with anyone else. That I hadn't been here pining over him, crushed and heartbroken because we had broken up. But the look was just a flicker and it was gone.

"You expect me to believe you've been with another guy? And you're having his baby?"

"That's exactly what I'm saying, Charlie. Now you need to leave and don't bother coming back."

Charlie stared at me, his brown eyes gleaming with dark irritation.

"Fucking slut," he muttered.

I didn't have a chance to say anything because Caleb grabbed him by the collar and shoved him out the door.

"You heard the lady . . . you need to leave. And if you call her a name one more time, I swear to God . . ."

Charlie ignored him and gave me a murderous look through the doorway. "I should've gotten rid of you years ago."

Before Caleb could do anything more to Charlie, I crossed the room and slammed the front door shut. It shuddered and then stilled, leaving Caleb and me standing there in a weird silence. Outside, a dog started to bark and I heard Charlie skid out of the driveway and roar down the street in his Mercedes.

It was Caleb who broke the silence.

"You're pregnant?"

I closed my eyes and nodded. I couldn't believe this was how he was finding out.

"With him?"

I had my eyes shut but I could tell he was looking at me. I shook my head and heard the hiss of his inhale.

"Is it mine?"

My throat felt like sandpaper, and my heartbeat was loud in my ears. He shouldn't be finding out this way, and it was all my

Biker Baby

fault that he was. If I had just kept my legs closed and stopped having sex with him, this wouldn't be happening.

"I'm so sorry," I whispered. When I opened my eyes, I grimaced at him. "I'm so, so sorry."

His brows pulled together. "Why are you sorry?"

"Because you shouldn't be finding out like this. I tried telling you sooner. But..."

"But?"

"I got distracted by all the sex."

His lips flickered, but then stilled. "Are you sure that you're pregnant?"

I sighed and crossed the room to the couch. I pulled the DO WHAT YOU LOVE EVERY DAY cushion to my chest and hugged it.

"The night I met you I had walked in on my boyfriend getting a blowjob off another woman. Turns out it was his girlfriend of five years and I was the other woman." I picked at the stitching on the cushion, unable to meet his eyes. "I went out that night to . . . I don't know, get over him by getting under someone else, I guess. It sounds crazy when I actually say it out loud, but I was upset. And then I met you . . ."

I exhaled deeply and looked up.

"Two days before I saw you at the clubhouse, I had an ultrasound. I needed to know who was the father. The ultrasound was conclusive. The dates aligned. You're the father, Caleb, not Charlie."

Caleb nodded and sat down across from me. He leaned forward and played with the big silver rings on his fingers absentmindedly.

"So what does this mean for us?" he asked.

"It means we're having a baby. It doesn't have to mean anything else." I felt sick. This wasn't how I wanted this to happen at all. "I don't expect anything from you. It doesn't have to be a big deal."

"You're having my baby, Honey. That's a big deal. "

I shifted forward on the couch and hugged my cushion tighter, aware of my raging pulse in my neck. "We don't need to figure this out now."

"I just found out you're having my baby."

"Exactly. And that's why we shouldn't talk now. You need time to process it. I think you should leave."

He looked surprised. "Leave?"

"You need to process the news. And that isn't going to happen with me standing over your shoulder."

He frowned. "I don't think I should leave. We need to talk about this."

My mind rolled back to when I was ten and my mom found out she was pregnant to some guy who worked the crap tables at one of the casinos on the strip. He said he was happy. Said he wanted to be a family. Talked about living in a house with a lawn and a swing set in the backyard. Two days later, my mom and I came home from doing the grocery shopping to find our TV and the roll of money we stashed in the freezer, gone. We never saw him again. And mom never had the baby.

I exhaled. Sadly, it wasn't the only time my mom found herself in that situation. I didn't have any brothers or sisters. And my mom never failed to remind me that it was because no man wanted an instant family. *The world isn't made up of Mike Brady's, Honey. No man wants to take on another man's responsibility. They don't want you, so they don't want me.*

I didn't know what man was responsible for me. I'm not sure my mom ever knew either. She was fifteen when he got her pregnant and then ran away. What I *did* know were the legion of unsuitable men who followed in his footsteps over the next eighteen years. The mechanic who moved us into his trailer and then kicked us out when Mom came home early from work and caught him in bed with the neighbor. The craps croupier with the lazy eye. The businessman who traveled a lot, but who actually had another family in another state. Then, finally, the one who decided he wanted to visit my room at night when I was twelve.

All of them made promises.

All of them broke them.

If my childhood taught me one thing, it was that rash decisions lead to heartbreak.

"We can't talk now," I said. "Not until you've processed it. If you stay, you'll make promises you can't keep because you've been caught off guard."

His eyebrows came together. "I'm not in a habit of doing that."

I stood up. "Please."

For some stupid reason I felt like crying.

Maybe it was my hormones. Or maybe it was because I was throwing him out of the house, when really, I wanted him to stay and rub my feet and tell me everything was going to be okay.

Or maybe, just maybe, I wanted to cry because no matter how much I wanted to deny it, I really liked him.

CHAPTER 12

CALEB

She's pregnant.

It was the one thought rolling through my mind as I rode through the early evening light. I didn't know where I was going, I just rode. Honey wanted me to process the news and she was right, I needed to work out what it all meant and how the pieces all fit together.

A baby.

It was so damn unexpected, I didn't know what to make of it. I mean, I loved kids. And I always knew I'd have a family of my own one day. But now?

I'd never even had any close calls. I didn't fuck without a condom. Not even with Brandi and she was the only girlfriend I'd ever had.

But now . . .

With the flick of my wrist, I rode farther into the evening. I considered dropping into Joe's, one of the local bars, to see some friendly faces, but decided adding alcohol to the mix wasn't going to make things any clearer. I thought about dropping in on

Cade and Indy, but Indy was only weeks away from giving birth to their first baby and I didn't want to impose. I thought about the clubhouse but I wasn't in the mood for the usual suspects and their antics, so I headed toward Cavalry Hill.

At the top of the old army fort, I parked my bike and lit a cigarette. Below, Destiny glittered with the first lights of the evening.

I thought about Honey. I was really into her. But trying to establish something while she was pregnant wasn't a good idea. There was more at risk now if things didn't work out. What we needed to do was focus on the baby and then see what happened.

A baby.

The idea ignited something in me and it took me a moment to realize I was smiling. Then I started to laugh. *Fuck yeah.* I was going to be a father.

In a few months, I'd be holding my own flesh and blood in my arms.

And I couldn't stop fucking grinning about it.

I drew on my cigarette. Was it a boy? A girl? Would he or she look like me, or Honey?

Fuck. A baby.

I laughed even harder and it echoed across the panoramic view of Destiny below.

I dropped my cigarette and crushed it with my boot.

What the fuck was I doing out here when the gorgeous woman carrying my baby was at home wondering what the hell was happening?

I climbed back on my bike and with a smile on my lips, I rode through the pink twilight back to Honey's apartment. When she opened the door, I lifted her up and twirled her around in my arms. She squealed and laughed, and I started to laugh, too.

When I let her down I took her cheeks between my hands and studied the face of the woman carrying my baby.

"Anything you need. Anything at all, I will give it to you." My thumbs caressed her cheeks. "We're in this together."

"I don't expect—"

I cut her off by kissing her, long and slow, savoring the softness of her mouth against mine.

It was the smell that ended the kiss.

Smoke.

"What's burning?" I asked pulling away.

Honey's eyes rounded. "Oh hell, the meatloaf!"

She ran to the kitchen. Smoke poured out of the oven when she opened the door, and the smoke alarm went crazy. After dumping the smoldering meatloaf onto the kitchen counter, she frantically waved the dishtowel in the air to disperse the smoke and to stop the alarm from screaming.

"Damn!" I said looking at the burnt meatloaf.

Honey shook her head and slumped her shoulders. "I told you I suck at cooking."

I couldn't help but grin. She was too cute. I slung my arm around her neck. "Come on. Let's go get dinner. My treat."

CHAPTER 13

HONEY

He took me to a small, out of the way pizzeria in town with bread sticks on the tables and red-and-white-checkered tablecloths. I wasn't able to keep anything down during the day, so by the time we got there, I was famished. Caleb ordered two large pizzas smothered in mozzarella and I tore into them.

"So what are we going to do?" I asked.

"We're going to work together to give Bump the best start in life as possible."

"Bump?"

He grinned. "Too lame?"

I smiled back at him. "No, I think it's cute you've already come up with a nickname." I rubbed my belly. Bump was hardly a bump yet, but you could definitely tell I was bigger than usual. With a deep exhale I looked up. "I think this *thing* between us has to stop."

"This *thing*? Do you mean the incredible sex we've been having?"

I don't know why I blushed but I did.

"I just don't think now is the time to explore anything between us," I explained, frowning as I focused on breaking apart the piece of pizza on my plate. "If we keep going the way we're going, it will complicate an already complicated situation, don't you agree?"

"Or it could bring us closer," he suggested.

"But what if it doesn't. What if someone's feelings grow while the other person's doesn't? Inevitably someone will get hurt."

"I'm not going to lie to you, I don't want to stop having sex with you. I like the way things are between us."

Lust pooled between my legs at his words.

"But if it turns sour, it could ruin everything. I mean, is now the right time to take that risk?" I shook my head already answering the question in my head. "My childhood was spent with a mother who continually took those risks. Moving from place to place. Hooking up with men who promised her one thing but always delivered something else. Dragging me back and forth, always chasing something but never catching it. She never put me first, and as a result I had a lonely and neglected childhood. I'm not willing to take those risks. I'm putting our baby first because I know what it means if I don't."

Caleb watched me intently, his brow slightly furrowed. "It sounds like you had a rough upbringing."

I frowned. My childhood was a lonely one because my mother indulged in one drama after another. And those dramas always involved men. Men who said one thing and then did another.

"My mom had me three days after her sixteenth birthday. I was born in a house for unwed schoolgirls, if you can believe it." I hated talking about my childhood because the memories still sent a cold ache through me. "They advised my mom to give me up. There were plenty of couples who couldn't have children who would raise me right, they told her. But my mom wasn't going to do anything other than what she wanted to do. So she ran away with me, and so began eighteen years of her reminding me what a mistake she'd made by not listening to them. What she didn't realize was that I felt exactly the same way. Just like her, I wished she'd listened to them." I shook my head and held up three fingers. "My mom taught me three things. How not to be a mother. How not to trust men. And how people say one thing but then do the other. I don't mean to sound like a Debbie downer, but I've seen what happens when parents put their own needs before their kids. I'm not talking about adult kids. I'm talking about the little ones. Their parents are their world. Their everything."

I huffed out a deep breath.

"Let me ask you this, have you ever been in a long-term relationship?" I asked.

He thought for a moment. "Not long term, no. I've never really wanted the commitment."

"And the only relationship I've had was with a loser who made me the *other woman* for two years." I sighed. "This would never work because you don't do commitment and I won't ever let myself be vulnerable again."

He frowned and picked at the label on his beer bottle.

"Okay, then," he finally said, lifting that vibrant blue gaze to me. "We'll reset our relationship. Dial it back and start over."

"You mean as friends?"

"Friends who are having a baby."

"And no sex?"

"Not by choice." He gave me a raised eyebrow. "But yes, no sex. Just friends. Let's start again. Take it from there."

I smiled across at him and when he smiled back I wondered if our baby would have the same captivating dimpled grin. I looked away because that smile was too enticing, and picked at a loose piece of mozzarella on my plate.

When I looked up, he was looking at me. "What?"

His bright blue eyes glittered across the table. "I just realized how very little I know about you."

"Likewise."

"And it seems crazy because now we're going to have a baby."

"What do you want to know? Ask me anything."

He thought for a moment, and I was struck by how handsome he was in the mood lighting of the restaurant.

"Okay, where were you born?" he asked.

"Vegas," I answered. "You?"

"Right here in Destiny. What's your birthdate?"

"July 30."

"You're kidding. I'm July 31."

"So we're two Leo's. See, it would never work between us."

"No?" he asked.

"Passionate and fiery. We'd never get out of the bedroom."

"Sounds pretty perfect to me." He grinned and desire swept through me.

My smile faded. How the hell was I going to keep things platonic when all I wanted to do was climb onto his lap?

"Tell me something about yourself that will surprise me," I said.

"Like?"

"Like . . . I don't know . . . have you ever been to prison?"

He paused and then shifted in the red vinyl booth, his attention dropping to the beer bottle in front of him. "Yes."

A strange tingle took up in the pit of my stomach. By the look on his face, he wasn't joking.

"Really?" I couldn't hide my surprise. The comment had been flippant. I didn't expect him to say yes.

"I got two years for assault and served eight months."

"I'm sorry," I said. "I didn't mean to—"

"Don't be sorry. I own what I did. And I would do it again."

I wanted to ask him why he was sent to prison but didn't want to make the situation any more awkward. Thankfully, he decided to share it with me anyway.

"I was in my second year of college. I was at a party when a douchebag by the name of Jesper Mitchell raped a friend of mine while she was passed out in a bed upstairs. I walked in on him raping her. She was out cold. He told me I'd have to wait my turn. He started swinging at me when I hauled him off her. So I swung back. I swung back until he was unconscious."

"And you did time for that?"

"No, those charges were dropped. It was when I defended myself against the police officer who turned up afterwards. He was Mitchell's uncle. He roughed me up, so I fought back. Unfortunately, the whole thing coincided with a 'more respect for the law' campaign being run by the local government. So the judge threw the book at me, and I got two years for breaking the jaw of a police officer."

"What happened to the man who raped your friend?"

"Nothing." Caleb's jaw ticked. "Not a goddamn thing. The investigation was a mess from the start. I was the only witness and I was a violent criminal, *apparently*. So it became a case of he said, he said. In the end, the judge threw it out of court for lack of evidence."

I shook my head. Sometimes the law didn't make any sense.

When I was in college, a similar thing happened to a classmate of mine at an off-campus party. She woke up to one of the football stars raping her. When she'd made an official complaint, the school and the student body wrapped themselves around the sports hero who was in school on a scholarship. He became the victim and she was ostracized. The police investigation was brutal for her and ended nowhere. She left college four months later and returned home to Iowa. A year later, the football player did it again. When the newest victim reached out to her, they joined forces and together they ensured he got what he deserved. He went to prison and they moved on with their lives.

"I'm so sorry that happened to you," I said quietly.

"Don't be." He smiled, and again I was swept away by how beautiful it was. Caleb Calley was gorgeous. "I put it behind me."

We were quiet for a moment. It wasn't awkward. It was almost as if we were somehow closer. More familiar. Our lives had collided like two atoms and now we were fusing them even closer together.

"Can you believe we made a baby?" I asked.

"It's blown my mind." He shook his head. "Especially when I know I used a lot of protection that night."

"Four condoms, if memory serves."

A smile whispered on his lips. "Man, we're greedy."

I dragged my teeth across my bottom lip wondering if he was concerned about the possibility of sexually transmitted diseases.

"I haven't been with anyone since you," I said. "And Dr. Perry tested for everything when he confirmed my pregnancy. Gave me the all clear. Thankfully. Finding out Charlie had been fucking other people for two years really scared me."

"I recently got checked. You're probably not going to believe me, but I've never had sex without protection."

We used four condoms the night we met. It was believable. But condoms weren't infallible, obviously, or we wouldn't be sitting there having this conversation.

"Not even with drunken encounters?"

"Nope. I grew up in an MC. I overheard things as a kid and decided early on I wasn't going to be getting shots of penicillin because I didn't wrap before I —" He stopped himself from finishing his sentence, realizing how crude it was. He gave me a crooked grin. "You get the picture."

I nodded and smiled, but then it faded when I wondered about how many women he'd slept with.

I looked at my watch. It was late. We'd lost almost three hours in the restaurant already.

"We should go," I said, standing up.

"Before we go, can I ask you something?" he asked.

He rose to his feet and the look he gave me was pure heat.

He leaned in. "Does your no-sex rule start tonight. Or do we have the rest of the evening to make the most of it?"

I knew I had to keep things platonic between us and end these insane sexual encounters, but I couldn't help but be enticed by my desire for him.

A wicked excitement lit up inside of me.

We had tonight, but come tomorrow we were nothing more than friends.

CHAPTER 14

HONEY

We drove back to my apartment as quickly as possible. Sexual tension filled the car with a thrumming pulse, urging us to get home fast. As he drove, Caleb slid his hand over my thigh and I parted my legs wider, welcoming the touch of his hands on my skin. As his fingers pushed beneath the satin of my panties a shiver rippled through me and I bit down on my lip, desperate for him to be inside me.

A groan left him when he felt how wet I was. "Christ, you're so wet just from me touching you."

His eyes were hooded. His lips wet from his tongue sliding across them. And when we stopped at a set of traffic lights he had to use his other hand to adjust the erection tenting the front of his pants.

As we left the lights, his finger slid into me, teasing my clit with tantalizing swirls, my body tightening around him when he pushed into me again.

"If you keep doing that, I'm going to come," I breathed. The tension was building in me with every maddening stroke against my clit, with every push of his fingers into my body. My feet dug into the floor of the car, my hands tightened around the seat. I parted my thighs wider and slowly rocked my hips to meet every torturous touch.

"Come for me, baby," he coaxed hoarsely.

He detonated my orgasm with one final press of his thumb against my clit. My head fell back and my eyes closed, my moans filling the car. Consumed by my climax, my hands gripped the seat so hard my fingers ached.

"You're fucking beautiful," Caleb moaned while expertly guiding the car through the streets toward my apartment. He rubbed the outline of his hard cock again. "I'm hard as fuck and I'm desperate to be inside you."

He pulled up into my parking space and we kissed passionately outside the car, then again on the stairs leading to the second floor. But we were both desperate to get inside, so we ran up the stairs and I hurriedly dug into my handbag for my keys.

Shoving the key into the door, I quickly unlocked it, but as soon as I stepped inside, I came to a stop.

Call it a sixth sense but somehow I knew someone had been in my apartment while we were gone.

I glanced around, looking for anything that might be out of place, but everything looked normal.

Yet...

"What's wrong?" Caleb asked.

"Someone has been in here."

Caleb's body language changed. He stiffened. His eyes darted around the room.

"Is something missing?" he asked, crossing the room to check the windows and opening the bedroom doors to look inside.

I glanced around and felt a shiver creep across my skin.

"No. It doesn't look like it."

Caleb checked the bathroom. When he came back into the room he shook his head. "Everything looks secure. Are you sure someone has been in here?"

Fear tickled my spine and I folded my arms across my chest. It sounded crazy, even when I could see nothing had been moved or taken. I just knew someone had been inside the apartment when we were out.

That's when I saw it.

Or should I say, *didn't* see it.

The meatloaf.

After burning it, I had left it on the counter to cool while we were out. But the meatloaf wasn't there and after looking around the kitchen, I found it in the garbage bin.

"Are you sure you didn't put it in there before we left?" Caleb asked.

Was I?

"I'm sure," I said. But even as the words left my mouth I started to doubt myself. Had I thrown it out and just forgotten? I was preoccupied, so it was a possibility.

Caleb checked the window overlooking the kitchen and it wasn't locked. It lifted up, and a cool breeze blew in from outside. We looked at each other. Someone could've easily gained entry by climbing through it.

But why break in to throw away a burnt meatloaf?

That would have to be the weirdest MO ever.

"Where do you keep your spare change?" he asked. "If it's missing, we'll know someone has been in here. Thieves aren't going to leave any available cash behind."

I kept my change in a pottery dish on the coffee table. The few dimes and nickels were still there, but my necklace, the one Autumn's mom had given me for Christmas a few years ago, was missing. And I distinctly remembered taking it off that afternoon and placing it in the dish.

My necklace is missing," I said. "It's a silver Tree of Life symbol surrounded by a circle of diamonds. I took it off and put it in there this afternoon because it kept snagging on my collar."

After checking my bedroom dresser, my jewelry box, and in the bathroom, there was no doubt it was gone. I looked at Caleb and couldn't hide the worry from my face.

"Someone has definitely been in here," I said, shakily. And they had deliberately thrown the meatloaf in the trash to let me know they had been. "Do you think it was Amy?"

He shook his head. "Not after the scare she got when three men in Kings of Mayhem cuts rode up on bikes and demanded all your stuff back."

"Then if it wasn't her," I couldn't hide my panic. "Who broke into my apartment and why?"

CHAPTER 15

HONEY

I lay frozen in my bed. My body stiff with fear. My limbs so rigid I thought they might snap. I heard the sound of glass breaking, more yelling, and then sobbing. It was my mom. She was crying again. Because he was hurting her over and over. With his words. And then with his fists. I wanted to go to her. To help her. But the last time I stood up to him I'd felt the back of his hand on my face and the cut from the skull ring on his finger. It had sliced into me and given me a cut on my cheek that needed five stitches. Mom had cried and told me she was sorry. But still she invited him back into the house the very next day when he turned up with a bottle of liquor for her and a stupid stuffed toy for me.

Now they were at it again.

I pulled the quilt over my head and pressed my palms over my ears.

When the air was gone and I needed to resurface for fresh air, I pulled the quilt down, and to my horror came face to face with the man who'd tortured my mom and me for the last six months.

Mom's boyfriend.

He was standing over my bed, smoking his cigarette and looking down at me.

"No," I breathed, terrified.

I could see it in his face. The gleam in his eyes. The energy radiating off him. I squeezed my legs together. I knew what he was there for and it terrified me. I was twelve and just waking up to what that look meant in the eyes of boys and men. I was well developed for my age. Mrs. Butler, our neighbor, said I was blooming.

Whatever it was, I hated it. Because it made boys and grown men look at me with that very look in their eyes.

"Go away," I demanded, shaking.

He just sucked on his cigarette and grinned, evilly. I could see the sweat beading on his forehead and dribbling past his temples, and when he smiled, his teeth were yellow. He snickered and flicked his cigarette onto the carpet. When his hands clamped over my mouth, I could smell nicotine and grease. I tried to fight. I screamed. I kicked. I fought with all my might, but it was no use. He was stronger and easily overpowered me. He held me down and stuck his disgusting mouth on mine. I thrashed. I snapped my head from side to side.

I. Fought. Hard.

But it wasn't me who stopped him.

It was my mom with a frying pan from the kitchen.

With an over-the-head whack, she knocked him out cold and he fell in a slump to the floor.

I went to her and threw my arms around her, looking for comfort, looking for reassurance. But she shook her head and pushed me away.

"Having a baby was a mistake," she said. "It ruined everything." And with that, she untangled my arms from her waist. "Come on, you can sleep at Mrs. Butler's tonight."

I sat up with a rush, thankfully in my own bed.
It took me a moment.
It was a dream.
A stupid, silly dream.
Except it wasn't.
My mom's boyfriend really had come into my room when I was twelve and tried forcing himself onto me. And just as I'd dreamed, my mom had knocked him out cold with a frying pan. She locked him in my bedroom and took me to Mrs. Butler's apartment across the hallway and left me there for the night.

I ran a hand through my hair and waited for my breathing to even out.

Having a baby was a mistake.
Those words cut me to the bone.
And the worst thing was, it wasn't the only time she had said them to me.

I exhaled in another attempt to calm my pounding heart, my head dropping to my hands as the pain of my childhood lingered around me. Sometimes in moments of heightened stress, the memories came back to haunt me.

The comforting stroke of tender fingers down my arm pulled me back to reality, and I looked up.

"Hey, are you okay?" Caleb's husky voice was warm in the cold darkness.

Last night after the break-in, I'd been rattled and worked up, anxious about a stranger invading my home. Caleb had comforted me, and tried to put my mind at ease by suggesting the break-in was probably just kids. Then he'd held me until I'd fallen asleep on the bed, wrapped in the security of his big arms.

I looked down at him and ached to feel those strong arms around me again.

"Bad dream." My voice was hoarse. Loaded with sleep and anxiety.

He rolled onto his back, and with a big, muscular arm, guided me down to the heat of his chest. Immediately, comfort wrapped itself around me.

"Want to tell me about it?" he asked.

I thought for a moment. Did I?

No.

What I wanted was him.

For him to chase away the demons lurking in the shadows.

For him to lead me further away from my past.

For him to hold me tight against his warm and powerful body, and to feverishly kiss the anxiety out of me.

I pressed my body against him.

For him to make love to me until the shadows were gone and I could breathe again.

CHAPTER 16

CALEB

I only meant to comfort her. She was shaken. Disturbed by the break-in.

But when my lips brushed against hers, the tenderness of our kiss quickly ignited into a roaring flame and it became less about comfort and everything about the desire tearing through me.

I kissed her hard and she whimpered against my mouth, moaning as she shifted around me in the bed. I could feel her hunger. Feel the pounding of her heart and the desperation in how she held my face to hers as we kissed wildly. The urgency of our earlier touching and teasing was back. But there was something else. Something primal roaring out of her, something she was running from, because she was running to me like she was being chased out of the shadows by a monster. I could feel her desperation, feel her need, her fear.

It made me pause to make sure she was alright. With my hand cupping her face, I pulled back to look at her. "Hey. Are you sure you're okay?"

Her hand slid down my belly and over the hard ridge of my cock.

"I need you," she breathed desperately. Fingers curled around me, gently pumping me, coaxing me, making me want to rip the bed sheets from us and devour her.

But I fought the voracious need in me to take her. Something told me she needed more than that. She needed something to cling onto in the darkness. With a groan I rose up onto my knees and flipped her onto her back. I started from her neck, at that soft area between her jaw and ear, and slowly worked my way down her slender throat. I trailed my tongue along her warm flesh, sliding it between her breasts and licking the skin of her cleavage as I grabbed a full, milky breast in my hand. I captured a tight, pink nipple between my lips and tortured it with my tongue until Honey was writhing beneath me, begging me to fuck her.

I released my hold on her breast as I worked my way farther south, my tongue and lips moving over the slight swell of her belly where my baby was growing, and I paused for a moment to marvel in that thought. That inside this beautiful woman was my baby. A baby I had put in there during moments like this. My cock throbbed and began to drip with pre-cum. It tilted and flinched, begging me to stop fucking around and to plunge deep and hard into her pussy. But I wasn't fucking around. I was savoring every inch of this goddess. I moved even lower, over her slim hips and along her firm thighs. When I reached the most sensitive part of her she gasped and tilted her hips toward my mouth so I could easily slide my tongue between the succulent, velvety skin. She gripped the headboard behind her, moaning my name and crying out with pleasure as the tension tightened and swirled within her. Within seconds, her body quivered against my lips as she started to come. I drove my tongue into her, teasing her pussy, torturing it as I lapped at her clit to draw out her orgasm so it was as sweet as it was long. Her legs shook and her toes curled into the bed as she cried out her climax into the bedroom.

When I knew she was done, I rose up on my knuckles to look down at her lovely face. My cock was pulsing, my balls aching to come. I couldn't help but press against her and was rewarded with a sudden flare of pleasure rolling through me.

"I need you inside me," she breathed.

I couldn't wait a moment longer.

Mindless with need and without thinking, I put on a condom and with one thrust I was inside her. The ecstasy was instant. My mind went blank of everything but pleasure. Making love to Honey and knowing she was pregnant with my baby blew my mind. She felt different. Warmer. Softer. *Like a goddess.* I took my time with her, kissing her deeply and moving into her slowly, restraining myself from losing it and fucking her hard and rough. I made love to her and lost myself in the magic of what we were doing. She writhed beneath me, moaning at what I was doing to her body, clenching me tight and gripping my hips with her thighs. She ran her fingers up my back and gripped my hips, holding me still as she chased her second orgasm. Grinding up against me and rubbing her creamy pussy against me as she bucked, her orgasm claimed her quickly and she climaxed beneath me, arching her back and moaning out my name.

It was too much. Engulfed in the heat of her body, I came hard, kissing her passionately on the mouth as my ecstasy took over and I pumped and pumped into her tight, beautiful body.

Collapsing against her, I rolled onto my back and pulled her to my chest.

"Damn! I'm not going to lie, Honey, I'm going to miss this," I said after catching my breath. And it was true. Sex with Honey gave me a satisfaction I'd never felt before.

Her warm breath tickled my skin when she laughed softly. "Don't worry, I'm going to be as big as a whale soon enough. You'll be pleased we agreed to stop."

My hand slid to her belly. I could hardly believe that my baby was growing there. I didn't care what size she got, she would always be sexy as fuck.

After disposing of the condom, I rolled her onto her back and bent my head to kiss the gentle rise of her belly.

"I don't care how big you get, you're always going to be sexy."

"You say that now, but you wait and see."

I pressed my cheek to her belly. The scent of her skin lulled my orgasm-soaked brain toward a peaceful place where everything was warm and relaxed. I felt her pulse against my cheek, and with the mind-blowing knowledge that my baby was so close to me, I felt myself floating on a hazy wave of contentment. It was a foreign, strange feeling, but definitely a feeling I could get used to.

"Caleb," she said my name with anticipation. And when I looked up from the warmth of her belly I saw the concern shining in her eyes. "Why did the person who broke into my apartment take just my necklace and nothing else?"

Wanting more than anything to remove the anxiety from the beautiful blue of her eyes, I pushed up on my arms and dragged my body along hers until I could look down onto her sweet face. *Christ, she was beautiful.* Her skin was slick from our lovemaking, smooth and shiny in the dim light. Gently wiping her hair from her cheek, I gave her a confident smile.

"They got interrupted, is all," I reassured her. "Thankfully, or else your TV and the rest of your jewelry would probably be gone, too."

"Do you really believe that?"

"I do."

Her eyes glittered up at me, reading me, trying to work out if I was telling the truth or just saying it to put her mind at ease. Then I felt her relax against me, and a small smile tugged at her lips.

"Thank you." She shifted gently beneath me, and her pussy brushed against my cock, sending an unexpected tremor through her. I saw the pleasure shimmer across her face as she dragged her teeth over her bottom lip, and it was all I needed. My cock began to swell again.

"Are you sure you want to stop?" I asked, in one last attempt to prevent the inevitable.

"I think it's best, don't you?"

"I will do whatever you want to do," I said, and then I gave her a heated, wicked look as I slid my hand between us and down to the warm slickness between her thighs. She hissed in a breath and moaned, squeezing her brows together and licking her lips, and my cock roared to life. "But not until tomorrow."

Using two fingers, I found and teased the little nub of nerves that loved to be rubbed and teased.

"You don't play fair," she breathed.

"You want me to stop?" I asked, my fingers swirling through her creaminess and sliding into her.

She gasped and writhed beneath me.

"Hell . . . no!" She moaned.

I smiled. Thank fuck. Because I was so damn hard again, it was enough to make me dizzy. I rolled onto her and put myself between her thighs. The moment she felt my cock pressing against her naked pussy, any reservations she had about having sex went out the window. *Hell, it fucking threw itself out the window.*

"No condom," she breathed in my ear, delirious with desire. "I want to feel you come inside me."

Her words made me see stars. And when she wound her lovely long legs around me, it was more than I could take. I pushed into her, hard and controlled, and *naked*, only to be overwhelmed by the feeling of her velvet, wet pussy swallowing my cock. Mind-blowing sensations stole the air from my lungs, and I had to pause for just a moment to catch my breath and stop myself from coming.

"Oh Christ, that feels . . . fuck, I've never . . ."

I dropped my head and claimed her mouth with a fierce and wild kiss, then spent the next hour driving home my argument for more sex and less talk about keeping it platonic.

CHAPTER 17

HONEY

I woke up to Caleb walking into the room carrying a cup of coffee. Dressed in nothing but his black pants and belt, he looked too damn sexy for words.

"I have news," he said with a delicious grin.

Sitting up, I looked at the clock. "It's not even seven o'clock and there is already news?"

He grinned again. Bright. Sexy. Perfect.

"I'm moving in," he said, handing me the cup of black coffee.

I looked at him over my cup. "I'm sorry, you're what?"

"I'm moving in." He sat on the edge of my bed. "You leave me no choice."

My mind scrambled. "Yes, I do. I leave you with the choice to *not* move in. Feel free to take it."

"I've already made up my mind."

I took another sip of my coffee. It was good. Strong, just how I liked it.

"Why?" I asked.

"Because you need me."

Biker Baby

"I need you?" I didn't mean to sound so disbelieving, but it was hard not to when he was standing there, *looking hot as fuck*, telling me I *needed* him.

"Yes. This apartment looks like it'd be expensive, so there's that. But I just spoke to Mrs. Lawrence from apartment seven, and she said there have been a rash of car thefts around the neighborhood lately. Plus, a few smashed windows. Probably kids looking for money."

"You've spoken to Mrs. Lawrence?"

"I ran into her in the hall. Asked her if she saw anything suspicious last night. She said she didn't, but mentioned the break-ins." He took a sip of his coffee, his big bicep flexing as he raised his cup to his lips. "I want you to be safe."

I rubbed my eyes, feeling a little overwhelmed. With last night's break-in still lingering, and the speed in which this was all happening, I felt a little anxious and out of sorts.

"We're having a baby," he said, soberly.

"But we're not together."

"No..."

"I mean, we just met and..."

Caleb smiled, and it was unfair, because that smile was damn disarming.

"Relax, Honey. This is a good thing. I can help you."

It was funny, but I hadn't stopped to think about how much Caleb would want to be involved in this pregnancy.

But was letting him move in a good way to find out?

If this was going to work, we needed to take a step back.

"I'll move into the spare room," he said.

I just stared at him. I could use help with the rent, but would it complicate things having him under the same roof? No one could deny we had some serious sexual chemistry going on... would living together be too much of a temptation.

"You know this is a recipe for disaster, right?" I said, yet despite my words, I was already warming to the idea.

"Maybe. Who knows? All I care about is making sure you and our baby are safe."

I watched him and sipped my coffee, his words ticking over in my mind.

Finally, I relaxed and smiled. "Okay."

His eyes lit up. "Yes?"

I nodded. "Yes."

He grinned and then did something completely random. He high-fived me.

"We're high-fiving now?" I asked, laughing.

He gave me an amused but wicked look. "It was either that or I rip those bed sheets off of you and give you an orgasm instead."

The muscles between my thighs throbbed and I had to bite back my urge to let him do just that.

"High-fives are good."

He sighed. "Why do I think I'll be high-fiving myself a lot over the next few months?"

He stood up. I watched him over my cup of coffee as he raised his arms above his head with a stretch and it struck me just how larger than life he was. His abdominal muscles flexed and dipped and just the sight of his impressive six-pack made me want to touch him.

If he moved in, would it complicate things?

And more importantly, how the hell would I stop having sex with him?

CHAPTER 18

HONEY

So Caleb moved in. Two Prospects brought his things over from the clubhouse, and by Saturday afternoon he was all moved into my spare room.

Despite my reservations about my new roomie, we fell into an easy, domesticated routine. He was an early riser and would have coffee ready for me by the time I got up for breakfast. He would also make me toast, and then we would argue about me eating it when I insisted I wasn't hungry. Then he would play the "you're pregnant with my baby" card and I would end up eating the damn toast. Eventually I stopped complaining, knowing I would lose the argument and end up eating whatever he put in front of me anyway.

When it came to housekeeping, he was tidy while I was prone to leaving my things where I dropped them. And when I came home after a day at work, our apartment was always straightened.

He was also a good cook. And sometimes, if his schedule allowed, I would come home to a home-cooked dinner.

Spaghetti. Roast chicken. Steak. Mashed potatoes. Which was good because we both knew how much I sucked at cooking.

Other nights, if he was home and not at the clubhouse, we would order in takeout and spend the night on the couch watching movies or we'd take his bike and visit the movie theater over in Humphrey.

And I had to admit, it was nice to come home after a long day at work where I slaved my ass off to make my business a success. I was on my feet all day, baking and making my popular cupcakes, while dealing with unreliable suppliers and sometimes hard-to-please customers—like the one standing in front of me right now, grilling me like a drill sergeant about today's cupcake special, the Marshmallow Madness Muffin.

Was it gluten-free?

Was the marshmallow sugar-free?

Was it an original recipe?

Why was it so dark in color, did I add preservatives to give it that look of decadency?

Um…what?

I smiled pleasantly, patiently, but she had almost exhausted my easy-going nature.

Eyes the color of whisky stared emotionlessly across at me as she waited for my response. Hair, like a silky auburn curtain hung perfectly past the shoulders of her Marc Jacobs silk shirt. She tapped one perfectly manicured fingernail on the glass display cabinet in front of me.

I gave her my biggest, brightest smile.

"I'm sorry, my cupcakes are quite simple. I mean, they look elaborate, but the trick to a really good cupcake is actually simple ingredients."

She looked at me blankly.

"So are they gluten-free or not?" she asked, irritably.

"Not," I replied, good-naturedly. "Nor are they sugar, dairy, egg or nut-free, but they are preservative-free. Guaranteed to mold up within a week!"

Not appreciating my lame attempt at lightheartedness, she looked at me with zero emotion. "You really should offer gluten-free options. And sugar-free."

Again, I smiled sweetly at her. Good customer service was the best marketing plan for any business. Mashing the goddamn marshmallow cupcake into that cold, indignant expression on her face was not.

So I bit back my loss of patience. "Would you like a sample? It might help you make up your mind."

It was already ten minutes past closing time and my feet were aching.

"Are you kidding me?" She raised an eyebrow at me. "Your pregnancy hormones must have gone to your head if you think I'm putting something like that in my mouth."

Whoa.

Pregnancy hormones?

"What did you say?" I frowned. How did this complete stranger know I was pregnant? And what was with the verbal attack? "How do you know I'm—"

"You keep rubbing your stomach," she interrupted, with an irritated eye roll. "And judging by how tight that apron is, you're either pregnant or you've been eating too many of your own cupcakes. If you're not pregnant, you really should go sugar-free."

I stared at her in utter astonishment.

But she didn't miss a beat. She simply pushed on her oversized sunglasses, picked up her Louis Vuitton handbag off the counter, and with an air of distain, took her two-hundred-dollar shoes and snooty attitude with her out the door.

Sailor, my *cowardly* assistant, swept into the room. He was cowardly because he'd been hiding in the back room while this positively painful customer had been verbally dissecting my marshmallow masterpiece. And then, apparently, my weight.

"Wow, that woman was absolute poison," Sailor said, flipping the open sign to closed. "Good riddance, sir."

"Nice of you to join me." I gave him a playful yet annoyed look which he simply waved off.

"Looked like you had that cutie pie all sorted," he said in his thick Louisiana accent. "You're the most diplomatic person I know."

I met Sailor my first night in Destiny. Back then he had been slinging beers at a gay bar on the outskirts of town. Dark hair. Dark eyes. Dark skin. Glossy lips. He was as handsome as he was dramatic, and next to Autumn, one of my best friends in the whole world.

"You've got to feel sorry for someone if they can't even enjoy a cupcake for what it is." I kicked off my shoes. My feet were killing me. "Why has society made things so complicated?"

"Girl, if I knew the answer to that I wouldn't be working in a cupcake store in downtown Destiny, Mississippi. I'd be selling the answer to that on Amazon and charging people five dollars a piece."

In a world that had gone crazy with *free* everything, my business was built on old-style baking delivered in a fresh, creative way. Chocolate cakes with gooey chocolate ganache covered in a sheen of flawless toffee. Classic vanilla with rich butterscotch chunks and sweet peanut brittle. Rich, red velvet sponge with a melt-in-your-mouth buttercream. I didn't do *free*. My business plan was built around enjoying the decadence of a good ol' fucking cupcake.

I knew it wasn't for everybody. But those who liked the idea came in droves.

Biker Baby

I smiled and slid my feet into a pair of slippers I kept behind the counter. I hated driving home in my work shoes, preferring the fluffy comfort of my well-worn Target loafers. "She said something really weird, though."

"Weird? How so?"

"Something about pregnancy hormones going to my head."

"She did? Did you ask her what she meant?"

"Yeah. She mentioned me rubbing my stomach a lot. Oh, and added, *you're either pregnant or you've been eating too many of your cupcakes. If you're not pregnant, you really should go sugar-free.*"

"Uh-hmm, Shorty got herself a mean girl mouth," he said dramatically. But then shrugged. "Crazy out of towner. Don't you worry about her. You look gorgeous."

He gave me a quick kiss on the cheek as he swooped past me to the display cabinet and began packing the leftover cupcakes onto a tray. We baked everything fresh first thing in the morning. Any leftovers were dropped off to the homeless shelter on my way home.

"I'm beat. Are you okay to close up and drop those at the shelter?"

"Of course. You got sexy plans with that hunky baby daddy of yours?"

I gave him a pointed look. "You know we don't do that anymore," I said, hanging my apron on a hook on the wall. "I'm just tired is all. They say you're supposed to lose the fatigue after the first trimester, but I think this baby wants me to stay home with my feet up. I'm exhausted."

"Sure thing, sweetheart." He gave me a wink. "You go."

It was just getting dark when I got home. Caleb wasn't home and it was funny, but even after living with him for such a short time, the place already seemed empty when he wasn't there.

As I placed my handbag on the kitchen counter, my phone buzzed with a message.

Caleb: *Not going to be home til late. Don't wait up.*
Me: *That won't be a problem. I'm beat. Going to soak in the tub and then head to bed.*
Caleb: *Bad day?*

I thought about the moody lady with whisky-colored eyes and auburn hair. Usually people loved my baking, so when I got an unhappy customer it really left me bothered. But tonight I felt even further unsettled. A strange feeling lingered inside of me when I recalled her comment about my pregnancy. She had brushed the comment off with some reasoning about me rubbing my belly, but something still felt a little off. I sighed. Maybe she was right. Maybe my pregnancy hormones *were* affecting me and it was nothing more than an accurate observation. I let it go and flicked Caleb another message.

Me: *All good. Have a good night.*

And he replied straight away.

Caleb: *You too. See you tomorrow.*

We hadn't touched each other since we'd agreed to keep things platonic. But it didn't mean I had lost my lust for him. I was so wildly attracted to him it was crazy, and the way I was in a constant state of arousal for him was pathetic. But I refused to show it. Caleb seemed unfazed by our no-sex agreement. He never pushed. And his easy-going nature was comforting. Some nights when he got home late I wondered if he had been with other girls at the clubhouse. He never mentioned anything and I refused to ask. If this was going to work, it was important that we kept things separate—he had his life and I had mine. We were in this for the baby only.

Yet the thought of him driving that big cock into anyone else made me nauseous. And sometimes I questioned how much I wanted to keep things platonic, or if somewhere along the way I was going to want more.

CHAPTER 19

CALEB

I hadn't lived with a woman since living at home with my mom and sister. I was used to living with men. Beasts of men who drank and smoked, and who worked out in the gym and left their stinking clothes on the floor in their room. I was used to testosterone. Grease. Dirt. And the smell of sweat, spilled liquor, and stale weed.

Living with a female was completely different. They smelled good. Looked good. Everything about them was good. But fuck me, they were messy keeping themselves that way. Honey had a bottle for everything. Hair care. Skin care. Hair removal. Skin removal. Makeup removal. Hair gel. Eye gel. Skin peels. *What the hell was a skin peel?* And they all cluttered the bathroom. Me, I had a toothbrush, a shaving kit, deodorant, hair product, and a comb. I was allocated one drawer. One drawer out of six. Whereas, Honey had an entire drawer for makeup alone.

Not that I was complaining. Living with Honey was a breeze. In fact, living with her was proving to be a lot of fun. We got along well. And the place seemed quiet without her if she wasn't home.

Since moving in I had gone along with her demands for keeping our relationship strictly *as friends,* but damn, if it wasn't for my right hand I'd be suffering the biggest case of blue balls known to man.

She was sexy as fuck. And because we lived together I'd accidentally caught her in various stages of undress a few times. Like last week when I'd walked in on her after a shower. Hell, I didn't know she was in there. I came around the corner and there she was, *butt naked.* Gasping, she'd quickly wrapped the towel around that beautiful body of hers while I'd made some witty comment. I mean, I think I did, to be honest I couldn't really remember because, at the time, all the blood in my brain had gone straight to my cock and all I could think about was making her gasp again.

Then this morning when we'd collided in the kitchen. She'd snuck out of her room wearing nothing but a tiny pair of panties and a tank top, thinking I was still in bed, and raced to the kitchen for a glass of water. But I was leaving the kitchen and we ran smack into each other. Literally. Our bodies collided. And I'm not going to lie. The sight of Honey in those tiny panties and the fleeting touch of her hips against the palm of my hand made me hard. And after an awkward apology, I'd returned to my room, closed the door, and jerked off.

It was going to take time to get used to not being able to touch her. And I was going to get some serious wrist cramps.

I hated the whole *friends* thing, but I wasn't going to pressure her when she had our baby growing in her womb. Stress, I was told, was no good for the fetus. So I made a vow to myself to keep my goddamn hands off her until the baby was born.

Instead, I focused on my work. Things were going well at the studio. My reputation as an artist was growing and I was frequently booked out. I was enjoying it. Some days I got to work on some really interesting pieces where I got to test my ability as an artist, as well as my skill with a tattoo gun. Other days it was standard designs, or something simple like quotes, birthdays, or song lyrics.

Like the one I was working on now. She was my last client for the day. Her name was Lulu and the tattoo I was inking into her skin were lyrics to a Justin Beiber song. I loved doing lyrics, it was interesting to see what songs and words spoke to people enough to have them permanently stained into their flesh. I'd done a lot of them over my ten years as a tattoo artist. But a Bieber song? Not until now. Usually the lyrics came from more classic rock 'n roll or grunge anthems—less pop and more cool. My own lyrical tattoo was down my left arm and quoted a line from Led Zeppelin's "Stairway To Heaven".

Lulu chose to put her Bieber lyrics down her right outer thigh.

After I finished, she stood in front of the mirror, admiring my handiwork. Her legs were long. Her dress short.

"I love it," she gasped breathlessly. "You're a genius."

"Thanks, sweetheart. Happy I could satisfy."

She climbed back on the bed so I could dress it. While I applied antiseptic cream and covered it in wrap, I went through how to look after a new tattoo, not that she needed it. This girl knew the drill. She had a sleeve and a massive dragon down the other thigh.

"All done," I said. "How does it feel?"

Dark brown eyes gleamed up at me. "It feels real good."

I stood up and went to my desk to gather the paperwork for her to hand to Pandora out at reception. But when I turned around, Lulu was off the bed and standing next to my ink station, completely fucking naked.

What the fuck?

"Ah, what are you doing, sweetheart?"

Biker Baby

She pulled her hair over one shoulder. "You don't like what you see?"

She had a banging body. Tanned. Smooth. Hard thighs and perky tits. But it didn't belong in my tattoo area fucking naked. She came toward me, her expression seductive, her lips slightly parted, one eyebrow raised. I raised one right back at her.

"Becky told me what a good lay you are," she said. "Told me all about that big cock of yours."

Becky? Who the fuck was Becky?

"I think there's been some kind of mistake, darlin', I don't know a Becky," I said.

"She came in here a few months ago. Heart tattoo. Just below her belly button." She indicated to the area on her body, drawing my eyes to the thin strip of pubic hair between her legs. I quickly lifted my eyes back to hers. "She said you were sure something."

I thought back to the blonde woman who I now knew was Becky. Fucking her on the tattoo bed had been a mistake. I'd never done anything like that before and I wasn't quite sure why I did it then. Only that life back then seemed out of control. Less anchored. A special kind of hell had hit the Kings of Mayhem in the form of Elias Knight only a few months before, and in the aftermath and carnage of his vendetta I did a lot of stupid shit. I acted out. Made poor decisions. *Like Becky on the tattoo bed.*

I made no excuses for it. I did it. I owned it. I fucked up.

But it wasn't happening again. Not at my place of work.

And definitely not while my baby grew in another woman's body.

"You do remember her, don't you?" Lulu asked, walking back over to the bed and sliding her naked ass across it.

"Of course, I do. Becky. Nice girl."

"She is. She's the nice one. I'm the *bad* one." She raised her eyebrow and opened her legs so I got an eyeful of pussy. A piercing of some kind glittered amongst the slick folds of flesh. I wasn't sure what it was. And I had no intention of finding out.

I walked over to her dress laying in a heap on the floor and picked it up.

"Not today, darlin'." I handed it to her. "It's a real sweet gesture but it ain't happening."

Lulu pouted. But her disappointment didn't stop her from making another attempt at getting what she wanted. She closed her legs and sat up, reaching for me and trailing a finger seductively up the zipper of my jeans. "I promise you, you've not had a pussy as fine as mine."

I stepped back. This wasn't happening. "You need to go."

She glared at me, her face tightening, her eyes sharpening.

Rejection can go two ways.

Clean or dirty.

One, the rejectee can get teary, hurt, apologetic. Or two, they can get angry and decide the only way to overcome the rejection is to rain down some kind of hellfire on their way out the door.

Lulu went with option two.

She shoved on her dress and then stormed out, swiping everything off the top of my ink station and calling me a pussy on her way out.

"Wow, what did you do to piss her off?" Pandora asked, appearing in the doorway five minutes later. I looked up from inspecting the scattered disaster of ink vials on the floor.

"Did she pay?" I asked.

"Hell yeah, she did. You think I'm going to let some crazy-ass bitch leave here without handing over the coin they owe?"

I smiled at her. Good old Pandora. She had a decent set of lady balls. Not a lot intimidated her.

"Good," I said, picking up three ink vials and a tube of antiseptic cream off the floor. Crimson ink spread in a puddle across the floor like a pool of blood. "Would you mind grabbing me the mop and bucket from the closet in the hall?"

"Sure thing."

When she disappeared, I picked up the remaining ink vials and the box of latex gloves laying on its side by the pooled ink.

"So, are you going to tell me what you did to make her so angry?" Pandora asked again, reappearing with a mop and bucket.

No. I wasn't.

"Here, let me do that," I said, avoiding her question as I took the mop from her. I looked at her outfit. She wore tight black jeans, grey knee-high boots, and a tighter-than-tight black t-shirt screaming *Baby Doll* across the front. "You look like you're extra dressed up. I don't want you to get ink all over your clothes. Is it date night?"

She grinned. "Roger is taking me to see a band over in Humphrey. He's on his way over to pick me up."

"Go. I'll clean this mess up."

"Are you sure?"

I nodded. "Go enjoy your night."

"Thanks!" She started to walk out but stopped and turned around, a mischievous grin spreading across her perfectly shaped red lips. "You know, we should have a code word for the next time a client hits on you."

She glanced at the CCTV cameras in the corner of the room and then grinned. "Have a good night."

CHAPTER 20

CALEB

The flowers turned up two days later. A dozen black roses with all of their heads chopped off and scattered around the thorny stems. They arrived at the studio in a long, gold box with a card attached that simply read *Caleb.*

The message was a dark one. Whoever was sending me these gifts was pissed.

At first I thought it was Lulu. Was this her idea of payback for turning her down?

But one look at the card and I knew the writing was the same as the card attached to the box containing the lacy thong and Polaroid.

Without knowing how, I'd pissed off my admirer.

"Wow, *she's* angry," Pandora said, walking into my office and perching herself on the end of my desk.

"Who's pissed off?" Cade asked, walking in after her.

"*Her*," Pandora replied. "His secret admirer."

"Stalker more like it," Cade said, looking at the box of severed rose heads.

"Who dropped the box off?" I asked Pandora.

"It was waiting by the front door when I opened up this morning."

"You want to take this to chapel?" Cade asked.

I cocked an eyebrow at him. "You're kidding, right? And get laughed out of the club because of a box of severed flowers? No, thanks. It's just some crazy Jane who will eventually own up or stop."

"Either that or she'll put your head in a box," Cade said with a frown.

"Well, I think it's sweet. I mean, not the dead flowers, but everything else has been nice." Pandora looked at the *Easy Rider* movie poster behind me. "Maybe the flowers are from someone else. Lulu, maybe?"

"I thought of that, but I doubt it. Lulu doesn't come across as being that committed to a cause."

"I don't know, she seemed pretty pissed off when she stormed out the other day."

Cade looked at me. "What did you do to Lulu?"

"He did nothing to her. That's the problem." Pandora pushed off the desk. "Anyway, I came in to tell you your last appointment has canceled."

My last appointment was a three-hour appointment to finish off a sleeve. The client was a regular called Kitty Kat who was a hostess over at the Red Room, a fetish bar in Humphrey. She was no stranger to a tattoo gun and I'd done so many of her tattoos she was like a walking portfolio of my work.

"Damn, did she reschedule?"

"Of course. But not for a couple of weeks. She's come down with mono."

"Okay. Send her some flowers with a note to get well." I was big on looking after my clients no matter how cheesy I had to be. "But not *flowery* flowers."

Pandora cocked an eyebrow at me. "Right. Flowers that don't look like flowers. That should be easy."

"You know what I mean. Something weird. Go with something *you* would like."

"What *I* would like?"

"Yeah, something, I don't know, *strange*."

Her red lips gaped at my use of the word strange.

"You know what I mean. Unusual. Interesting. She's a dominatrix, for heaven sakes."

Cade held up the box of decapitated black roses and shook it.

"Not my style," Pandora said, unimpressed.

I took the box off my brother and threw it in the dumpster in the alley behind the studio. When I came back inside, Pandora had returned to the front counter but Cade was still in my office, leaning against the tattoo bed, his legs crossed at the ankles.

"The new girl you're seeing, do you think she's involved with these gifts?" he asked.

"Who says I'm seeing anyone?"

"You suddenly move in with a girl none of us know anything about and you seriously want me to believe she is your roommate and nothing else?"

I shrugged it off. "I couldn't live at the clubhouse forever."

He gave me a *don't bullshit me* look. "Try again, little brother. That doesn't make sense. There has to be another reason—"

"She's pregnant," I interrupted him.

I didn't see the point of lying to him. He would find out soon enough.

Plus, I wanted to get home to Honey. She was home because she'd had a couple of big days at the store and was exhausted. Now that Kitty Kat had cancelled, my afternoon was free and I figured maybe we could spend some time together.

I looked up to see Cade's jaw drop. Slowly his brows rose and he let out a deep breath. "And it's definitely yours?"

Biker Baby

I explained the situation to him. The one night in the motel. Her roommate stealing all of her stuff. Honey's determination to keep things uncomplicated by not being romantically involved. I told him about the break-in and my priority in keeping Honey safe, and he listened quietly, then slowly nodded in agreement, because put in a similar situation, my brother would do exactly the same.

"Have you told Honey about the gifts?" he asked.

"Are you kidding me? She'd freak out."

"She deserves to know."

"Maybe if she wasn't pregnant." I opened my scheduling book on my desk and checked my appointments for the next day. I had a late start. "I don't want to stress her out unnecessarily."

"Fair enough. But if the gifts get any more sinister, you'll need to come clean."

"The gifts aren't going to get anymore sinister," I said, snapping my appointment book shut. "Look, we're not telling anyone about the baby until after Tully's wedding next week. Honey wants to meet the family first, so try and keep this to yourself before then."

An amused smirk spread across my brother's face and a roguish gleam took up in his eyes. Trying not to chuckle, he patted me on the back. "Just make sure I'm there when you tell Mom. I wouldn't miss that for the fucking world."

He started laughing as he walked away.

"Asshole," I muttered.

Twenty minutes later I finished up in the studio and headed for home.

CHAPTER 21

HONEY

I stood under the spray of warm water and let the gentle needles of warmth crash against my skin and spread their calm over my body. Slowly my muscles began to relax. The last few days had been tiresome. It felt like I was on my feet and at the bakery all the time. The store was doing well, and Sailor and I seemed to always be rushed off our feet, which was awesome for the business account, but hell on my body.

Knowing I was exhausted, Sailor insisted I take a day off. And I'd known Sailor long enough to know he'd just nag at me until I did.

Now I had a day of nothingness stretching out before me. Nothing to do but put my feet up and forget about cupcakes and customers, and running around trying to make everything work and ensure all the pieces to fit.

I sighed and lost myself in the relaxation as the water pounded over my shoulders, the steam seductively drawing me into a euphoric trance.

Despite my exhaustion, my body ached with longing.

Biker Baby

Weeks of no sex was playing havoc with my body, and it was tight with need. I let my hand slide between my legs and felt the flare of pleasure as my fingers brushed over my achy clit. I exhaled deeply and moaned as another surge rolled through me. My fingers were a poor substitute for Caleb, but they would have to do because I needed an orgasm, and as soon as I pressed against my clit, I knew it wasn't going to take long. I bit down on my bottom lip and closed my eyes, letting my mind wander free. Letting it imagine whatever it wanted. With whomever it wanted.

And apparently that was Caleb.

Caleb touching me.

Caleb claiming my mouth with his mouth.

Caleb touching my body with his body.

I pictured him in the bathroom with me. His glorious body naked amongst the steam. His face dark with heated promise, his eyes molten with desire. Beneath his touch my body creamed. Desire roared through me. My body trembled and I started to come. I fell against the wet-tiled wall and cried out, my orgasm slowly sending me to the floor of the shower in a weakened, quivering mess.

I took a moment for my heartbeat to calm and my breathing to even out. And then I started to laugh. Loud. I felt relieved. The tight, antsy need was gone, and in its place were softened, loosened limbs and a mind lost in a post-orgasmic haze.

Feeling deliciously content, I peeled myself off the floor and got myself dried and dressed, ready to make some dinner and settle in front of the TV for the rest of the afternoon.

To my surprise, Caleb was in the kitchen when I came out of the bathroom. I was surprised because I hadn't heard him come in. Standing at the kitchen sink, he was shirtless and in nothing but a pair of jeans sitting low on his hips. He was drinking coffee, his broad back to me, his big muscles pulling and tensing with every movement.

Even after the delicious orgasm I'd just had, my clit throbbed and my muscles ached to be fucked.

I stopped walking and my cheeks reddened, the thought just occurring to me. Had he heard me moan in the shower? The walls were paper-thin in our apartment, I knew this because Caleb didn't realize I could hear his moans when he jerked off in the shower in the mornings. And I had been quite vocal mid-orgasm.

"Hey," I said, leaning a hip against the counter.

He turned around and his hard chest and ridiculous six-pack gleamed in the late afternoon light.

"Hey, yourself." He smiled. "Coffee?"

I pulled a face. "No, thanks. If I have even a drop it'll make me vomit." I rubbed my belly. Last week I couldn't get enough black coffee. This week, not so much. "Your baby is fussy."

At the mention of his baby, his grin got even bigger but he didn't say anything. He just stood there looking hot as fuck.

And I was no match for that damn smile.

My pussy throbbed, my clit ached.

Self-gratification and fingers be fucked. I needed cock.

With one thing on my mind, I went to him and mashed my mouth to his, completely taking him by surprise. He moaned, and for a moment he hesitated, but as my tongue swept into his mouth and my hard nipples pressed against the thick muscle of his naked chest, he dropped the cup into the sink and wrapped his powerful arms around me. He kissed me hard. Groaning into my mouth. Making me wet. Making me dizzy. I didn't know what was wrong with me. It was like my hormones had flipped some kind of concubine switch inside of me. I wanted sex. And I wanted it all the time. With him.

Thankfully, Caleb wanted it, too, judging by the hardness pressing into my shorts as he carried me to his bedroom. When he set me down on the bed, I wasted no time unbuckling his belt and getting him out of his black pants.

I wasn't supposed to want this. We'd agreed to keep things nonphysical and stop having sex, yadda fucking yadda, but I was powerless against the force of him.

"This isn't us keeping it platonic," he said against my lips.

"I don't want to think about it," I replied, lost in the sensation of his skin against my skin and the desperate throb between my thighs. It'd been weeks since he'd touched me, and even though I knew it was wrong, my body was desperate for the relief only he could give me.

Just one more time.

"We suck at this no-sex thing," he said, caging me in his big arms as he looked down at me.

I pulled him back down to me. Mindless. Primal. Powerless.

"Less talking, more fucking," I said, gripping his ass as I pushed his giant cock into me.

The light snapped on, illuminating the room and waking me up.

I opened my eyes. "Mom?"

"Yes, my sweet-faced girl. It's your momma," my mom sang as she swept into the room.

I sat up, confused. It was the middle of the night.

"Is everything okay?" I asked, rubbing my sleepy eyes.

"Things are more than okay, my darling girl." She went to the small wardrobe up against the wall and pulled down an old suitcase. "In fact, things couldn't be any better!"

"What are you doing?" I asked.

She smiled happily and dropped the suitcase. Crossing the room, she sat on the edge of the bed and drew me close to her.

"How would you like to live in a house, Honey? With two bathrooms and your very own room?"

She was beaming.

"My own room?"

"Yep. And a pool in the backyard."

My eyes widened. That sounded like a dream.

"But how?" I asked.

Her smile grew even bigger. In this light, her gold jewelry gleamed but it was nothing like the gleam in her smile.

"Oh, my darling, his name is Henry and I am in love with him. So very much in love with him. And he loves me." She wiped my fringe out of my eyes. "And he will love you, too."

"Who is Henry?"

Mom hadn't mentioned him before now.

"He is a lovely man Mommy met at one of the places she visits, you know that. I've mentioned him before."

She hadn't. But I nodded anyway. Because I liked when Mom was in one of her good moods and I didn't want to upset her.

"He wants to marry me. And we are going to live in his big, beautiful house. I've been there before. Oh, you should see it, Honey. It's so wonderful. Like one of those houses you see in the magazines. It's white with little blue shutters on the windows, and rooms the size of our entire apartment." Mom was excited, I could tell, because her eyes were wide and bright. "He's coming to pick us up in his car tonight, Honey. So we need to pack all of our things, okay."

She pulled me into her arms and squeezed me against her until I could barely breathe.

I loved my mom when she was like this. Happy. Fun-loving. Affectionate.

But it never lasted.

I climbed out of bed and packed up all of my things out of the wardrobe I shared with my mom. It didn't take very long because I didn't own very much. In fact, it all fit into the one little suitcase. But it was fun, because Mom was singing as she packed up her belongings, and she would talk about all the things we had to look forward to. A new home. Garden parties. A real family.

Once we were packed up, we sat at the little table where we ate our meals. But the minutes ticked by slowly and I grew tired waiting for him to show up, and my body started to ache for sleep. Not that I showed my mom. Because she was already beginning to look sad with every minute that passed.

In the end, Henry never turned up that night.

Or the next day.

In fact, he never showed up ever again.

A few days later I came home from to find my mom sitting at the small table again, smoking her cigarettes and crying. She held a glass of liquor in her hand and ice tinkled every time she raised it to her painted red lips. She was dressed in her tight red dress and her gleaming red high heels with her hair swept up off her face. But as I got closer I could see her mascara had run down her face and her fake eyelashes were coming off one eye.

She was slurring.

I joined her and dumped my school bag on the table, awkwardly climbing onto the chair because I was only seven years old and sometimes I still had difficulty moving heavy things like the chair. Mom sniffed and took another sip of her drink, then sucked back more of her cigarette. Beside the ashtray was a pamphlet for a clinic somewhere in town. Family Planning, it said. I didn't know what it was for or why my mom would need it, but I didn't ask.

"Never trust a man, Honey," she said bitterly. "They always say one thing but then do another. They'll tell you what they think you

want to hear. They don't want to be assholes so they'll say one thing knowing full well they're not going to follow through. It's about saving face, you see. When confronted with a situation, they want to be the good guy. The hero. But then reality sinks in and they forget all of that the first chance they get."

She stubbed out her cigarette in the ashtray and drained her glass. Then rising unsteadily to her feet, she wobbled across the small apartment and disappeared into the bathroom, slamming the door behind her.

My eyes snapped open, startled awake by the slamming of the door in my dream.

Never trust a man, Honey.

They always say one thing but then do another.

I sat up

My mom resented having me.

On her thirty-fourth birthday, she let me go. Sent me out into the world and told me it was time to fend for myself.

And I had been doing that ever since.

I never saw my mom.

She was somewhere in Vegas. Smoking her hand-rolled cigarettes and visiting another bottle of bourbon, no doubt, while dressing up in her shortest outfit and visiting the local casinos and bars always on the hunt for another date and another drink. From the moment I was born she resented me and never missed a chance to remind me how I'd ruined her life.

When I met Autumn, life took an upward turn. Her family became my family and I was given a sense of what *family* meant. Holidays. Vacations. Christmases spent making snowmen in freshly fallen snow and drinking eggnog by a roaring fire. Support. Love. Laughter. Her mom became the mom I never had, and ten years later we were still close. She was the reason I was well-adjusted and remained relatively unscathed by my childhood.

Biker Baby

I sighed, my heart heavy. As much as I tried not to think about growing up with my mom, the pain lingered.

I glanced at Caleb lying next to me. He was sound asleep, the sheet wrapped around his hips and his glorious torso exposed.

He will resent you.

I heard my mom's voice as plain as if she was in the room with me.

You're forcing him to be with you.

I pulled back the sheets and climbed out of bed.

Having a baby was a mistake. It ruined everything.

And I walked out of his room and into mine.

If this was going to work, I had to keep Caleb at arm's length and not confuse the situation with emotions. We weren't together. We were two people who happened to be having a baby together.

Nothing more.

And I was best to remember that.

CHAPTER 22

HONEY

I placed the piece of paper down on the table in front of him.

"What is this?" Caleb asked, his coffee cup paused halfway to his mouth.

"It's a contract," I said. "A fully non-negotiable, fully binding contract."

"A contract for what?"

"Read it."

He picked it up and began to read. "I, Honey Bee Scott, hereby agree that I will not have anymore sex or heavy make-out sessions with one Caleb Randy Calley." He looked at me over the paper. "You really wrote and signed this?"

I nodded. "Keep reading."

"I, Caleb Randy Calley, hereby agree to not have anymore sex or heavy make-out sessions with the above, Honey Bee Scott." He shook his head. "I'm not signing this."

"You have to!"

"Why?"

"So we stop having sex!"

He cocked an eyebrow at me. "That's the worst argument ever. I love sex. And I love having sex with you."

"We have to stop or we are going to seriously fuck things up." I folded my arms across my chest and leaned against the counter. "And clearly I can't be trusted to control myself. These hormones are making me crazy. Crazy for sex. I need help."

It was a ridiculous concept. The contract. But I was desperate. I needed someone to help me keep my hands off my ridiculously fuckable roommate.

He stood up and took a step toward me. He wore his usual pair of belted black pants sitting low on his hips. Heat radiated off his naked chest and a pulse took up between my thighs as he stepped between my knees.

"It hasn't complicated things so far," he said.

My arms fell to my side. "Caleb . . ."

I went to protest, but without a word he cupped my face in his big hands and pressed his lips to mine. I refused to kiss him back, no matter how much I wanted to, and kept my lips glued shut.

"Kiss me . . ." he whispered against my lips.

I opened my mouth to argue, but his tongue swept in and his lips took command. And because I have absolutely zero self-discipline whatsoever, I melted against him, my body begging for more. I was so damn turned on it was ridiculous. He hoisted me up onto the counter and pressed himself against me.

"We shouldn't," I moaned against his mouth, while at the same time fumbling with the buckle of his belt.

"Yes, we should," he breathed, his hands holding my face to his. "I haven't signed your damn contract yet."

He swooped me up in his arms, kissing me fiercely as he walked us out of the kitchen, through the living room and to his bedroom. At the doorway I wriggled to my feet and took a step away from him. I put my hand on his broad chest to keep some space between us, and shook my head.

"I mean it, Caleb," I said breathlessly while looking at him pleadingly. "We have to think seriously about what we're doing."

"I am thinking very seriously about what I'm doing." He raised an eyebrow. "And what I am about to do."

His black pants were tented at the front, his desire on full display, and my insides throbbed with need.

"Please," I begged. I could barely breathe with want.

He scrubbed his hands down his face. "Fine."

"Really?"

He stepped back to me and put his hands on my shoulders. "We'll do it your way. For now."

CALEB

I was hard as fuck and Honey was standing there in a tiny pair of shorts and a barely there top, telling me we couldn't take this any farther. Jesus Christ, talk about blue balls. I sighed. Even after a full night of lovemaking the night before, my body still ached for her. I didn't know what it was about Honey but it was fucking hard work keeping my hands off her.

But she was insisting we remain friends, not lovers, and I sure as fuck wasn't going to press her about it. If she wanted to keep things platonic, then I was going to respect her wishes.

For now.

But once our baby was born, I was going to be merciless in my pursuit of her.

Frustrated, I took a shower. I stood under the water feeling hot and prickly, and had to take care of my raging hard-on myself. With one hand pressed against the shower tiles and the other wrapped around my cock, I began to stroke. It didn't take long, and my knees went soft and my climax hit me like a truck. I groaned and it reverberated around the bathroom as thick ropes of cum shot out of my cock and onto my fisted hand.

It was never as good as the real thing, though, but something told me I'd be doing a lot of this until Honey got over this platonic bullshit.

CHAPTER 23

CALEB

On a Saturday about five weeks after I moved into Honey's apartment, Tully married Heidi, one of the actresses from Head Quarters.

Now, when you belong to an MC, getting married is a big fucking deal.

We might be bikers and we might be rough. Hell, we might be so far from what you might think is suitable in society. But whatever you thought of us, the Kings of Mayhem knew how to throw a fucking party.

And Tully and Heidi's wedding gave us the chance to throw a huge one!

Tully, our Coke-bottle glasses wearing club member, was in a seventies' tuxedo, a powder-blue polyester get-up with wide lapels, a ruffled shirt with frills, and a black tie. While his wife-to-be towered over him in a barely there, tight white dress, her hem high and her long legs traveling on forever. Diamonds glittered in a garter wrapped around a smooth, exposed thigh.

Biker Baby

And she carried a bouquet of black roses Mrs. Stephens had ordered in from New Orleans.

Cade and I stood beside them in our black suits, white shirts without ties, and suspenders. While Heidi's two bridesmaids wore what Honey would call romper suits. They were made out of some black, flimsy fabric, were short, and showed a hell of a lot of boob.

Officiating the ceremony was Father Murphy, the kindly priest who had married and buried members from the Kings of Mayhem for as far back as I could remember. He was a cool dude. Not judgy or ready to rain down fire and brimstone at our morally corrupt ways. He took everything in with quiet acceptance. He knew what we were. What we did. And there was no judgment. Although I often saw him do the sign of the cross whenever something rattled his moral compass. And let's face it, today he was marrying an adult entertainment actress to a biker in a room full of MC family and friends, as well as people from the porn industry. There was going to be a lot of cross signing.

Watching Heidi and Tully exchange their vows, I looked out over the sea of faces watching the ceremony and scanned them for Honey. She was sitting next to Maverick toward the back of the room. He had asked Autumn to be his plus-one, but so far she had avoided his pleas for another date. I looked at Honey sitting there in her breezy yellow dress and couldn't help but smile. I don't know why. Just that whenever I saw her, it made me feel good.

She smiled back and I gave her a wink. It felt good bringing her. She was in her second trimester and her belly was swelling more and more everyday. We'd agreed to wait until after the wedding to tell my family about the pregnancy. Honey wanted to meet them at least once before we told them. And I wanted to play it anyway she felt comfortable with. So the wedding was a good opportunity to introduce her to my family, to my world.

We hadn't touched since the afternoon she'd pounced on me in the kitchen. I had waited for, hoped for, more *pouncing,* but since she'd created those ridiculous rules, I had to settle for getting up close and personal with only Mrs. Palmer and her five daughters.

Which was slowly driving me crazy with need.

When Father Murphy pronounced Tully and Heidi husband and wife, the public display of affection that followed was all tongues and shameless chemistry. Father Murphy looked a little squeamish, but everyone else in the room cheered and whistled, some bikers taking their own old ladies in their arms and kissing them senseless, too.

The ceremony was followed by a reception in one of Head Quarters' large studios used for shooting some of the bigger scenes where more space was required. It was a huge room that opened up to a veranda overlooking the river cutting through the property.

Waiters roamed through the throng of wedding guests carrying trays of food and glasses of champagne. Beer bottles were opened, Patrón was shot and bourbon was swilled. From a state-of-the-art sound system, music filled the room and drifted out over the veranda.

The party had begun.

I found Honey filling a paper plate with food from a passing waiter.

"Sorry, I got caught up with the bride and groom." I ran a gentle hand down her slender arm. "Are you okay?"

Her eyes sparkled with happiness. "Yes, so far I've met Indy and Cade, a guy called Hawke—who might or might not have a crush on me now that he knows I bake cupcakes for a living—oh, and a guy called Matlock who has the filthiest mouth I've ever heard!"

She was right. Matlock couldn't talk without cussing.

"Oh, and your uncle, Bull. He came over and introduced himself." She bit into a piece of southern fried chicken. "He has very nice eyes."

Bull had freaky-as-fuck eyes. But for some reason, all the chicks dug them.

"You want to meet my mom?"

"You know, every single person I've met today has asked me if I've met your mom, yet and when I tell them no, they laugh. I get the feeling you're not telling me something. Is she that scary?"

I couldn't help but grin. "Yeah. She's *that* scary."

Honey rolled her eyes. "I'm sure she's lovely."

"You ready?"

"With sauce all over my face and teeth. Hell yes, I'm ready." She winked and grinned. She did in fact have sauce on her lips, and when I reached up and wiped it from the corner of her mouth, her eyes danced across at me. She put her plate down on a nearby table and used a napkin to wipe her mouth. "How do I look?"

She showed me her teeth. They were spotless. And she was perfect.

"Beautiful," I said.

"You're just saying that to butter me up before I meet your scary mom."

It was my mouth that opened to reply. But it was my mother's voice that interrupted. "Oh, I don't know if I'm that scary, am I?"

Honey and I both jerked our heads to find my mom standing two feet away from us. With a head of raven back curls and deeply hooded eyes that could reduce any man or woman to a smoldering, combusted mess at her feet, my mom was as intimidating as she was beautiful.

Honey looked horrified, but I had to stifle back a laugh.

"Oh my God—" Honey breathed desperately.

Mom came closer, her biker chick walk in check. Her eyes glittered up and down Honey, her expression pure poker faced.

"Relax, if my reputation hadn't preceded me then I would worry I was losing my touch." She offered Honey her hand. "I'm Ronnie, Caleb's scary mother."

Honey took it and shook it rigorously. "I'm Honey, Caleb's disgraceful plus one."

The two women smiled at one another and something about the moment resonated through me. And it took me a while to understand what I was feeling. But then it hit me with absolute clarity. Honey *belonged* here. With us. With *me*.

My mom turned her attention to me.

"I'm going to steal your date away. Tully needs you over at the bar for some best man duties or something. I'm thinking it's probably shots. Although, considering the bar is currently holding him up, I'm not sure if that's such a good idea." She smiled but I knew she was up to something. "So while you take care of your groom, I'm going to take *your date* over to meet a few of the ladies. Don't worry, she'll be safe. I promise I will be on my best behavior."

She said the words sweetly. But my mom didn't do sweet, so she was lying. Mom was taking this opportunity to find out what she could about my *date*.

I gave her a raised eyebrow, but Honey brushed a reassuring hand across mine as she passed by. "I'm sure I'll be fine."

Watching my mom lead Honey away, I couldn't help but smile. Something very real was happening inside of me. Something I'd never felt. Never known.

"She's beautiful," Cade said, joining me.

I couldn't drag my eyes off her. "Yes, she is."

"You know Mom's going to know everything there is to know about her in the next five minutes."

"Yep."

Biker Baby

"And if she finds out you've been keeping her a secret, there'll be hell to pay."

"Yep."

My brother chuckled and tapped me on the arm, finally dragging my attention away from Honey. "Come on, Tully wants us at the bar. He wants to celebrate with his groomsmen."

Tully was hammered already. While his bride was outside on the veranda smoking cigarettes and a joint with her bridesmaids, he was inside getting plastered. He was a mess and already had a liquor stain down the front of his ruffled shirt.

He was also at the *I love you* stage and slung an arm over my shoulder.

"You gotta find yourself a good woman and let her make an honest man outta you. Because it's the best feeling in the world." He slumped against me and I had to hold him up. Something told me his bride was going to be doing all the work later. "You gotta find a nice girl—or a bad one— and settle down."

"I'll take that under consideration," I said to him with a grin.

"There's no feeling like that smooth, warm body of your hot old lady filling the bed next to you," he slurred, his eyes hooded. He struggled to focus on his wife out on the veranda. "Tonight, I'm going to give her a baby."

I couldn't help my chuckle. I doubted he was going to give her anything in his state.

"In fact, I'm gonna go give her one right . . . right, now." He released me and stumbled out onto the veranda and into the arms of his brand new wife. I turned away just as Cade slid another shot along the bar. I shook my head.

"No more," I said. After two shots of Patrón, I was done. I ordered a bourbon. I wasn't going to get hammered, not when Honey was with me.

I watched her from the bar across the room, my bones aching to touch her and claim her as mine. My heart bloomed with pride because that beautiful woman over there talking to my sister-in-law was carrying my baby in her belly.

Fuck it. I didn't want to be over here at the bar. I wanted to be out on that dance floor with her in my arms. Because dancing with her was the only way it was going to happen.

I put down my glass, wandered over to her, and extended my hand. She looked up at me, grinned, and accepted it, then followed me out onto the dance floor. Stevie Ray Vaughan's "Mary Had A Little Lamb" filled the room and everyone on the dance floor danced away to the bluesy number like they didn't have a care in the world. And as I danced with her, we laughed and enjoyed the night, and it felt good. It had been a good night. Hell, it had been an amazing night. Being with her. Seeing her relax and be at ease in my world; watching her talk and laugh with the old ladies like she was one of them.

When Gary Moore's "Still Got the Blues" took over, the mood on the dance floor changed and I wondered if Honey would walk away. But she didn't. Instead, she smiled and let me pull her closer so I could wrap my arms around her waist and hold her against the body that was aching for her touch. For her closeness. For her. It had been weeks since our last encounter, and my body was screaming for her to touch me.

A sheen of sweat shone on her beautiful face as she smiled up at me. The song was intimate. Full of emotion. A song about longing. And longing was something I knew something about. She looked up at me, and for a moment I was lost in the vibrant blue of her lovely eyes. Emotion shimmered across her face and she licked her lips as she leaned into me and laid her cheek against my chest. My heart beat wildly. This was torture. Absolute torture. Being this close to her, holding her close and feeling the gentle swell of her belly pressing into my stomach.

Across the room, Cade danced with his wife on the dance floor. She was heavily pregnant and he did nothing but dote on her. Now he held her close, his hands cupping her face as he kissed her gently. Together they swayed to the music, their love vibrant, their future certain. I felt Honey shift her head and knew she was looking at them, too.

Suddenly she straightened, a big smile spreading across her face. She grabbed both my hands and placed them on her curved belly.

"Did you feel that?" she asked, her face open, her eyes shining.

And then it happened. Right there on the dance floor, I felt my baby move in Honey's belly. The world around us fell away as our baby moved about, awake and active, shifting in her. We both looked at each other and laughed.

"Holy hell," I said, sliding my hands over the curve of her stomach.

Something in me shifted. Feeling my baby. He never seemed more real to me.

Oh yeah. We were having a boy. I just knew it.

I looked up from her belly to her beautiful face. I wanted to kiss her. I wanted to pull her to me and slam my mouth to hers. I wanted to take her home and peel those clothes off her, piece by piece, and make love to her right through the night until dawn. Hell, I wanted to scream to the heavens about how much I wanted this.

Instead, the moment was broken by my mom's surprised and very loud voice.

"You're pregnant?" she exclaimed.

Both Honey and I turned our heads to look at her. Standing only a few feet away and holding a glass of champagne in each hand, my mom stared at us in disbelief.

"Oh, crap," Honey whispered.

"Guess the cat's out of the bag now," I replied out of the corner of my mouth.

"What do you mean?"

"In about sixty seconds this entire wedding reception is going to know about this."

Honey jerked her head to look at me, her eyes wide with concern. "What do we tell them? How do we explain us to them?"

"We don't have to explain anything to them." We both looked down at my hands on her stomach and then back at my mom. "We were kind of hoping to keep it to ourselves for a bit."

But Mom didn't hear anything other than my confirmation that yes, Honey was pregnant.

"A baby!" She looked at me. "Is it yours?"

"Jesus, Mom. Yes, it's my baby."

Her smile started in her eyes and finally broke on her lips. She handed the champagne glasses to a passing waitress and walked over to us.

"A baby, well, color me surprised." She pulled me into a hug, squeezing tight. When she released me, she did the same to Honey.

"You're okay with it?" I asked.

"Another grandbaby, of course I'm okay with it." She smiled, but it was dubious. "But you better tell your grandmother and pray no one gets to her first."

CHAPTER 24

HONEY

It was a crazy night from that point on.

Our secret was out and what followed was a lot of congratulations and a lot of questions.

Overall, people seemed really excited and enthusiastic, especially some of the old ladies who crowded around me and started with the questions about names, due dates, OB-GYNs, and was I getting the right prenatal care. They circled me like a wolf pack, protecting one of their own.

Others didn't seem too interested, namely the older club members who simply patted Caleb on the back and moved on.

Indy, who looked like she was about to pop, was excited about a cousin for her baby. Ronnie was thrilled with the idea of another grandbaby. Although, beneath the façade of joy I could see a simmering doubt in those sapphire blue eyes of hers. She didn't know me and I didn't know her. And if I was honest, she kind of intimidated me. She was a tough biker queen. The widow of the murdered President, sister to the current President, and mother to three Kings of Mayhem club members. Going by some of the conversations I'd heard, she was the one the other old ladies either feared or looked up to. I glanced over at her. She was having a quiet one-on-one with Caleb. Probably asking him what the hell he was up to and making sure he hadn't lost his mind.

But I couldn't blame her for being doubtful. Or guarded about me. Tonight was the first time she'd met me, and two hours later she found out I was pregnant and her son was the father. Getting to know each other was going to take time. I glanced around the reception area full of Kings and their Queens. This whole environment was going to take time to get used to.

Needing to use the bathroom, I excused myself and walked along a long hallway until I found it. Inside it was empty and I was relieved, after the frenzied attention from everyone at the reception I needed five minutes of peace and quiet. I took a moment in the stall to catch my breath and close my eyes against the world. This was happening. I was becoming a part of this MC whether I'd planned to or not. If the last twenty minutes had shown me anything it was that I might not be a member of the club but I was carrying a King's baby and that made me someone in this club. I thought of Caleb and smiled. Through all the craziness, his attention never wavered, always casting a protective eye in my direction, even when the old ladies swarmed around me and separated us, he'd maintained a watchful eye over me.

I exhaled and felt any reservations about Caleb leave me. I felt good. Happy. And for the first time, relaxed and confident that we knew what we were doing and nothing could stand in our way.

When I left the cubicle, I noticed a blonde girl at the sink, checking her make-up and fixing her long hair. As I washed my hands, our eyes met in the mirror.

"I think you're very brave," she said.

Her tone grabbed my attention.

"Excuse me?" I asked.

Her eyes dropped to my stomach and then returned to mine in the mirror.

"Caleb isn't known for his commitment. He loses interest real quick, if you know what I mean." She flounced her hair and adjusted her large boobs in the low-cut top she had on. A gold necklace with the name *Tiffani* glinted in the harsh fluorescent light. "He's always been that way. Always looking for new pussy. I mean, we thought that maybe he had changed when he hooked up with Brandi. But, well, not even she could tame him."

She stepped away from the mirror and turned to look at me. Again, her eyes swept over me, one eyebrow lifting. "And if Brandi couldn't keep him interested, what chance do you have?"

My jaw dropped.

"Oh, don't look so shocked. I'm simply keeping it real. Telling you how it is. You know, girl code and all that."

There was absolutely no girl code in anything she had just said. It was pure vitriolic bullshit. Probably motivated by a burn from the man himself.

"So when did he turn you down?" I asked casually, drying my hands with a paper towel.

Her glossy lips parted with a scowl. "Come again?"

"Caleb. When did he turn you down? Or has it been so many times you've lost count?"

Her confidence slipped, only briefly, but long enough for me to know I was right.

Her eyes narrowed and she dug her tongue into her cheek as she smirked. "Don't think for a moment that this baby changes anything. You're nothing more than a passing hobby. He'll move on. Trust me. You're just another notch on his bedpost, darlin'."

This girl was a real bitch.

And I had a real short wick when it came to this type of bitchiness.

"It must really suck wanting something so much and knowing you can't have him," I said, scrunching up the paper towel and throwing it in the bin. "But if you ever want to know how good it feels to be fucked by him, you know where to find me. I'll be the one riding him later tonight."

It was a lie. No one knew we weren't anything more than friends. But this bitch needed to be put in her place, and despite being a little bit rocked by her attack, I felt up to the task.

Her eyes narrowed and her smirk disappeared, replaced by a face full of thunder. Obviously, I'd struck a nerve.

But Tiffani was a girl with goals. She had done what she had set out to do so she flashed me a nasty smile, pushed up her boobs a bit more, and threw her little handbag over her shoulder. "He'll break your heart, darlin'. Don't say you weren't warned."

She walked out first, while I leaned against the sink and tried to collect my emotions. I felt sick but refused to let her rattle me.

I straightened. Girls like that, they got their satisfaction from the pain of others. But I wasn't going to give her anything to fuel it. So I shook it off and left the bathroom, determined to put Tiffani behind me.

Caleb found me before I found him. He was waiting for me outside the bathroom, a glass of sparkling water in one hand and a bottle of beer in the other. I wondered if he'd been there in time to see Tiffani leave, but she wasn't draped all over him like I'm sure she would have been if she'd seen him.

"Hey, you," he said with that killer smile of his. He handed me the glass of water. "I figured you'd be here, you know, that dime-store bladder of yours."

"It's dime store because your baby is bouncing on it." I smiled up at him as I took the glass from him. "Thank you."

"Want to get some fresh air?"

After the mean girl attack I was ready for lots of fresh air.

"Please, it's a bit chaotic out there at the moment," I said.

"Sorry about that." Again he smiled but it was softer. "When you're a part of an MC, you're a part of a huge family. Your business quickly becomes their business. You tell one person something, and before you know it, ten people know about it. You'll get used to it."

A strange sense of belonging unfurled in me.

"You think they'll like me?"

"They already do."

Caleb took my hand in his and we walked down to the river and sat down at the end of the pier. Twilight slowly darkened to night and moonlight danced on the water. It was a clear night, crickets sung in the shadows and above us the stars twinkled in brilliant starshine.

"So tomorrow I'm going to meet your grandmother," I said.

"Are you ready?"

"I don't know what to expect."

He chuckled softly. "There aren't any words I could use to prepare you, believe me."

I'd heard talk about his feisty grandma. She was one of a kind, they said. She wasn't here tonight because she'd broken her foot and was resting at home.

"How do you think she'll react, you know, when she finds out about the baby?"

"She'll be thrilled. Like my mom, family is everything to her." His finger brushed mine. "And she'll love you."

The touch of his finger against mine sent a wave of longing through me.

I raised my face to the moonlight and inhaled a deep breath of fresh night air and it raced through my mind like a cool breeze, bringing with it a beautiful sense of calm.

When I glanced back at Caleb he was looking at me. Our eyes met and the moment became excruciatingly intimate. I licked my lips and his eyes darkened as he watched my tongue slide across them. His Adam's apple bobbed and his lips parted. Emotion was all around us. Attraction. Longing. Need.

He swallowed deeply and the St. Christopher on the choker chain around his neck glinted in the bright moonlight.

"I like your St. Christopher," I said, breaking the spell.

He reached up and touched it.

"My granddaddy gave it to me when I was young. It was his. He wore it in the war. He said it kept him safe through two tours of Vietnam." He ran a finger over the tarnished silver. "It's the most precious thing I own."

"Even more than your Harley?"

He gave me a lopsided smile. "A Harley you can replace. This is irreplaceable. I never take it off and it'd kill me to lose it. It's the last bit of him I have, you know."

"You were close?"

He nodded. "Growing up, he was my best friend. When he died suddenly, it felt like my whole world fell away."

"How old were you?"

"He died three days before my ninth birthday."

Feeling his sorrow, I thought for a moment and then said, "It must've been nice growing up with grandparents." *With family.*

"You're a part of this now, too," he said.

It was a kind thing to say and it warmed me because I knew he said it to give me the sense of belonging that I'd missed out on as a kid. Caleb was a lot of things, I was learning. Strong. Sexy. Fiercely protective of what was his. Generous. He was all that, but he was also incredibly thoughtful. Considerate.

We looked at one another. Across the water, the band was singing the old Poison hit "Unskinny Bop" and a bunch of drunk bikers and their old ladies sang along. Their loud, off-key voices dipped and waned on the breeze.

I didn't tell Caleb about the girl in the bathroom. I didn't want to ruin the night. Because aside from my mean girl encounter, the night had been perfect.

"What do you think, time to go home?" he asked, draining his beer bottle.

I was surprised. The party didn't show any signs of dying down.

"You don't want to stay here and hang out with your buddies? It sounds like they're having a good time."

He shook his head and his eyes were a beautiful blue in the dim light of the night. We looked at one another for a moment longer.

He didn't try to kiss me.

But it lingered in the air between us.

"Come on," he said, finally breaking eye contact. He rose to his feet and offered me a hand. "Let's go home."

CHAPTER 25

HONEY

The next day, Caleb took me to meet his grandmother. She lived in the historic part of town where the homes were built during the nineteenth century and once upon a time served in the Civil War as hospitals and outposts.

The old home with the wraparound porch was off Magnolia Street and was partially hidden from the road by a well-looked-after garden. As we walked through the little gate at the front and along the path to the steps, the sweet scent of roses greeted us.

Caleb led me by the hand as we climbed the steps. Potted ferns and flowers hung from the eves and bright red trumpet flowers festooned the railings, their vines weaving through the wrought-iron balustrade. Farther along the porch, sitting on a comfortable-looking chair with her left booted ankle resting up on a stool, was an older lady with flaming red hair. She was wearing a vibrantly colored caftan, bright red lipstick, and a pair of black biker sunglasses.

She was also sound asleep.

As we stepped onto the porch she didn't stir.

"Grandma Sybil," Caleb said gently, so as not to startle her.

She didn't move. Her head was tilted back and her red lips were slack. Gold-ringed fingers rested on her chest, her long nails as brightly colored as her outfit.

"Grandma?" Caleb said again, this time a little louder. But again, the old lady didn't stir.

Caleb released my hand and gently nudged her, but when the old lady didn't move, he nudged her again.

"Grandma." His voice took on a sharper tone and a prickly sensation took up in the base of my spine. "Sybil. Wake up."

His fingers curled around her wrist as he gently shook her. He leaned down, his face coming close to hers, and I realized he was checking to see if she was breathing.

"Grandma?" He sounded alarmed and gave me a worried glance over his shoulder.

And just when I thought he was about to ask me to call an ambulance, a devilish grin spread across the old lady's lips.

"Boo!" she said, startling the life out of Caleb.

He jumped back in surprise. "Jesus Christ, Sybil!"

When he straightened, she lifted her sunglasses and started laughing.

"I thought you were dead!" Caleb exasperated.

"Of course you did. That was the point!" The old lady chuckled.

"Do you want to give your youngest grandson a freaking heart attack?"

She waved off his comment. "I'm stuck on this porch like an old lady because I broke my foot. I'm bored. Give me a break and stop being a pussy." It was then she noticed me and her face lit up with curiosity. "Well now, who do we have here?"

"Grandma, this is Honey," Caleb said, still riled by his roguish grandmother.

"Hi, Grandma Sybil," I said, stepping forward and giving her a warm smile.

She reached for my hand and placed a second hand on top of it.

"Well, aren't you just the prettiest thing." Her wise old eyes glittered over my face before she indicated to the wicker chair next to her. "Please, have a seat."

I sat down and immediately felt welcomed by the old lady.

"Caleb, there is a fresh batch of lemonade in the ice box. Will you fetch us a glass each, please?"

"Sure." Caleb glanced at me and then back at his grandmother. He raised a dark eyebrow. "Play nice."

Sybil gave him an innocent look.

Once he was gone, she focused on me, her bright blue eyes taking in every inch of my face.

"So how long have you and my grandson been an item?" she asked.

"Oh, no, we're not together," I said, slightly wilting under her gaze. "I mean, we're friends . . . but . . ."

She tilted her head to the side, ever so faintly, those eyes trying to work me out.

"Hmmmmm . . . what a shame. You certainly look like you're *something*. The way he looks at you. Hmph. I suppose I'm just being a foolish old lady."

Her eyes sparkled over at me with something I couldn't put my finger on. It was almost like a secret knowledge. I shifted uncomfortably. There was nothing foolish about Sybil Calley.

Caleb returned with three glasses of lemonade.

"Did you put a little sugar in it, Caleb?" Grandma Sybil asked.

"You know you're not allowed any liquor while you're on those painkillers the doctors have you taking."

"Oh, fooey!" Grandma waved off the comment as if it was a ridiculous idea. She winked at me. "Ain't nothing like a little sugar to make the afternoon a little more interesting."

"Yeah, well, that sugar is not happening when you are taking drugs for pain."

Grandma Sybil rolled her eyes. "I was a child of the sixties, sonny. You think I'm going to let a couple of Advil and a splash of bourbon push me around? What about some weed? This drought is making me crazy. I heard Hawke had some insane buds, is that true?"

"You're not having any liquor *or* any weed when you're on medication." He paused in front of her. "And no damn peyote either."

Again, Sybil rolled her eyes.

"This is delicious lemonade," I said, interrupting their war of wills.

"Jury made it this morning before heading off to work," Grandma Sybil explained. "Used the lemons from the lemon tree out the back. It's over a hundred years old, you know, and gives us some of the finest lemon juice in the state. Jury says it's all in the way you squeeze the juice. You gotta do it right with your hands, coax the juice out real slow."

"Jury is Grandma's boyfriend," Caleb explained.

"Yes, and he's very good with his hands," she said with a playful wink.

Caleb paled at his grandmother's innuendo.

"How did you hurt your ankle?" I asked, suppressing a smile at the old lady's mischievousness

"Sex act," she said, taking a casual sip of her drink.

My lemonade caught in the back of my throat and almost exited out my nose.

"Jesus Christ," Caleb said, looking pained.

"We have a chair," she started to explain. "A recliner. Big enough for two people—"

Caleb stood up. "I think I'll fetch some of that banana loaf I saw in the kitchen."

He hastily made his escape off the porch and out of earshot of his feisty grandmother. When I looked over at Grandma Sybil, an amused grin curled on her lips and a mischievous glint sparkled in her eyes.

"Now that we've gotten rid of the fun police, pass me that box on the table over there, will you, sweetheart?"

She nodded toward the wicker and glass table beside me. On top of it was a vintage wooden box, intricately carved and about the size of a jewelry box. I handed it to her and watched on, amused, as she pulled out a silver hip flask. Unscrewing the lid, she poured a decent nip of liquor into her lemonade, then offered me the flask. I shook my head.

"Caleb's a good boy. Sweet. But damn if he's not infuriating, fussing over me like I'm an old woman. I broke my foot in two places having some rather fun sexy time with my man. Don't mean I have to sit here in purgatory until I can walk again. I like my liquor and I like my weed. And I usually like them together. When you get to my age, you'll see, you won't be told you can't have either." She added an extra nip to her lemonade and rescrewed the cap. Placing the flask back in the box, she handed it back to me, just as Caleb came back into the room with a plate of banana loaf. She winked at me. We had a secret.

"Is it safe to come back out?" Caleb asked.

"Just having some girl talk," Grandma Sybil replied. She raised her drink to her bright red lips, but Caleb smoothly glided past her and took it out of her hand before she had a chance to take a sip. He smelled it and gave her a filthy look.

"Seriously, Sybil?"

She glared at him and smacked her bejeweled fingers against the arms of her chair. "Goddamnit."

"If you've got to have something, you're better off having a joint than mixing this with your meds."

"Fine. Get me some weed and I'll gladly give up the liquor."

"Now where in the hell am I going to get you some weed when the whole goddamn south has run dry?"

"You can visit your granddaddy's cabin. Last time I was out there I saw a few plants growing rather nicely down by the river. I'm not sure if they would've survived when the river got high last winter, but it's worth a look."

"I doubt anything survived the flood," Caleb said.

Grandma Sybil turned her attention to me. "Did my grandson tell you I used to look after the weed production for the Kings in the 1970s. We grew the best buds in the South. Plump. Aromatic. With a purple-tinged hue. It was potent. Sweet and smooth. We had a roaring trade, earned the Kings a fortune. Of course, this was in the day before they shifted their focus to pussy and pornographic movies."

Hearing the words pussy and pornographic almost sent another spray of lemonade out of my nose.

"Wait, I thought you said the Kings weren't involved with drugs."

I said it to Caleb. But it was Grandma Sybil who replied.

"Hutch never worried about weed. He enjoyed it. More than alcohol. He always said liquor was worse than cannabis. It was the heroin and the opiates he despised. The shit he saw destroy his fellow comrades in the war." She smiled, her eyes fading as she recalled her memories of times long past. "He encouraged it, you know. The cannabis fields. Taught me everything there was about growing a crop. From sewing it to cultivating the plants into fat, bud-producing plants. He was a purposeful man, my Hutch. He was a gentle man with gentle ways. He saw the merit in those plants, so he loved them—gave them life, if you will—then gave them to me to raise." She shrugged. "And I turned them into a money tree."

"So what happened?" I asked, intrigued.

"It was a deal the Kings struck with the Knights in the early eighties. By then, the weed industry wasn't as profitable as *other interests*," Caleb explained, rather diplomatically. "It became a pawn in our negotiations with the Knights."

"And I got shut down," Sybil added. "The eighties were all about coke—grotesque and garish, if you ask me. Weed wasn't as in demand. What was once the shiny jewel in our crown somehow became nothing more than a rough pebble in our arson of collateral with the Knights."

She looked at her grandson. "So, my favorite grandson, will you visit granddaddy's cabin and see what's growing out there by the river?"

Caleb and his grandmother shared a challenging stare before Caleb finally broke. "Fine, I'll go and have a look."

I saw Sybil's eyes brighten with a mysterious glint. "Good!" She smacked her hands together. "Now that that ugly business is sorted, which one of you is going to tell me when my great-grandbaby is due?"

Caleb and I both looked at her, our mouths dropping open.

"You know?" Caleb asked.

"Oh, son, please. The MC grapevine is faster than any form of communication on this planet."

"Who told you?"

"I ain't no rat." She raised an eyebrow at her grandson. "But get me some ganja from the river, and I might be open to bribery."

CHAPTER 26

CALEB

We drove out to my granddaddy's cabin.

It was a simple cabin built by a man who appreciated and saw the value in simple things. One main room with a kitchen, two bedrooms, a bathroom, and a small laundry off to the side. Hutch Calley had built it in the seventies when he had a wife and two little boys. He and Sybil made plans here. Built the Kings of Mayhem here. Raised my dad and uncle here.

We climbed the steps to the back door and I unlocked it using the spare key I found in the terracotta planter on the porch. Inside, it was stuffy. It'd been a long time since I'd been out here. Months. Maybe even last year sometime.

As a kid I used to spend a lot of time here fishing with my brothers, running free through the fields of untouched land, racing our dog, and climbing trees. Granddaddy built us a treehouse on the far side of the property, and me and my brothers used to spend hours there, reading comics, telling stories and eventually smoking cigarettes stolen from the packets that were always lying about, begging to be taken by curious kids.

It was one of those cigarettes that saw the demise of the treehouse by fire when I was eight. We weren't sure who was responsible, but I always suspected it was probably me. My daddy had been furious, but not my granddaddy. I think he knew I was responsible and didn't want me feeling bad.

We were close. I used to love coming here and spending time with him. I was so much closer to him than my father, and I learned more from him than anyone else.

I opened the sliding door and stepped out onto the veranda and the sappy aroma of marijuana hit me right away. Walking to the railing I stared out at a sea of shamrock green leaves gently swaying in the late afternoon breeze.

Honey came up behind me and gasped, stunned at the sight of so many marijuana plants. "So this is what your grandma was talking about."

"I don't think she realizes how many there are," I replied, just as stunned.

Timber floorboards creaked as I crossed the veranda and took the steps down to the riverbank. Here the plants thrived in the loamy soil. It was rich and super fertile, enhanced by wild bat guano and nutrients from the river water. The plants stood as tall as me, gently swaying in the late afternoon light.

"These plants are massive," Honey whispered in awe and I turned to her. She ran a delicate finger over a huge, furry bud. "I feel like I'm in Jurassic Park."

I grinned at her, a little in awe of the plants myself. There had to be at least thirty or forty of them, all fat and plump with emerald leaves and dark purple heads. The air was warm and heady with their pungent aroma.

When a gentle ripple of wind lifted the sweet aroma closer, an idea hit me.

"Come on," I said, taking Honey's hand in mine. "I'd better cut down some of these buds and get them dried out before Sybil decides I'm taking too long and starts self-medicating with bourbon shots and peyote chasers."

HONEY

Despite the marijuana plant being in the trunk, we still drove to Grandma Sybil's with the windows down because Caleb was worried about the affects the aroma would have on the baby. You know, essential oils and all that. I tried to reassure him that it was fine, that I was fine, that the baby was fine, but he insisted. And then when we got to Sybil's, he also insisted I wash my hands because I had touched the impressive buds on one of the towering plants.

When I told him I had wiped my finger on my skirt right away, he looked at me with a pained expression. "Please, baby girl, will you just do this for me?"

It was hard to not do as he asked when he was looking at me with pleading eyes and a furrowed brow.

"Fine," I said, surrendering to his adorable good looks. When I glanced over at Sybil she was smiling back at us and I had to turn away, afraid my eyes would betray me and she would see through the thin veil of my façade. That despite what I said about being just friends, my heart still wanted something very different.

CHAPTER 27

CALEB

I was late to chapel the next day.

With good reason.

Everyone was seated when I walked in and threw the massive marijuana plant down on the redwood table.

I had their attention.

"Gentlemen, here is the answer to the southern weed drought," I said.

Immediately, the air became ripe with the sweet scent of pot.

"Fuck me, look at the size of those buds!" Hawke said with a lovesick cadence only a marijuana fiend could understand. "They're the size of my fucking fingers!"

"Where the hell did you get this?" Bull asked.

"And give me the directions because I'm ready to ride out there now," Matlock added, eyeing the plant like it was a priceless object.

He went to touch one of the buds, but I stopped him with a warning. "You touch it and I'll break every one of your fingers."

Biker Baby

"You got some secret nirvana where the marijuana grows like trees?" Vader asked with a gleam in his eyes.

"Kind of, I found these out at the Calley cabin. There has to be thirty or forty plants just growing wild by the river." I looked at Bull. "Remember Sybil's marijuana crops of the seventies?"

"Of course. This clubhouse is standing on the land we bought from the profits."

"These plants are from those crops. She kept the seeds and grew a few plants for her own purpose. But she hasn't been out there in nearly a year and a half. Didn't realize these had even survived or repopulated. Or how many there were."

"So what are you proposing?" Cade asked.

My older brother hated the drug trade. Just like our granddaddy, he hated the heroin and the meth, hated what it did to people and what those people did to others. But he wasn't averse to smoking a joint.

"Things have been tight since Head Quarters burnt down and we lost five months of production. I propose we recoup those lost earnings by supplying weed to the Knights."

We had lost close to three-million dollars thanks to a psychopath with a vendetta against the club. He'd burned down the studio as part of his plan to get my brother and cousin out on the road in the early hours of the morning. Then he had lain in wait and assassinated my cousin with two bullets from his sniper rifle.

"You mean go into business with those fuckers?" Hawke asked, clearly disgusted. "No fucking way. The Knights are a bunch of motherfucking cunts. You can't trust them."

As clubs went, the Kings were bigger. The Knights were a younger, broken fraction of a now defunct club from the north. They were growing in size but they lacked the finesse and discipline of the Kings of Mayhem. Their rules and our rules greatly differed.

"The Knights have trade in place. It would take months for us to set something like that up. I say, take advantage of their network and let them distribute it. We'll grow and supply, for an attractive cost, of course."

"Yeah, but trading with the Knights? Come on, man." Tully had the same look of disgust as Hawke.

"I don't know, I think it's worth thinking about," Maverick said, eyeing off the furry buds.

"What's to stop them from cultivating their own crops?" Vader asked.

"Different county, different law enforcement," I explained. "We have Bucky. They don't."

Sheriff Buckman had been in our pocket since day one. He would turn a blind eye. For a hefty fee, of course.

"Besides, they've kept their fingers out of the porn business," I reminded them. "They've kept their hands off our trade."

"This might just work," Bull said, staring at the massive plant on the table in front of him. He looked up at all the men gathered around the table. "All of us in favor of the Kings reaching out to the Knights and offering a supply deal, say aye."

The room reverberated with sixteen men saying aye.

All except one.

Hawke pouted like a petulant child.

"Hawke?" Bull questioned.

"I hate the idea of doing any business with those fuckers," he sneered.

"We're just reaching out. We'll need to finalize how much we can supply, how much setting up the production will cost. But before that, we'll need to know if they're even interested in a supply deal."

"You've got your numbers. Sixteen votes to one." Hawke continued to look pissed.

Biker Baby

I moved to stand behind him and put a hand on his shoulder. "We're not giving anything away. And they're not taking anything from us that we don't want to give."

Two years ago, Hawke's wife had left him for a Knight. She'd been sneaking around behind his back before clearing out their apartment and moving in with her new biker boyfriend. In Hawke, the betrayal still ran deep.

He looked at me and then around the table. Then slowly he nodded.

"Aye," he finally said and the other Kings banged their hands on the table in approval. It would've been hard for him to give his approval, and we all knew it. "Now can we dry some of this fucker out and get to smoking it?"

Three days later, the deal with the Knights was in place. We would cultivate and supply the marijuana for a tidy sum. And they would create extra security to ensure no more heroin or other chemicals made it into our town.

Our deal wouldn't end drugs in Destiny.

But supplying weed was the lesser of two evils.

"Nicely played, Caleb," Bull said, cupping my shoulder and patting my back as we left the deserted cinema where we'd made the deal. It was located on neutral territory and was the perfect location, out of town with no one around. "You just made the club rich, and I'm pretty sure when Sybil calls you her favorite grandson, from now on she might just mean it."

CHAPTER 28

CALEB

It took me a month to set up the weed fields.

Bull put me in charge—with Grandma Sybil's help, of course.

It was four weeks of organizing land clearing, procuring reliable staff, sourcing equipment and labor for the construction of a lab, and cutting a deal with our friendly, albeit corrupt, sheriff.

We were using almost four-and-a-half acres of land the Kings had purchased out by the watermelon fields. Back in the sixties and seventies it had been a canning factory, now the old warehouse was a massive hydroponics lab.

With everything in place, I was able to take a step back. Setting up the weed fields had been an interesting and rewarding project, but tattoo artistry was my real passion. I was pleased to hand over the cannabis production to our newly employed project manager and get back to what I enjoyed more.

It also meant I could spend more time with Honey. It felt like weeks since I'd spent any time with her. She was just over five months pregnant now, although in some dresses she wore you

Biker Baby

could hardly tell she had a baby bump. She was still insisting we kept things platonic, while I still prayed she'd wake up from that madness and want more someday. I won't lie. It'd been weeks since I'd had sex, and my balls were aching for it. So when I saw her and she looked all glowing and beautiful, and when she smelled so good and felt so soft, it was like my balls were in a vise. My left hand was getting boring. My right hand had retired from overuse.

Now I was back at work in the studio, and things were getting back to normal.

Today was my first day back, and I was completely booked. Once people heard I was back, Pandora said the bookings kept coming.

This morning had been all about simple designs that required very little expertise. Now I was working on something a little more fun. The tattoo was intricate. An elaborately detailed crown that tested both my creativity and my dexterity. But I pulled it off, just like I always did, with absolute fucking skill. I'd been a tattoo artist for almost ten years and there wasn't a lot I couldn't do. Give me a picture of what you wanted and I could create a masterpiece.

This beauty belonged to Maverick. It was a skull wearing a crown, and beneath it were the words *I wasn't given my kingdom, I took it.*

I was just wiping it off when Pandora walked in, dressed in a tight rubber dress and looking more like a dominatrix than the office manager of a tattoo shop. The dress was new with a neckline cut so low you could almost see her nipples.

"You almost done, Caleb?" she asked. "You have a visitor."

"Who?" I asked as I dressed Maverick's tattoo.

"Brandi."

Both Maverick and I looked up at the mention of Brandi's name, and Maverick raised his eyebrows because he knew the trouble that might walk through that door.

When my ex-girlfriend and I broke up a few months earlier, she didn't handle it very well. Actually, that's an understatement. She didn't handle it at all. There were a lot of tears and meltdowns and tantrums, with middle-of-the-night phone calls that swung between tearful and sad to angry and accusatory. One night she turned up at the clubhouse naked beneath her coat and cornered me in my room, begging me to fuck her. When I turned her down, her meltdown was epic. She slapped my face, kicked over my bike, and told me my cock was too big.

I hadn't seen her since. Realizing she needed help, she left town for a renowned clinic that treated people for everything from depression and personality disorders, to alcohol and drug dependency.

Now she was back.

"Send her in," I said to Pandora, who raised an eyebrow at me, but didn't say anything as she left the room. She didn't need to. Her look said it all. *Are you sure this is a good idea?*

Maverick rose and gave me an amused grin.

"Think I will leave you to deal with that nightmare all on your own," he said, patting me on the back and chuckling to himself as he disappeared out the door and down the hallway.

While I waited for my ex-girlfriend, I tidied up my tattoo station. Sitting on top, next to a box of unopened latex gloves was a bottle of Jack Daniel's single barrel whisky, courtesy of my secret admirer. It had arrived by courier earlier that morning. Pandora said she had pressed the courier driver to tell her who the sender was, but he said it was against company policy, and even if it wasn't, he was never given those details anyway.

I picked it up and looked at it. Judging by the label, it promised to be good. But I didn't know how I felt about drinking it. I didn't know who was sending me all this stuff and what she had in mind, or what she expected from me. Had she tampered with it?

I was putting the bottle away in my desk drawer when Brandi appeared in the doorway.

"It's a bit early for that, isn't it?" Her velvet smooth voice said.

I looked up. Seeing her standing in the doorway was a surprise. After the way things ended, she was the last person I ever thought I would see again.

"Is it ever too early?" I joked.

She smiled warmly. She looked good. Hell, she looked real good. Her flowing auburn hair gleamed like a halo around her beautiful face, and her eyes were warm like a good whisky. She really was a beauty.

"Hey," she said softly, leaning against the door jam.

"Hey, yourself."

When she was like this I remembered why I'd dated her in the first place.

She put a hand out as if to calm me. "I promise, I come in peace."

I couldn't help but smile, and when she crossed the distance between us and hugged me, I relaxed. This was a very different Brandi to the one yelling at me for breaking up with her. She held me to her. Her perfume subtle and tantalizing as I held her in my arms. I stepped back and looked into the gorgeous face of the woman whose heart I had broken. It looked as if she was in a much better place. "It's good to see you."

"You, too." Her eyes twinkled with a confidence I hadn't seen in a while. It made me feel better. I'd always felt guilty about breaking her heart. But at the time she'd wanted me to love her and I knew I never would. It was kinder to let her go. So I broke it off with her.

"So what brings you to this part of town?" I asked.

Her beautiful face frowned and she looked sad. "It's Jasper. He passed away yesterday."

Jasper was her dog. An old staffy who was as affectionate as he was obedient.

"I'm so sorry," I said. "He was a very cool dog."

Tears glittered in her eyes as she nodded.

"I had to have him put down. The vet said he was in pain."

"It's a hard thing to do," I said.

"The hardest," she sniffed. Then she straightened and sighed. "To be honest, I don't know why I came by to see you. I guess Jasper's death has inspired me to fix things. To apologize, I suppose. I'm sorry for what happened when I last saw you."

"It's okay." I moved away from her and leaned against the tattoo bed. "You're looking a lot happier. Despite Jasper and his passing."

"You're being too kind," she said with a teary smile. "I was a psycho. But then, you always brought out the crazy in me."

"I'm sorry I did."

Again she put her hand out. "Please don't apologize. I'm the one who lost her mind. I kicked over your bike. Did I do much damage?"

Thankfully, no.

"Nothing Picasso couldn't fix up."

She grimaced. "Jesus, what a crazy bitch."

We both looked at each other and then we laughed. The ice was broken.

"Does that mean I'm forgiven?" she asked through her laughter.

"Of course."

Biker Baby

She smiled brightly and flicked her long hair over her shoulder. "How about I buy you lunch to say thank you. I'm heading to Los Angeles tomorrow and I'd like to say goodbye on a more positive note."

I thought about it. I felt better knowing she was in a better place.

"Sure," I said. "It sounds like a great idea."

CHAPTER 29

HONEY

"Oh my God, look at all those penises!" Sailor exclaimed as he walked into the kitchen of my bakery.

I was bent over one of the stainless-steel tables, applying star-shaped icing borders to thirty-nine cupcakes decorated with sugar penises.

"They're for Barbie Elliot's bachelorette party tomorrow afternoon," I explained, not looking up. I was on my last row of cupcakes. Two more borders and I was done. I could grab some lunch.

"Why are there only thirty-nine? Why not forty?" Sailor asked. Then he gasped. "Please tell me your pregnancy hormones didn't kick in and you had to devour one. I know you said you couldn't help yourself when it came to cock, but girlfriend, this is taking it too far. What will Barbie Elliot do without all of her penises?"

I rolled my eyes. I knew I'd regret telling Sailor about my overactive hormones and sex drive.

Biker Baby

I finished the last icing border and straightened. "It was deliberate. Barbie Elliot found out one of her bridesmaids is dating her ex-fiancé. So the bridesmaid got booted from the wedding party, because according to Barbie, she'd broken girl code."

Sailor's eyes lit up. "Oh, a scandal. I love it."

"Barbie insisted I only deliver thirty-nine. She wants everyone to remember that someone is missing. And she wants them all to remember why."

"Ugh. That woman is so totalitarian." Sailor waved it off. Bored.

"Can you do me a favor? Can you pack all of these up in those boxes we keep for bachelorette parties? I'm going to get some lunch."

"Want me to go pick some lunch up for you?" he offered.

"No, thanks. I need to stretch my legs. I've been bent over thirty-nine penises all morning."

Sailor's eyes lit up with glee. "Oh, darling, sounds like a Friday night at my place."

Outside it was warm, and the midday sun felt good on my skin. I took my time, enjoying the walk to Mickey's, the popular pizzeria Caleb had taken me to the night he'd found out about the baby. Mickey's made the best wood-fired pizzas in the south, and when the cravings hit, wild horses couldn't hold me back. As I neared, the delicious aroma of hand-tossed pizza dough, rich marinara sauce, deli meats, and a thousand different cheeses wafted out onto the street, and my stomach began to growl. When I walked in, I started to salivate.

I didn't need to think about what to order. I was a regular now, so when Mickey saw me walk in, he winked and told me one mushroom margherita pizza was coming right up.

I leaned against a dark timber pole as I waited and started scrolling through Facebook on my phone.

It took me a while before I saw them.

In fact, it was only by chance that I looked up and there they were.

In a dark, shadowy corner of the room, sitting close to one another.

My throat tightened and I immediately wished the floor would open up and suck me down to the bowels of Destiny where I could make my escape. Unfortunately, I had already ordered. So making any kind of mistake would mean relinquishing my fifteen-dollar pizza. Not to mention, it would be rude. So I decided my best option was to hide behind a dark timber post and wait for my pizza, completely hidden from view. Which totally would have worked if Caleb hadn't looked up at that exact moment.

His face lit up when he saw me, but then he frowned as if something suddenly occurred to him. *Like how to explain to his date that his roomie was knocked up with his baby.* The girl with him saw us looking at each other and frowned. It made Caleb act.

"Honey!" he called out.

Reluctantly, I approached their table.

"Hey, what a surprise seeing you here," I said, trying not to notice how attractive his date was and how put together she seemed. I smiled at her. "Hi, there."

"Brandi, this is Honey. My roommate."

Brandi visibly relaxed. "Oh, right. The one you were telling me about."

My ears perked up.

"I told Brandi how I'd moved in with a friend because I needed a change of scenery," Caleb explained.

Emotion spun through me.

A change of scenery?

What. The. Fuck?

Everybody knew about the baby, why not this woman?

"Sure, yes. Of course," I squeaked. It was hard to talk because a big ball of cold had lodged itself in my tight throat. My eyes reached for him, questioningly, but he was too busy keeping it cool to notice.

And that was the moment, right there. The moment I realized I was living a lie. I could no longer hide my true feelings for Caleb and I felt angry at myself because of it. This was exactly what I had wanted to avoid. *Feelings.* Undeniable feelings for Caleb.

And now they were all up in my face as I stood there in front of him and his *date*.

A *date* who looked vaguely familiar but whom I couldn't quite place.

Whisky-colored eyes. Auburn hair. I tried to place her but I was too busy being hurt to retrieve the memory.

"Of course, I didn't believe him when he said he was just friends with his female roomie," she said, breaking my train of thought. "But now that I've met you . . . it all makes sense."

Whoa. What?

She laughed. "Oh, Jesus, that sounded awful. I didn't mean it like that."

Yeah, she did.

"Well, it was really lovely to meet you, Brenda," I said.

"Brandi." She corrected me.

But I ignored her and looked at Caleb, surprised I could even open my mouth to speak because my face was so stiff. "Enjoy your date."

Caleb frowned at my comment and his eyes darkened. But I didn't give him a chance to respond. I took my mushroom margherita pizza and my angry little heart, and I left.

CHAPTER 30

CALEB

Honey was chopping up salad vegetables when I walked in, and the way she was executing them with the knife confirmed my earlier suspicions that she was upset about Brandi.

"You want to talk about it?" I asked, leaning a hip against the counter.

"About what?" she asked angrily, guillotining a bell pepper with three whacks of the sharp blade.

"Brandi."

At the mention of Brandi's name, the poor pepper copped it with another whack of the knife.

"You're pissed," I said calmly.

"I'm not pissed," she replied. She put a carrot on the chopping board and began to wail down on it. "I'm *super* pissed."

"At me?"

"Why didn't you tell her about the baby? Why everyone else and not her?" she asked suddenly, sending a second carrot to the same fate as the first. But she didn't give me a chance to answer.

"And why was she in my store a few months ago giving me a hard time?"

That threw me. "What do you mean?"

"Just after we started living together she came into the shop and was a prized bitch about me not having gluten-free cupcakes before basically implying I was either pregnant or too fat eating too many cupcakes."

"You're saying Brandi came into the shop and gave you a hard time?"

"Yes. And she was a real pain in the ass!"

"Are you sure it was her?"

"Yes, I'm sure it was her. Obviously, she was dressed differently today. Dressed down even. But it was her. I'm sure." She frowned and bit her bottom lip. "I mean, maybe."

I stood behind her and placed my hand over hers, calmly guiding the knife down onto the chopping board. I turned her around. The urge to kiss her beautiful mouth swelled in my chest but I ignored it, just like I did every other damn day.

"Brandi and I broke up almost six months ago. She's been out of town for months."

Surprise registered on her face. "She's your ex-girlfriend?"

I nodded. "And she didn't take the break up very well. She went to a real bad place in her head afterwards. Said some crazy shit, did some crazy stuff. She doesn't handle disappointment very well and it really fucked with her."

She pulled away and walked over to the couch, slowly sitting down. "How long were you with her?"

"About six months."

She nodded, processing what I was saying.

"Can I ask why you broke up?"

I pushed off the counter and walked over to where she sat on the couch. "She wanted something I just couldn't give her. I thought what we had was something simple and easy, but she thought it was something else. When I realized what she wanted, I knew I didn't want the same, so I broke it off with her." I sat down next to her and took her hand in mine. "She and I—we're done. But today was the first time I'd seen her since she had a big meltdown and went away to get some help. When she showed up this afternoon she seemed better. Calmer. Happier. I wanted to make sure she was really doing okay. When she suggested lunch as an apology for her meltdown, it seemed like a good idea."

"Of course, I understand." She pulled her hand free to wipe her hair from her face. "Oh, crap, I'm such a douche."

Which wasn't what I was expecting her to say.

"What do you mean?"

"Of course you should've gone to lunch with her. Made sure she was okay. I'm just being ridiculous."

"No, you're not. If the roles were reversed, I'd feel the same way."

"You mean you'd act like a jealous loon if you were fat because you were pregnant with my baby and saw me all cozy with a guy in a dark restaurant?"

"For starters, you and I both know that I'd be a hot pregnant man. Secondly, I wasn't cozy with her at all. And thirdly, you're not a jealous loon. A little wacko, but not a complete loony tune." I grinned at her, because even when she pouted she was adorable. I took her hand back and I wasn't going to let it go. "I want you to know that nothing is happening between her and me. And I'm not going to be with anyone else while you're pregnant."

"Really?"

I reached over and cupped her jaw in my hands. "No."

"But you have this huge sexual appetite—"

"Says the girl who wouldn't stop having sex with me long enough to tell me about her pregnancy." I smiled and she laughed softly. My thumb grazed her cheek. "You and this baby, you're my priority, okay? Anything else will just have to wait. Plus, there's something to be said for using your left hand."

She smiled, and again I had to resist the urge to kiss her. I licked my lips, feeling the temptation roll through me. And for the briefest moment I wondered if we'd gotten it all wrong. If we were being too cautious. If being together was something we should be running toward instead of running away from.

Why couldn't we be together?

Because you don't do commitment and I won't ever let myself be vulnerable again.

Honey's words came back to remind me.

Her past was holding her back.

So I would ride out the pregnancy.

But then when our baby was born, I was coming for her.

In every way imaginable.

CHAPTER 31

HONEY

"You know this is crazy, right?" I laughed, touching the bandana Caleb had wrapped around my head to cover my eyes.

"You need cheering up. That's exactly what I am doing."

"It looks like you're kidnapping me."

"How would you know how it looks? You're blindfolded."

I laughed and touched the bandana again. But Caleb quickly told me off. "No looking!"

"That's like saying don't eat the cupcake and then putting the cupcake right in front of me."

"Why do all your analogies involve food?"

"Because food is my obsession at the moment. I don't know if you've noticed, but I'm pregnant and this baby is practically holding me hostage, forcing me to seek out calories in every situation." I let my hands drop to my lap. "I'm pretty sure Bump's father is an eater."

"Bump's father is an incredibly handsome guy, or so I've heard."

I grinned again, and when I touched my blindfold Caleb brushed my hand away.

"Do I need to tie you up, too?"

Lust pooled between my thighs at the thought of Caleb tying me up. Because it had been weeks and weeks since we'd had sex, and sometimes it felt like I was in a permanent state of arousal. I licked my lips and clenched my thighs together. And living with Caleb didn't help. Not with him walking around shirtless all the time, with those black slacks and belts hanging low on his hips, and that impressive six-pack and deeply carved chest always on display.

But now my body was positively aching for it. If I wanted an orgasm I had to give it to myself, and it seemed so unfair when I lived with such a sexy beast.

I exhaled deeply and decided to change the subject.

"So where are you taking me?" I asked for the hundredth time since he had picked me up from work and told me he had a surprise for me. He had put the blindfold on me and very carefully led me out to the car.

"You really don't like surprises, do you?"

"I love them—when I don't have to wait for them," I replied, fighting the urge to lift my chin and sneak a peek out of the bottom of the bandana wrapped across my eyes.

I heard Caleb chuckle as he pulled the car over and killed the engine.

"We're here?" I asked.

In response, Caleb climbed out of the car, and a few seconds later my door opened. He gently guided me out of the car, careful to make sure I had my footing right so I didn't fall over. I didn't have a clue where we were. It was somewhere with people because I could hear cars coming and going, and I could feel people around us.

"You're going to be arrested for sure," I joked as he closed the car door behind me. Caleb's hand was warm around mine as he led me along what I guessed was a sidewalk.

"People can see us, can't they?" I asked.

"Yep."

"They can see I'm blindfolded, can't they?"

"Yep."

"Do they look alarmed?"

"Nope."

"Geez, people. What if I was being kidnapped and brought here against my will?"

He stopped walking and turned me to face him.

"I'm taking you inside now," he said, with a hint of amusement in his deep, rich voice. "Everything is going to make sense in a minute, okay, beautiful?"

Beautiful. My heart curled at his use of the word. I nodded and let him lead me through a doorway. Immediately the outside noise was replaced by the gentle lullaby of store music.

Where the hell were we?

"Ready?" he asked.

I nodded and Caleb peeled the blindfold from around my head.

"Open your eyes," he said.

As I did, the inside of the store came into focus. For as far as the eye could see there was baby furniture, baby strollers, baby clothes, and accessories, as well as linen and bedding. The store was huge.

"You brought me to a baby store?" I whispered in disbelief.

Caleb's smile was big and his blue eyes were bright in the store light. "Well, I'm not sure if you noticed, but you're actually having a baby. And that baby is going to need stuff."

"Stuff?"

"Yes. Stuff. And today we are going to pick up a fuck ton of... stuff."

I couldn't help but smile. But it was short lived. I didn't have the money for stuff. I reached for the price tag of the baby crib I was standing next to and my heart dropped to my toes.

"I could probably afford a couple of things," I said softly. At least I had a bit left on my credit card.

Caleb reached for my hand and brought it to his lips, kissing the top of it. "This is my treat."

I opened my mouth to protest, but he cut me off. "Please, Honey. You're having my baby. It's the least I could do."

"But you've already done so much."

Caleb's face softened and he pulled me to him. He didn't put his arms around me—because that would be crossing boundaries—instead, he put a hand on each shoulder and looked at me.

"I could spend the rest of my life buying you things and it would still fall short of giving you what you are giving me." His brow furrowed. "You're growing my baby in your belly. Let me do this."

He seemed so earnest. So genuine. So I gave in and nodded.

"You'll just go ahead and do it anyway," I said as if there was no point in fighting. But the truth was, I was touched. And so incredibly grateful for the gesture.

I spent the next hour picking out *stuff*. We wandered through the store and Caleb would point at things, pick them up, feel them, try and guess what they were for, get it totally wrong, and then be totally surprised or squeamish when he found out what they were. Like mesh underwear. I'm not sure *what* he thought they were, but he lost a little color when I held up a pack of postpartum pads and told him what went where and why.

It was fun. *He* made it fun. And I was so grateful for all the effort he was making

A few times he had to leave and make a few phone calls, or take a phone call, but for the most part he was by my side through the whole process.

It felt good.

Yet, at the same time it made me feel a bit weird. We weren't a couple. We were friends who were having a baby. He wasn't my boyfriend, or my lover. And tonight while I was sitting on the floor trying to piece together the brand new crib, he would be free to be wherever and with whomever he wanted. And no matter how hard I denied it, the thought of him being with another woman made me feel weird.

Sure, he said he wasn't going to be with anyone.

But how long could I expect him to hold back?

When he went to make a call, I picked up a baby blanket. It was made from the softest fabric, and the moment I brought it up to my cheek, the memory washed over me.

I was three. My mom sat me in the corner of the living room in our one-bedroom apartment and switched on the TV.

"Now don't you move until mommy comes back into the room," she said. She put her finger over her lips. "Not a word now."

I nodded wishing she'd join me on the couch and cuddle me while we watched cartoons. But she didn't. Instead, she went to the door and let her friend in. He was a lot older than her and he seemed nervous when he saw me. Like he didn't know what to say, so he didn't say anything. He followed my mom into the room and I watched the big hand on the clock move around from the five to the eleven, as muffled noises drifted into the room through the closed bedroom door. When the shouting started, I lifted the blanket to cover my face.

"Why would I leave her and my kids for someone else and her kid?"

Biker Baby

The door ripped open and he stormed past me, stuffing his shirt into his pants as he disappeared out the front door.

Mom stared at me for a moment from her bedroom door, crying, her face dark and resentful, and then she slammed it shut.

"Are you okay?" Caleb asked, when he found me staring off into space with the baby blanket pressed against my cheek. He had just walked back in.

I exhaled deeply, trying to shake off the memory.

"Just a bit tired," I replied hoarsely, putting the blanket back. "I think I'm about done."

"Are you sure?"

I looked at him. He was so handsome. So big and strong. Any woman would be lucky to have him.

It made me want to cry.

Which was just stupid.

Instead, I forced a smile and joked, "Boy, I could use a drink."

We headed toward the sales counter to pay for everything. "Good. Because that's the second half of your surprise."

"There's a sequel?"

"Baby, I don't do things in halves." He grinned and then winked at the sales assistant who was ringing up our things.

"What about all the stuff we just bought?" I glanced around at all the items stacked up on the counter.

He waved it off. "They're going to deliver it tomorrow."

Caleb handed the sales assistant his credit card and they exchanged a look. She looked away with a flirtatious and knowing smile and my stomach knotted with jealousy. I glared at her but she was too busy ringing up the sale to notice.

I was being ridiculous, so I turned away and leaned my back against the counter.

"So does part two involve a blindfold, too?" I asked sheepishly.

"No." He gave me a sideways glance. "I mean, if you want it to . . ."

I rolled my eyes but smiled. "No, I'm good."

"Thank you very much, Caleb," she said as she handed him back his card.

Again, he winked and again I felt it stab at my heart when I noticed the chemistry between them. "Thanks, darlin'."

I followed him out of the store, silently chastising myself for hating on the sales girl so much. It wasn't her fault she was young and pretty, and just his type.

"Where to now?" I asked as we climbed into the car.

"Like I said, it's a surprise."

I rolled my eyes and put on my seatbelt. My mood was getting flatter by the minute because my hormones were all over the place like they were on some kind of amusement park ride. I was a slave to them and their ridiculous thoughts.

"Everything okay?" Caleb asked, glancing over as he steered the SUV through traffic.

"Just tired, I guess." It was a lie. I was busy thinking about him having sex with the sales girl and it was slowly making me insane. And I hated how insane I was being. One minute I wanted us to be friends, and just friends. The next, I wanted to wrap him up and keep him all to myself.

Clearly I was falling for him.

And insane.

Maybe it was because I was about to have his baby

Or maybe I was genuinely falling in love with him.

Either way, it was bullshit. A big, pile of bullshit. Nothing good could come of whatever my heart was up to, and I had to stop it before it went any further. I could hear my mother's voice echoing through the years to reach me. *"Don't trap a man with a baby, Honey. He'll just end up resenting you."*

Biker Baby

I looked over at him driving and my chest tightened with longing.

He glanced over at me, then suddenly pulled the car off to the side of the road and killed the engine. He rested a strong, muscular arm across the steering wheel as he turned to face me.

"Okay, what's going on?"

I looked at him blankly. "What do you mean?"

"Ever since we left the store you've been . . . flat."

"Really?"

I tried to sound surprised.

Because there was no way in hell I was admitting anything.

But Caleb wasn't fooled and cocked an eyebrow at me. "Nuh-uh. Something is going on with you. Now spill."

The sudden urge to cry hit me like a wall of water and it was impossible to hold back.

"Do you want to date her?" I blurted out, knowing I sounded like a jealous, crazy lady but unable to stop. Because apparently, I no longer had a filter.

Caleb looked mildly perplexed. "Date who?"

"Old Sally smiley face back there!" I exclaimed.

Caleb's mild perplexity turned to outright confusion. "What the hell are you talking about?"

"Don't act like you don't know what I'm talking about."

"But I don't!"

"The sales assistant! The one with the big boobs and the flirty eyes!" I cried. "The one you couldn't keep your eyes off."

"The girl in the baby store?"

"Yes, *the girl in the baby store*! Could you have been more obvious about wanting to fuck her?"

Caleb looked at me like I'd spoken to him in Dothraki. But I ignored him and continued headfirst into my meltdown.

"Admit it. You can't wait to get me home so you can turn back around and go fuck her."

"In the store?"

"No, on a date, you ass!" I exclaimed. "You're going to dump me home and then call up fucking... whatever her fucking name is... "

"Sally Smiley Face, if memory serves," he said calmly.

"Yes, fucking Sally fucking not pregnant Smiley face!" I wailed.

"That's a pretty long name to cry out when I come. You know, since I'm going to be fucking her later."

My eyes turned to saucers. "See! I knew it. You do want to fuck her."

"I do not want to fuck her," he said calmly.

"Oh, sure. Then why did you get her number?" I asked.

I wasn't a hundred percent sure he had gotten her number but I was almost sure that he had. He basically confirmed my suspicions when he didn't deny it. And for some stupid reason I was determined to make him admit it.

"You're being crazy," he said unfazed.

"Don't change the subject. Did you get her number or not?"

"Yes, I got her number. Technically."

My heart sank.

"Thank you," I said, trying to stop my quivering chin. "For proving my point."

Caleb sighed. "I'm not sure what point you're trying to prove. But if it makes you feel better—"

"Just take me home!" I said, shoving my arms across my chest and turning to stare out the window. My heart beat wildly in my chest.

Caleb looked at me for a moment, probably trying to work out my special brand of crazy before sighing and easing the car back into the traffic. A horrible tension sat between us like a brick wall. I glanced over and noticed his jaw was ticking. He was wearing sunglasses so I couldn't see his eyes, but he was gritting his teeth so I knew he was pissed. Or frustrated. Or both. And I couldn't blame him. He'd knocked up a psychopath.

CHAPTER 32

HONEY

We rode home in awful silence which was only made worse by my desperate need to cry. My face was stiff with the cold ache of unshed tears, but I refused to cry in front of him.

As we pulled into the parking space outside our apartment, the car was barely stopped before I climbed out and started across the parking lot.

I felt worked up.
Confused.
Jealous.
Insane.
And—
Whoa.
My baby moved like she was doing tumbles in my tummy.
"Wow!" I said.
Caleb came up behind me. "Are you okay?"
Again, our baby moved and my meltdown was completely forgotten.
"I think your baby is an acrobat," I said.

Caleb smiled and it glittered in his eyes. I took his big hands and spread them across my baby bump. But nothing happened. When it looked like our baby had gone back to sleep and wasn't going to move again, he let his hands drop to his side.

"I'm sorry you didn't feel it," I said softly.

"Seems my boy is active. I'm sure we're going to feel him more and more."

"You're calling Bump a boy. Is that wishful thinking?"

He smiled. "You keep referring to him as a her."

"Well, one of us has to be right, I guess."

He laughed. "I suppose you're right."

The frost between us began to thaw.

"I'm sorry for arguing about the sales girl," I said, casting my eyes down at my feet. I don't know what had come over me to make me feel so *vulnerable.*

He lifted my chin. "You don't need to say you're sorry."

"I'm not usually so difficult."

"It's okay." His face was gentle, and in his eyes was an unbearable tenderness. "Remember what I said, I'm not going to be with anyone else."

"I know." I sighed and relaxed. It was easy to forget all the reassurances he gave me when my hormones were doing mini drive-bys past my sanity.

"Are we good?" he asked.

"Yes, we are."

"Good. Now are you ready for the second half of your surprise?"

I nodded. Unsure of what I was agreeing to.

"We're going to dinner." He gave me a broad grin as he gave me his arm. "Let's go enjoy ourselves before you get too big and I can't get you out the front door."

He winked but I punched him in the arm anyway.

He took me to Catfish Kelly's, which despite its name was a very upmarket restaurant in town where bookings were hard to come by. We ate over-the-top hamburgers and ridiculously-priced sweet potato chips, while sitting out on the deck overlooking the water. I was relaxed and he was happy. It was easy between us again and my meltdown over the sales girl was forgotten, although the fact he got her number still lingered. But our conversation was easy and comforting, and in my heart I knew things were going to be okay. Somehow.

After our hamburgers, he didn't seem to be in a rush to get home, so we drove up to Cavalry Hill and sat under a starlit sky, watching the twinkling lights of Destiny below. It was a magical night, and he told me stories about his granddaddy, and how when he was young, his granddaddy would take him out to the cabin by the river and teach him how to do all sorts of things, like fix engines, build forts, cultivate marijuana plants, and how to use a slingshot.

"But the best thing he ever taught me was how to draw," Caleb said.

"He was an artist?"

"He had a sketchbook, and when the noise in his head got too much he'd sit out on that porch by the river and draw. I can't tell you how many nights we sat out there, an old man and a boy, just quieting the noise in our heads with our pencils and sketchbooks."

Later, when it started to get cold, we climbed back into this car and he drove us home.

When we pulled into the driveway, I noticed the light was on inside the apartment.

"Did you leave it on?" I asked, suddenly worried.

Ever since the break-in, I was on edge about someone getting inside the apartment again.

But Caleb simply gave me one of his disarming smiles.

Biker Baby

"Relax, it's not what you think," he replied calmly.

Confused, I climbed out of the car and followed him inside. Right away, I could tell things had been moved about the apartment, and as I stepped farther inside I could see all of Caleb's belongings, like his bed, blankets, and boxes of his clothes in the corner of the living room. Alarmed, I glanced at him, but he seemed perfectly at ease.

"What's going on?" I asked, looking at him suspiciously.

He smiled and turned me to face him. "Do you trust me?"

"Caleb—"

"Do you?"

I nodded.

"Then relax and close your eyes."

I looked at him questioningly but relaxed and did what he asked. I closed my eyes and let him guide me across the room. When he told me to open them again, I was standing in the doorway of his dark bedroom.

"Ready?" he asked.

I nodded and he flicked on the bedroom light.

And a gasp fell from my lips.

Before me, his room had been magically transformed into the most beautiful nursery I had ever seen. Everything I'd picked out earlier that day at the baby furniture store was assembled and in place. The crib. The chest of drawers. The changing table. Shelving.

"Oh my God, Caleb . . ." I walked into the room, gazing around me, slowly absorbing everything. "How—?"

"While you were walking around the store picking things out I asked the sales girl if I could have two very mean looking Prospects come and pick it all up."

"That's why you got her number?"

"The one and only reason. I gave it to the Prospects so they could organize the pick up and bring it back here. My mom, Indy, and Cherry met them here and helped them put it all together."

I gazed around the room, dazed and slightly overwhelmed by the gesture. In my chest, my heart overflowed with appreciation.

"I don't know what to say." Tears welled in my eyes. "It's so beautiful."

"You like it?"

"Like it, Caleb, it's the most beautiful thing in the world."

I wanted to cry. This man. This rugged, handsome, beautiful man. He was so thoughtful and kind.

"Thank you," I whispered.

He smiled and it was devastating. This whole fairytale moment was so completely and utterly devastating. How I could I not be in love with him?

I couldn't.

Because the truth was, I was crazy, madly, deeply head over heels in love with him.

"But what about you? Does this mean you're moving out?"

My heart sank at the thought.

"No," he said, reassuringly. "I'm going to take the couch for a while."

"You didn't have to give up your room."

He came toward me and put his hands on my growing stomach. "My baby needs his own room. I can sleep anywhere."

I couldn't find the right words to thank him. None of them seemed right. So I leaned up and kissed him on his cheek. "Thank you."

He smiled down at me, and the moment got weird. His smile faded and so did mine, and when his eyes dropped to my lips, I couldn't help but lick them. My heart stopped. My breathing, too. And I had to swallow deeply to get them both moving again.

"You're welcome," he said, finally, moving away from me. He headed for the bathroom. "I'm going to take a shower."

While he was showering, I stole another few minutes in the nursery, wandering around the room and taking it all in and appreciating all the hard work that had gone into it. I couldn't believe he'd corralled everyone to come over and get it set up as a surprise. My heart twisted. Even the little mobile with the bumblebees and teddy bears was in place and dangling down over the crib.

When Caleb came out of the shower, I was already dressed in my pajamas and in bed, sitting up against the pillows. He appeared in my doorway, dressed in a pair of boxer shorts and a white t-shirt.

Again, a sense of longing spread through me.

"Good night," he said.

"Thanks again for today."

His grin was beautiful, his voice husky and warm. "It was my pleasure." He winked. "Good night, Honey."

"Hey," I called out to him. "Don't take the couch. You can sleep in here. For tonight, you know, until we get the couch sorted."

The couch was currently piled high with his belongings.

"You sure?"

In response, I pulled back the covers and patted the bed next to me. "After what you did today, I'm not having you sleep on the floor."

He climbed into bed next to me, and I mashed the covers down with my arm, making a barrier between us in the sheets.

Darkness engulfed us as he turned off the lamp on the bedside table. He smelled soapy and warm, and I couldn't lie, him lying next to me was comforting and nice.

"What you did today was one of the nicest things anyone has ever done for me," I whispered. "Thank you, Caleb."

"You're welcome."

I felt him shift next to me.

"Was this just a ploy to get into bed with me?" I asked in the darkness.

I couldn't see him, but I could feel him grinning.

"It worked, didn't it?"

CHAPTER 33

CALEB

A noise woke me a little after 2 AM.

And for a moment I had no idea where I was. But as the cobwebs of sleep slowly cleared, I realized I was in bed with Honey and she was curled up behind me, her long legs tangled around mine. She was warm and soft, and I had a raging wood throbbing in my shorts.

My phone vibrated on the bedside table next to me and I realized it was what woke me. I reached for it.

It was Cade.

"Get over to Mom's now," he rasped. "She just got a call. It's Chance. He's been injured."

I sat up. "What happened?"

Ice ran through my veins.

"His unit was caught in an explosion. They're not sure if there are any survivors."

My brother's words were like a sword running through me.

"What do you fucking mean, Cade? What the fuck?"

Honey stirred and woke up, blinking her eyes and looking up at me from the pillow.

"Just get over here. Mom's on the phone with the military now. We'll know more by the time you get here."

Cade hung up.

"What's wrong?" Honey asked, slowly sitting up. "Are you okay?"

No. I was fucking far from okay. I was stunned. Nausea pulsed in my stomach and fear crept up my spine. I ripped off the bed covers and reached for my black pants on the chair next to the bed.

"Caleb?"

"It's Chance. He's been injured or . . . " I shook my head. No. I wasn't going to go there. My older brother was not about to become another fallen hero. "I've got to get over to my mom's."

"I'm coming with you."

"No. You sleep. I will call you when I know something."

But Honey was already climbing out of bed. She came to me and took me by the hands.

"You need to stop. Okay? Catch a breath before you drive over to your mom's." Her big blue eyes were full of concern. "Let me come with you. And whatever happens, I'll be there for you, okay."

Honey was the calm to my storm and I loved her for it.

She moved away from me, and for a moment, I did what she said. I paused and took a breath. And I watched her slip out of her pajamas, her sexy body six months pregnant with our baby, her breasts swollen, her belly round, and in my chest my heart filled with an immeasurable love for her. Slowly, my racing heart began to calm and the tingle of foreboding at the base of my spine was slightly tempered, although not completely gone.

I crossed the room to her.

"Stay here and sleep." My voice was husky because I was tired and anxious about Chance. But also because being this close to her, I longed to touch her, hold her and feel the calming thump of her heart against mine. I slid my hands over her belly where our baby was growing. "You need to rest."

She looked at me, her eyes searching my face, and then she nodded. "Okay, but you call me when you need to."

My hands lingered on her for a moment longer. "I will."

In five minutes, I was gone, riding into the darkness and toward something I had to accept may change everything forever. A numbness spread through my chest as I pushed the Harley farther into the night, memories of my eldest brother playing in my head. Of us as kids. Of him teaching me to ride my first bike when I was four. Of him showing me how to bait a hook and cast a fishing line, of the hours we spent down at his favorite fishing spot on the river. Of him yelling at me for borrowing his Tom Glavine baseball card, only for him to come into my room later that night and slip it into my hand while I slept because the next day I was going in for my first operation on my ears.

My jaw ticked and I bit my teeth together. With a jerk of my wrist I roared faster through the deserted streets of Destiny.

Growing up, I spent more time with Chance than anyone. Cade was always with Indy but Chance was a loner, preferring the quiet solitude of home where he could play his guitar, or fish down by the river. When he was in high school, I guess you could say he got popular. Girls were always calling our house. And he was always going off to parties. But no matter how popular or busy he became, he still had time for his kid brother.

When he left for the Navy SEALs, his absence was loud in our house.

He left because of our father. Because he didn't want to grow into the kind of man our father turned out to be. He never told me what he saw, or why it messed him up so much, but he did warn me to get as far away from our old man as I could.

But I didn't need to heed his warning. Because someone murdered our father before I needed to.

Chance came home for the funeral. But he didn't cry. It was his duty, he said, to come home and be there for his family. But as for his old man, as far as he was concerned he could rot in hell.

And then he was gone again.

I missed him.

I still did.

Fifteen minutes later, I pulled into my mom's driveway. All the lights were on in the house. I parked my bike, briefly wondering if old Mrs. Baker from across the road would call my mom and complain about the rumble of a Harley at two thirty in the morning, before I bounded up the front steps to the porch.

Inside, Mom was on the phone, smoking and pacing across the kitchen. Cade was also smoking and pacing across the kitchen, while Ari, my mom's boyfriend, sat calm but concerned at the twelve-seater dining table.

"What do we know?" I asked, walking in.

Cade came toward me, his face grim. "There was a bomb blast. The details are fucking sketchy. But he survived. Five out of his eight-squad didn't."

"Jesus Christ." I ran a hand through my hair. "When did it happen?"

"Two days ago."

"Two—why are we just finding out about it now?"

Cade shook his head, agitated, concerned. "Probably because of where he was, which of course is fucking classified."

Mom hung up from her call and slowly sat down at the head of the table.

Biker Baby

"He's okay," she said, her usually calm voice was shaky. "He's on his way back home. They needed to stabilize him before they could evacuate him."

Cade lit her a cigarette and handed it to her. She accepted it and drew in a heavy breath, exhaling it as if she was trying to exhale her pain.

"Did they say what his injuries were?" he asked.

"They're bad." Mom's chin quivered and Ari reached over, placing his hand on top of hers. "He's burnt. Badly. Second and third-degree burns to thirty or forty percent of his body."

I heard Cade exhale deeply next to me.

"What does that mean for him?" I asked.

"Months of rehabilitation. Surgery. They don't think he'll lose any of his limbs. It's going to be a slow healing process."

Heartbreak and rage crashed violently through me.

"The person I spoke to on the phone said he also had some bad shrapnel wounds. Lacerations, including a life threatening one to his skull." Tears glittered in my mom's eyes but she fought them. "They're taking him to a naval hospital in Maryland. He'll arrive tomorrow. I'll get the next flight out."

"I'll get it organized," Ari said, picking up his cell phone and scrolling through flights.

"I'm coming with you," Cade said.

"No, Indy is about to have her baby any day now. You're needed here." Mom drew shakily on her cigarette. "Besides, they won't let anyone into see him but me."

"Let me go with you," I said to her. "Even if I can't see him."

"You have a pregnant girlfriend," she reminded me.

"And she would insist I accompany my mom to visit my injured brother."

"You both have women carrying your babies. You both need to be here. Not across the country."

"I'll go with her," Ari said, getting up from the table. "I'll go make some calls."

Mom tried to swallow back her worry. She was a strong woman, but her Achilles' heel was her family. We meant everything to her, and if anything happened to any of us, she felt it right through to her soul.

I placed a reassuring hand on her shoulder. "He's alive. And when he's well enough, we'll bring him home."

She patted my hand. "I hope so, son."

Cade sat down at the table next to her. "I'll ride up to the university tomorrow and tell Chastity."

"No," Mom said. "She has exams coming up. Let's just wait and see what happens before we tell your sister."

When Mom decided to lie down, and Cade headed home to Indy, I rode home in the darkness with a cool, pre-dawn air whipping at my face. Once home and inside our apartment, I tried to be quiet so as not to wake Honey. I slipped off my hoodie and shook off my boots, and instead of heading for the couch to sleep, I decided to check on her. Seeing her sleeping so soundly made my chest ache with longing. In another time, I would've slid into the bed next to her and lost myself in her warmth and the creaminess of her body as I made love to her. Comfort would have been found in making her cry out my name before I lost myself in the pleasure of coming inside her. But those days were past. Now I had to settle for sitting on the edge of the bed and taking a moment to watch her.

She was perfect. *Fucking perfect.* And during the maelstrom going on around me, I was just grateful she was there to temper the storm.

She stirred and slowly blinked awake. "I didn't hear you come in. Are you okay?"

I nodded, and despite my heavy heart, smiled. "I will be."

"Is Chance okay?"

Christ, I hope so.

"He's on his way back to the US now. They're taking him to a naval hospital in Maryland. Mom is flying out tomorrow, but they won't let anyone else in to see him."

She sat up and leaned back into the pillow, looking crumpled and sleepy. *And adorable.* She reached for my hand and pulled it into hers. "How bad are his injuries?"

"He suffered some burns and shrapnel injuries. We'll know more tomorrow once Mom has been to see him. But he's alive and we have to hold onto that thought."

Fuck.

Now I felt like fucking crying.

Feeling emotional, I rubbed my eyes.

Honey squeezed my hand. "You look tired."

"I'm fucking exhausted."

She glanced out the window. It was still dark out, but in an hour it would be light. "You should try and get some sleep."

She was right, but I knew I wouldn't be able to sleep. There was too much going on in my head. "I don't think I can."

She ran a tender hand up my back and I closed my eyes at the comfort funneling through me. It was like the anniversary of my father's murder when she'd come to the clubhouse and soothed me into a deep and peaceful sleep.

"Just lie down for a bit," she whispered, gently coaxing me down onto the bed. She wrapped her arms around me, and I got lost in the warmth of her holding me against her body. I got lost in the happiness of feeling her round belly pressing into my back and in the comfort of her soft breaths against the back of my neck. Before I realized it, sleep overcame me and the agony of my brother's tragedy was momentarily lost in a heavy and dreamless slumber.

CHAPTER 34

CALEB

I awoke with a start several hours later. Looking at the clock, I was surprised to see it was almost lunchtime. Next to me, Honey was still sound asleep, on her back with her arm limp over her swollen belly.

Careful not to wake her, I slipped from her bed and went to the bathroom for a shower. The noise was back in my head, and the fear and anxiety of my brother's injuries flooded every cell in my body. I needed an escape and knew the perfect place.

After a shower, I packed an overnight bag, and after leaving Honey a note, left our apartment and took off on my bike. I dropped into my mom's to check if there was any more news about Chance. He was still en route to the US and there had been no change in his condition. However, one of the other two survivors had passed away from his injuries. The news was gut wrenching. Another family was going to receive the news we were praying we never heard. It was also a sober reminder that Chance was still critically wounded, and until he was home on

US soil and given the necessary time his body needed to heal, he wasn't out of the woods.

Cade and Indy arrived and Indy filled us in on some of the realities of burn injuries. He might have survived the initial injuries, but infection was a real concern. He would have to recuperate in a sterile hospital room and the recovery would be long and often painful.

"We'll bring him home," Mom said, barely holding back her tears. "And we will look after him."

When she said *we*, she meant the whole club.

Indy slid her hand over hers. "It will be a while before he is released. I want you to be prepared for it. What it is. What it means. How he looks. It's going to be difficult."

Mom looked at her through her unshed tears, her eyes as bright as sapphires.

"Baby girl, my whole life was built on difficult. Why the hell would this be any different?"

There was nothing left to do but wait.

But I needed to get away. I needed to stop the noise in my head. Mom was fine, soothed by some of Sybil's stash and a shot of Patrón. It was time to head out to my granddaddy's cabin for the night and spend some quiet time on the porch overlooking the water. I climbed on my bike and took my time riding through the golden light of the afternoon, arriving at the cabin just as the sun began to set.

Inside, I dumped my overnight bag by the bedroom door but didn't switch on the light. Dusky light from a dying sun streamed in through the kitchen window, breaking the shadows in the room.

As I passed a wooden hutch, I paused to look at the photos spread across the dark wooden shelves. Years of family memories captured in time. Photos of a young Hutch and Sybil when they were building the cabin. Of two blonde-haired little boys fishing by the river's edge taken sometime in the early seventies. Of my mom and my dad when they were so young and naïve, their arms around each other as they posed awkwardly for the camera before heading off to prom. Of Sybil and Hutch's six grandchildren, the twins Abby and Isaac, and me with my brothers and sister. All of us young and smiling.

I picked up a silver framed photo of me and my granddaddy. It was taken just before he passed away. I was only eight but we'd already formed such a close bond. Sybil once told me that Hutch had admitted to her that he felt closer to me than he ever did with my father. My daddy, he said, wasn't interested in him right from the very beginning. But in me, he'd found a kindred spirit, and I felt exactly the same way. Losing him had punched a hole right through my heart and I'd never gotten over it.

I picked up a second photo. It was of Chance and me taken a week before he was shipped out. Chance was in his Navy uniform and smiling broadly for the camera. I was a geeky fourteen-year-old with no muscles, no facial hair, and no idea I was going to watch my father die in front of me in a matter of months.

Our family had lost so many. Not just our biological family, but our MC family, as well. Losing Chance was not an option.

I thought of Honey and our baby, and a calming warmth swept through me. I put the photo down and took a deep breath. Pulling my sketchbook and pencils from my overnight bag, I stepped out onto the back veranda overlooking the water and sat in my granddaddy's chair. Looking for some peace and quiet from my own head, I opened my sketchbook and began drawing.

I'm not sure how long I was out there, but it grew dark so I had to turn on the porch light. I took a beer from the refrigerator in the kitchen and lost myself deeper into my art. Frogs croaked down by the water, and bugs buzzed in the air. Farther down the river an owl hooted, calling out to her mate.

When a set of headlights broke through the darkness of the trees, I realized I must've been out on the veranda for hours. I got up, the chair creaking and moaning as I climbed out of it to see who was here.

Just as I stepped inside, there was a knock on the door.

It was Honey.

Love bloomed in my heart when I saw her standing there on the doorstep looking unsure and a little vulnerable. She wasn't sure if she should have come, but she was here just in case. For me.

Without saying a thing, I pulled her into my arms and held her tightly to my chest, burying my face in the warmth of her neck as all my emotions surged to the surface. Until I'd seen her, I didn't realize how much I needed her right now.

"It's okay," she whispered.

I didn't want to let her go. I wanted to stay engulfed in her. But I broke away and stepped back to let her inside.

"I wanted to check on you," she said, placing her handbag on the small, round dining table. "I hope that's okay."

"You're a sight for sore eyes," I said. I was tired. Emotionally wrecked. Having her here made me incredibly happy. I sat down on the couch and she sat across from me, her legs curled underneath her, the swell of her belly obvious in the dress she wore.

And that was how we sat for hours. Talking. About everything. About Chance and his injuries and what it would mean for him now. She asked about him and I told her how he'd joined the Kings of Mayhem while on a break from his Navy duties before heading into the more specialized field of the Navy SEALs. How he bought me my first tattoo gun.

And in turn she told me about her childhood. How when she was growing up she wanted to be a part of a family because she was always lonely for company when her mom was never home.

And when she told me that, I longed to tell her that she could be a part of the biggest family in the state if she would just let me in and give me a chance.

But I didn't.

Because I wasn't in the mood to hear her answers.

Not tonight.

Realizing it was after midnight, we moved to the bedroom and my body ached with fatigue, my mind even more so. Moonlight streamed into the room and cast the shadows in a milky white glow, making her skin as smooth as marble. She moved across the room and kissed me chastely on the cheek, wrapping her arms around me as she gave me a warm embrace goodnight.

"You're not sleeping in here?" I asked wearily as she moved away.

She paused and stood across the room looking at me, thinking. Her eyes gleamed like big shiny orbs. I sat on the end of the bed wanting her to join me. Wanting to fall asleep in her arms. Wanting her. Needing her. But not wanting to hear her say no.

Without a word, she came to me and pressed her lips to mine. It was a closed lip kiss, but it lingered as if we were frozen in time. And when I parted my lips, they parted hers and my tongue moved into her luscious mouth.

For a moment there was hesitation. But then she exhaled breathlessly and her tongue brushed against mine and a soft moan caught in her throat.

In an instant, desire replaced reminiscence. Lust replaced pain. Action replaced hesitation. With a hiss I pulled her onto my lap and held her to me, my eyebrows slammed together as I kissed her with every part of my soul. The pain of my brother's accident nipped at my heels, but when Honey kissed me it was like we were flying so high nothing could catch me.

Without words, I undressed her, slowly, savoring every reveal of exposed flesh as I peeled her clothes away from her beautiful body. She was so tanned, so smooth, and the way she slid her hands around my neck and kissed me passionately had me so hard it hurt.

I was so lost in desire it barely registered when she climbed onto my lap and sank down on my cock with a deep, breathless moan.

With a slow rise and fall of her hips she rode me, her head tilted back, her milky, slender throat smooth and creamy, her heavy belly rubbing against the bumps and grooves of my stomach. She closed her eyes and her plump, delicious lips parted as she moaned with the pleasure she was taking from me.

She arched her back, allowing me easy access to her perfect breasts. I took one in my hand and enclosed my mouth over her perky, pink nipple, sucking it into my mouth and lapping at it with my tongue. She moaned and lost herself in the sensation, my name falling from her lips as her eyes found mine.

And suddenly we weren't fucking. It was so much more than that. There was real emotion and it filled the room and wrapped us in its arms as Honey moved slowly against me, gently rolling her hips over mine. My climax was building, but I wanted this to last because this was like nothing I'd ever known. The warmth. The emotion. The electrical charge in the air.

Honey's eyes held mine as she placed a cool hand on my shoulder to steady herself, and I couldn't look away. There was so much more in those smoldering blue eyes than lust. When she closed them I felt her clench tightly around my cock and I groaned as the pleasure swelled in my balls, and again I had to resist the urge to give in to my orgasm. She dropped her head back and moaned, her pussy gripping my cock as she started to come. And Christ Almighty, she looked like a fucking angel. So creamy and smooth. Her beautiful, long hair swirling around her polished shoulders and tumbling over her breasts as she took everything my cock had to give her. Her breathing hitched and she cried out, her tight pussy milking me. Her muscles tightening around me, her body quivering and trembling as her orgasm tore through her. That was it. There was no point fighting it. No point resisting. It was a slow build but it erupted into a giant supernova, ferociously consuming me with a force I'd never known. Blinded by ecstasy, I grabbed her face and smashed my mouth to hers, kissing her wildly as I came hard inside her, my hips thrusting, my cock violently ejaculating with months of pent-up desire.

Breathless and my mind blown, I fell back onto the bed and pulled her down with me and into my arms, my heart thundering as I savored the sensation of her naked skin against mine. I kissed the top of her head and closed my eyes, my mind wiped clean of the darkness brought on by Chance and the uncertainty of his survival. This woman. This angel. The mother of my child. She'd given me a small space of time free from the torment of worrying about my brother by loving me with her beautiful body and soothing me with her gentle touch. She fought off my pain as fiercely as if it had been her own, and the strongest of emotions bloomed in my heart because of it.

I held her close and got lost in the warmth of her sweet body covering mine. It had taken a while, but we were finally where we belonged.

Together.

CHAPTER 35

HONEY

"So what was it like this morning when you woke up in his arms?" Autumn asked.

We were climbing the stairs to my apartment. I was carrying two bags of groceries while Autumn was breaking into the box of pepperoni pizza she was holding.

"I didn't hang around long enough to find out," I said, ashamed.

"You mean you didn't stay?"

"I had an appointment. I had to leave early."

She stopped on the step in front of me, the slice of pizza in her hand paused halfway to her mouth. "What are you talking about? We've been at the mall all day."

"It felt weird, okay. I had to get out of there."

"Weird?" Her eyes searched my face and I could see the moment she realized the truth. "Are you in love with him?"

I swallowed thickly. Yes, I was in love with him.

I sighed and walked past her, ignoring her look of disbelief as I made my way to the front door. I shoved the key in, hating the hot prickle of shame creeping up my spine and flushing across the nape of my neck, as I pushed the door open.

"So you told him you had an appointment and bailed on him?" she said, following me inside.

I dumped the groceries on the counter. "Please don't, Autumn, I already feel bad enough."

And I did. It felt like I had abandoned him.

She sighed. "So, you're not together. But do you want to be?"

She put the open box of pizza on the table and moved to the kitchen to get some plates.

"No." I glanced away, afraid she would see the uncertainty on my face, as I put the cold groceries in the refrigerator.

Autumn sounded surprise. "No?"

"Caleb is amazing." Amazing? Hell, my heart *craved* him. "But we're complete opposites. I don't fit into his world."

I thought about my first night at the clubhouse and the girl passed out at the base of the stripper pole, and the larger lady bent over the pool table as an older biker slapped into her from behind. I thought about Caleb's father and how his fourteen-year old son had watched his murder unfold before him. I thought of going to the bathroom at the clubhouse and walking in on a yellow-haired girl giving a biker a blowjob. I thought about Tiffani and the string of other scantily dressed women who were eager to warm the bed of a King.

And then I thought of Caleb and my chest squeezed with longing because I wished our worlds were somehow compatible.

"His world?" Autumn raised her eyebrow.

I shook my head and grabbed two plates, taking them to the dining table and sitting down. "The club life. The parties. The *women*."

"But from what you've told me, he hasn't been with any women since... well, you know... since you guys made a baby."

Biker Baby

"Yeah, but what about afterwards? When our baby is here and life settles into boring, domesticated routines of baby naps, feeding times, and diapers. What happens when my boobs spring a leak and I'm exhausted from sleep and I don't feel like making love? Have you seen those girls who hang around the clubhouse? They're eager. They're willing. They're a temptation. And after Charlie . . . " I shook my head. "I don't want it, Autumn. I don't want that life for me or the baby."

I put a piece of pizza on my plate but left it there. Autumn was making me feel even more guilty about the night before in the cabin and my appetite was gone.

Since leaving the cabin I'd been consumed with guilt. I'd broken my own rule. The sex had been great. I mean, the sex had been *really* great. And after I'd fallen asleep in his arms, he'd woken me up with the most tender of caresses in the middle of the night. Moonlight had streamed into the room, casting an ethereal light into the room where we made love without words, our bodies speaking the only language we needed. He had taken everything from me, and I had given it to him willingly, lost in the sensation of his body and what it did to me. But the spell had been broken with the harsh morning light. Already feeling the onset of guilt and regret, I'd fled the cabin, lying about an appointment.

Like a coward.

Why? Because we'd crossed the line.

One I'd been too terrified to cross by myself.

And I needed to process what I'd done and what it meant.

Oh, I knew I was in love with him. That was probably the only thing I did know.

But what I was going to do about it was a complete fucking mystery.

"What's the point in starting something with someone I don't see a future with?" I said sadly.

"The way I see it, you've already started something. You just can't see it."

"I can't be with him, Autumn."

"Then why did you make love to him last night?"

"I shouldn't have done it," I said quietly. "It was a selfish, stupid mistake."

The creak of the floorboard turned both our heads, and to my horror I saw Caleb standing in the doorway to his bedroom.

Oh, Jesus. I didn't know he was home. I thought he was still out at the cabin.

Heat rushed up my spine and spread across my face and neck.

He looked at me. He was still. His face as dark as thunder.

"Hey, I didn't know you were back," I said, alarmed, wondering how much he'd heard. I stood up with a rush. Guilt rolled through me as I watched him shove his arms into his cut and grab his keys off the kitchen counter. "We got pizza, are you hungry?"

Caleb's face was set. His eyes were hard and his jaw tight. He smashed on his aviators and brushed past us to the front door. "I'm done."

Without another word, he ripped open the door and slammed it behind him.

Autumn and I both jumped.

"How much do you think he heard?" I asked Autumn.

"Based on that exit . . . pretty much everything about how unsuitable he is and nothing about you being in love with him."

I grimaced and slowly sat back down again. "He's going to completely misunderstand."

My best friend gave me a sympathetic look. "Then tell him, Honey. Let him know how you feel."

She was right, I needed to tell him, but when I rang him it went to voicemail. So I texted him, asking him to please call me. I wasn't going to tell him I was in love with him over a text message. He needed to hear me tell him face to face. And then we could talk. But he never replied.

Autumn did her best to try and comfort me, but it was a losing battle, because no matter how you looked at it, I'd just pushed Caleb away.

After she left, I rang him again, but like the first call, it went to voicemail. He was ignoring me and I couldn't blame him. I could only imagine how hurt he felt.

It got late and I tried to sleep, but the minutes ticked over with excruciating slowness, and lying in the dark, I couldn't help but listen for Caleb's bike. But it never came. Sometime after 3 AM I fell into a restless sleep only to wake up with the sun breaking through the dawn. I pulled back the covers and tiptoed to the living room, hoping he'd snuck in after I'd fallen asleep. But his blankets were still folded up on an empty couch.

Unease began to tingle at base of my spine.

Where was he? Was he okay?

I checked my phone, but there were no messages.

Before going to bed I had sent him a second message.

Me: *I'm sorry. Please call me.*

But he hadn't replied.

Feeling drained, I showered and forced down some breakfast. Now that I was in my second trimester, the nausea was only minor and I was able to keep food down. So I brewed some tea and fixed some toast, and tried to ignore the growing anxiety in my chest. I told myself I had nothing to worry about. We had Bump's sonogram at nine, and there was no way he would miss it.

But by eight o'clock, my worry replaced reasoning.

Had he been in an accident?

Was he lying hurt somewhere?

Was he with another woman?
No. Caleb wouldn't do that.
He told me he wouldn't. Gave his word.
I rang him again. And again there was no answer.

So I sent him another text message, even though by then I didn't expect an answer because I was convinced something was terribly wrong.

I could feel it.

I went to my sonogram appointment, saw our baby, and was relieved when the doctor confirmed everything was progressing nicely.

"Do you want to know the sex?" he asked.

I thought about it.

Did I?

Did Caleb?

No, he didn't want to know. Because if he did he would have been there.

When I left the doctor's office, I stopped by the Kings of Mayhem clubhouse to see if anyone had heard from him.

By then, worry had morphed into anger.

My guilt into hurt.

And when I pulled up beside to a familiar Harley sitting next to a pink Mercedes in the clubhouse parking lot, a prickly anxiety began to tingle at the base of my spine again.

Crossing the compound, my knees went weak. And when Tiffani walked out of the clubhouse, barely dressed in her almost non-existent Daisy Dukes and looking like the cat that ate the cream, I began to feel like I might throw up my breakfast right there on the pavement. Her heavily made-up eyes swept up and down me, and she smirked.

"Sorry, Honey, but you can't keep a good man down," she said as she walked past me, swaying her hips.

Before I could reply, Caleb appeared at the door and my skin went cold. I glanced at Tiffani and back to him. For a moment my heart stopped beating and my lungs emptied of air as I realized what had happened. Last night, while I was lying awake, unable to sleep because I was consumed with guilt and worry, Caleb had been here, balls deep in a blonde girl with double Ds and a smug smile. One look at him and I knew it was true.

Seeing the look on my face, Tiffani laughed and slunk away. I turned back to Caleb. Tears stabbed at my eyes and heat flared in my cheeks. I wanted to do so many things in that moment. Cry. Yell. Throw something. Cry. Ask him why he picked her over *us*. Cry.

Instead, I pulled the sonogram out of my handbag and smashed it to his chest.

"You missed it," I said. Then turning away, stormed off.

Realizing what I had given him and what he had missed, he growled and chased after me.

"Honey, wait!"

But I wasn't about to listen to anything he had to say. If he wanted to fuck her, then she could have him. I was right to think we were worlds apart. I was right to think things could never work between us. I ran to my car and climbed in, fumbling with the keys in the ignition. I tried to close the door, but Caleb's big hand clamped down on it and wrenched it wider.

"Will you stop!" he begged.

"Leave me alone! I've got nothing to say to you." I looked away from him because tears stabbed at my eyes and it would be a cold day in hell before I let him see them. "You clearly have more important things to do."

"I'm sorry I missed the appointment."

"Don't bother." I grabbed the door and tried to close it, but again Caleb stopped it.

"Please just tell me, is everything okay with the baby?"

I narrowed my eyes and snatched the sonogram out of his hands. "What baby?"

Then, yanking the door closed, I gunned the engine and sped out of the compound.

CHAPTER 36

CALEB

"You're a fucking idiot," came the voice behind me. I swung around. Cade was walking toward me.

"Don't start," I warned, turning away because my head was pounding like a motherfucker and I didn't want a verbal beat down from my older brother.

But Cade wasn't about to let it go.

"What the fuck are you up to?"

"I fucked up. I get it."

"Do you?"

"Yes, I get it. I fucked up."

"Then where are you going?" he asked as I headed toward the clubhouse.

"I'm hungover. I'm tired. I'm going back to bed."

He swung me around. "That woman you just reduced to tears is carrying your baby. You go after her, brother, and you make it right."

I shrugged him off. "She hates me."

"So?"

"So . . . she doesn't want anything to do with me right now." I ran a frustrated hand through my hair. "Don't you think I would go after her if I thought she wanted me to? Believe me when I say, she doesn't."

Cade nodded toward Tiffani who was leaning up against her car smoking a cigarette. "Tell me she's not involved."

I turned away, ashamed, and headed toward the clubhouse.

"You fucking douche," Cade muttered.

"It's not what you think."

"No?"

I swung back to face him. "No!"

"So you didn't fuck that little skank while your pregnant girlfriend was at home wondering where the fuck you were."

He looked at me like I was scum. And even though it wasn't what he thought, he was right. I was a fucking douche. I had let Honey down.

"She's not my girlfriend," I yelled. "And if you want to know why, go and fucking ask her. She has a whole list of reasons why I'm so fucking unsuitable. Yeah, she's carrying my baby, but it turns out she doesn't think that much of me after all. Apparently, I'm biker scum. Our worlds don't gel. I'm a nice guy, but fucking hell, I'm not good enough to be with her."

But Cade wasn't buying any of it. He shook his head and gave me a dark look. "Stop being such a fucking pussy and go make it right."

Turning, he walked away, leaving me in early morning sunlight feeling like the biggest piece of shit in the world.

A simple apology wasn't going to do it.

Biker Baby

So I rode into town for flowers. I knew she liked sunflowers, so I headed into the little village near her home on Chamomile Street, where she said a flower shop carried them all year round.

As I was leaving, I saw Indy walking across the road toward me. Heavily pregnant, she was carrying a paper bag of baguettes and groceries from the bakery behind her.

"Hey!" she called out.

I pulled down my aviators and inwardly groaned. This was going to hurt. Indy didn't tolerate bad manners.

"Hey," I mumbled.

Just as I predicted, she let me have it.

"You asshole! What the hell is wrong with you? I just got off the phone with Cade and he told me what you did." She hit me with one of the baguettes. "What's gotten into you? Have you lost your fucking mind?"

I squinted in the bright sunlight. "You're assaulting me with bread, and I'm the crazy one?"

She paused mid-hit. "Yes, you are! Because to do what you did you must be fucking crazy."

She hit me again.

"I get it. I'm scum."

"You're not scum, Caleb. What you did was scummy."

"It's not what you think."

Again, she whacked me with her bread bat.

"It's *always* what we think. You guys think you can just say that and we'll believe you—"

"I didn't fuck her," I interrupted her.

She stopped the bread assault and looked mildly surprised. "You didn't?"

"No. For fuck's sake, I might be an asshole but I'm not that much of one."

"Then, what?"

"I missed the sonogram. I promised her I would be there every step of the way but I missed the sonogram because I was so fucking pissed at her for what I overheard. I let her down, okay, but I didn't let her down by fucking someone else."

"So you didn't get balls deep in some club skank?"

"No." I frowned. Why did everyone think I was such a douche? "Tiffani tried. She will *always* try. When she didn't get any interest out of me, she spent the night with Grunt. He's still passed out at the clubhouse. Ask him yourself."

"Then why did you let Honey think you did?"

"Because if she thinks I am capable of doing that, then what's the point in trying to convince her otherwise? She's already made her mind up about me. I told her I wasn't going to be with anyone. Yet she thinks the first chance I get, I go running in the direction of another woman. If that's what she thinks of me—"

"Jesus Christ, Caleb, stop being such a fucking pussy," she snapped, echoing her husband's words of less than an hour ago. "You go and see your girl, and you let her know that you didn't do anything with Tiffani."

"She doesn't want to hear it, Indy. She doesn't see me as anything more than the sperm donor of her baby."

Indy rolled her eyes. "When did you become such a fucking princess?"

"Harsh," I replied.

My hangover was really ramping up in the heat of the day. My head pounded and I had to squint because everything was fuzzy.

"Oh, fuck . . ." Indy's eyes suddenly went round. She paused and then grabbed the front of my t-shirt. "Oh, no, no, no, no, no, no..."

"What?" I asked, a little confused.

She looked at me and then to the ground. My eyes followed and saw the puddle of water on the pavement.

"My water just broke!"

It took a moment for her words to register.

Then they hit me like a punch to the face.

"Fuck!" I had no idea what to do. "I'll call an ambulance."

But Indy didn't hear me. She was bent over with pain and let out an almighty cry.

I dropped the sunflowers and searched for my phone, patting my cut and hoping like hell I hadn't left it in the clubhouse.

Indy bent over in pain again. "Oh God!"

My phone was in the back pocket of my jeans and I quickly dialed 911.

"There's no time ... this baby ... it's coming ..."

"Don't say that!" I looked at her, alarmed. "I'm calling an ambulance."

Her hand bit into my shirt. "You listen to me and you listen to me good, Caleb Calley. Your niece or nephew is about to spill out onto this goddamn pavement." She gritted her teeth. "Now get me inside that goddamn florist before I give birth out here in the street!"

CHAPTER 37

HONEY

"You know, he didn't sleep with that girl," Indy said. She was resting in her hospital bed with her newborn son cradled in her arms.

For someone who'd only given birth three hours earlier, she looked incredible.

"He didn't?" I asked, trying not to sound hopeful.

Indy shook her head. "No. Grunt did."

"Then why did he let me think he did?"

"He overheard you talking to Autumn. Heard what you said about him not being suitable. It hurt him. More than he thought, I guess, and he didn't know what to do with it so he went and did what he has always done . . . get drunk and hang out with his club brothers."

"Can I ask how you know all of this?"

She looked sheepish. "I might have assaulted him with bread."

I laughed. "I don't even know what that means, but it sounds awesome."

She smiled. "I saw him, not long after you did. By then Cade had already told me what had happened at the clubhouse between you and him. So when I came across him at the market, I attacked him with my baguette."

"That's got to be the best thing I've ever heard."

"He told me what really happened." She smiled. "And then my water broke on his boots."

We both laughed, and when River squirmed in her arms and made some of those cute baby noises, Indy looked down at him and began to gently rock him.

"You know, Caleb's a good guy." She looked up again. "And I've never seen him as into a girl as he is with you."

I couldn't help but smile.

"You should give him a chance," she said lightly. "You make a good couple."

"It's not that easy," I said.

"It never is." She laughed softly. "He feels bad about missing the sonogram. But that's all he did. Go easy on him. He's a Calley. They're smart sonsofbitches, but when it comes to affairs of the heart they do really stupid shit. You'll learn. Caleb has a big heart. I don't think he'd hurt you for the world."

I appreciated her words. "Thank you. But I'm not here to talk about my pitiful love life. I'm here to ooh and ahh over this handsome little man. Are you ready to hand him over, or do I have to bribe you?"

"Here, take him." She handed me her newborn son. "But just so you know, bribery works, too. I'm feeling generous today, but next time bring cake."

For the next ten minutes we ogled over little River Isaac Calley until Cade turned up. He'd been down at the cafeteria getting his wife coffee and a chocolate fudge brownie. He took his son from me and cradled him in his big arms. He wasn't wearing his cut, and I realized it was the first time I'd ever seen him without it. He looked like any other new father, his eyes misty, his face soft with a never experienced before love that only came with holding your newborn baby in your arms.

"I'm going to go," I said to them, feeling it was time to leave them to it. You could feel the love in the room and they needed alone time with their son.

"Caleb's out in the hall," Cade said, glancing up from gazing at his son. "He's waiting for you."

My stomach knotted.

"Remember what I said, go easy on him," Indy added. She was already breaking into the brownie. "He made a mistake and I'm sure he's paying for it."

She was right. He really hadn't done anything wrong. *Like getting ten-inches deep into that club skank.* And the relief I had was insane. I felt let down that he'd missed our sonogram, but it didn't even come close to how I felt about him fucking Tiffani. I wasn't going to keep this going.

Which was all well and good until I actually saw him.

He was waiting for me in the corridor looking so damn rough, but at the same time, so damn delicious, and my heart spun on its heels with all the pain and worry from the night before.

He looked up when he heard me and the tension stretched out between us.

"I didn't touch her," he said.

"I know."

He came toward me, cautiously. He looked like a wreck. Messy hair. Pale skin. Scruffy jaw. "I'm sorry I missed the sonogram."

"Why did you?"

"Because I made a mistake." His jaw tightened. "Listen, Honey. I get it. You don't want me. All those reasons why you don't want to be with me—"

"I'm so sorry I said those things."

"You're only sorry I overheard you."

"No, I'm sorry because I said them. I can only imagine how it felt. Especially after . . ."

"After—"

"What happened in the cabin, I didn't mean to make it sound like it meant nothing."

"Did it?" he asked. "Mean nothing?"

"It meant something." I struggled to find the words that could somehow make this better. That could somehow take away the hurt. "It meant more than it ever has meant."

I watched his throat as he tried to swallow.

"I can't keep doing this," he breathed.

"What do you mean?"

"This. Us. Waiting for you to want me. To want us."

"We both decided that—"

"I don't care what we decided then. It's changed. For me, anyway. I think we were wrong."

"Obviously we weren't . . . look at last night, you didn't even bother to come home. This is exactly why we made the decision to keep it platonic."

He looked tired. "I made a mistake."

"Is this how it would be? You running off to your clubhouse every time something goes wrong?"

"No. I fucked up. But I didn't do anything with Tiffani."

"Not this time. But what about the next?"

"There won't be a next time." He looked at me and his jaw ticked. "Because I'm giving you what you want."

Alarm sizzled at the base of my spine. "What do you mean?"

"I'm done. You've made it perfectly clear you don't want me."

"Caleb—"

"I'll be gone by tonight."

He walked away and my heart broke.

I had pushed him away and it was exactly what I didn't want to do.

It was time to stop running.

Stop pushing him away.

Stop letting my stupid past get in the way of what was good for me.

As I watched him moving farther away from me, I finally decided to face my fears and take back my power from them.

Fears be damned. This man deserved better from me.

"It's a girl," I said suddenly, my voice echoing down the hospital corridor.

Caleb stopped walking and slowly turned around. He frowned as he absorbed what I'd just said.

"A girl?"

I nodded, feeling the tears stab at my eyes. "I hope you're ready for it. If she's anything like me, we're in for one hell of a ride."

His eyes glittered across at me, and as the realization sank in, the shadow slowly lifted from his face. With hasty strides he crossed the distance between us and gently took me by the arms. He looked at me in wonder. *Stunned* wonder. "We're having a daughter?"

I nodded and tried to hold back my tears. But the emotion in his voice made it impossible, and quite suddenly I started to cry. Without a word, he pulled me into his arms and held me to his broad chest, and my body softened in surrender against him. I could feel the wild beating of his heart and closed my eyes, allowing myself to be lost in the warmth of his embrace. Being in his arms, it was where I belonged.

"Darlin', don't cry," he whispered, pressing a kiss to my hair. "I won't let you down again. I swear on my life." He pulled back to look at me and I could see the sincerity on his handsome face. "I'm going to take care of you both. You have my word."

Biker Baby

I smiled through my tears. "Don't pay any attention to these." I pointed to the tears rolling down my cheeks. "Apparently this is a thing now. I cry at everything."

He took my face in his big hands and his eyes reached right into mine. And in the bright blueness there was a tender warmth. "Be with me," he rasped in his deep, rich voice.

"What?"

"Fuck everything else, Honey. Be with me. I want this. I want you. I want us. Give me a chance." His thumbs caressed my jaw. "Baby, say you'll be my girl."

He kissed me, and it was a slow, desperate kiss full of promises and hope.

When he pulled away, his fingers raked through my hair as he searched my face for my answer, and his eyes were so full of emotion, I started to cry harder.

"Yes." I nodded, as more tears streamed down my cheeks. "I think I'd like that."

He smiled and it was huge. Happiness lit up his tired eyes. "Yes?"

I nodded and started to laugh through my tears. "Yes."

He exhaled harshly and kissed me again, his big hands cupping my jaw and holding me to him as his lips and tongue took command of mine.

"Let me take you home," he whispered against my lips. "Let me show you how good this will be."

When I nodded, he slung a big arm around my shoulders and led me down the corridor and out of the hospital.

CHAPTER 38

HONEY

My heart felt light, my head full of happiness as we drove home. It felt right. Doing this. Taking the chance and being together. Sometimes the greatest rewards were born from the highest risks and I knew this one was going to end in our favor.

Once home, I led him to the bedroom and we took our time undressing one another. We kissed, tenderly at first, before our desire detonated and we fell to the bed, our bodies crying out for more. I lay down with my head in the pillows, my body open to him as he crawled along the length of me, his eyes wild with desire, his cock hard and big as it slid across my belly.

He bent his head, and his tongue led a trail along the smooth curve of my throat, his lips devouring the flesh at the base of my jaw. I gasped at the pleasure. At the tenderness. At the way his body blanketed mine. At the touch of his erection as it rubbed against my clit, teasing me, torturing me, making me so wet I could barely stand it. I was so aroused I was trembling beneath his touch, writhing, the muscles between my thighs aching to be stretched and filled. He leaned into me, his muscular body blanketing me in a delicious heat and smooth skin as he positioned himself between my open thighs. Taking himself in his hand, he slid the wide crest of his cock through the most sensitive part of me, his face shimmering with pleasure, his lips parting, his eyes hooded with rampant desire as he rubbed himself through my flesh, torturing and teasing me before pushing hard into me.

My breath left me as it left him.

Our eyes met.

Emotion crashed around us.

He thrust in again, a desperate moan escaping his parted lips as he found his rhythm and began to make love to me. Beneath him I fell in tune to the way he loved my body, my legs wrapping tightly around his muscular waist as our bodies began to move in perfect synchronicity.

It was beauty. It was euphoria. It was the summoning of magic. Every delicious stroke and touch, every erotic tangle of our limbs, every soft slide of warm skin against skin, they pulled me deeper and deeper into an abyss of sensation until I was completely, and utterly, lost. My climax was a slow burn. It came from the very core of me, sweet and warm, a sugary bliss spreading through my body, moving slowly until it rose like a wave and crashed over me with such force I cried out with unrestrained ecstasy.

Caleb rose up on his big arms to look down at me, emotion raw and naked on his face, his eyes vibrant with everything he was feeling. Lust. Desire. *Need*. He thrust into me again and his eyes closed briefly with the pleasure. My name fell from his wet lips in a desperate breath. In response, I moved beneath him and it was his undoing. A tremor ran through him and he gripped the bedding around my head as he cried out, his eyebrows drawn together, his body driving into mine—one, two, three times more, before he stilled and I felt his powerful cock ejaculating violently into me. Slowly, he brought his body down to rest against mine, his skin hot and slick, his wild heartbeat a soft pulse against me. His breathing slowly evened and cooled on my heated flesh.

When he was ready, he raised his head and looked into my eyes. "This is right. And if I have to spend the rest of my life proving it to you, then I will."

CHAPTER 39

CALEB

Life got busy.

Only a few months ago I was filling my days with tattoo work and filling my nights with drinking, hanging out with my brothers, and losing myself in the body of a woman I would never see again. I didn't realize it then but I realized it now, I had been lonely. Now I knew what I had been missing out on and the thought of going back to that lifestyle was unappealing, uninviting, and made me wish I'd met Honey sooner.

Now, months later, I barely had time to breathe. Between dividing my time at the studio, working for the club, and spending time with Honey, there didn't seem a moment to spare. And there wasn't a second that I didn't love it.

The weed fields were well underway. Sybil was thrilled that her pot production was back in play and she was a regular visitor to the fields, although I'm not sure our production manager, Luther Barbosa, didn't want to see her as frequently as he did. Not that he wasn't more than equipped to deal with her sharp-tongue and cyclonic personality. He was a lawyer. He was used to arguing and bamboozling, and in a weird way, I think he enjoyed debating with my feisty grandmother.

Things were going really well at the tattoo studio. I had more clients than ever, a lot of them regulars or people who'd heard about me through word of mouth. I'd even won a couple of awards for my work, which thrilled Ari because now he could use the words *award-winning* on all our marketing and social media advertising.

And Honey. Christ, I was falling hard for her. Everyday I woke up next to her, our bodies entwined, and I had to check that this was really my life. It was good. Almost too good to be true. The due date of our baby girl was only eight weeks away, and I was growing more and more excited with each passing moment.

The only shadows on the horizon were two things I had absolutely no control over. My brother, who was still in a bad way in a Maryland military hospital. And my crazy-ass stalker who seemed to be getting crazier by the day.

I stared at a pair of Bob Seger tickets sitting on my desk in front of me, courtesy of my bipolar secret admirer. It was a concert I'd really wanted to go to, but the creepiness left me at odds with going. I picked them up and stared at them. They were expensive seats.

My stalker. I didn't get it. One minute she seemed smitten, head over heels for me. The next, the pendulum swung in a different direction and she hated me. Like when she sent me the black roses with all the heads cut up and chopped off.

But this week, according to the Bob Seger tickets in my hand, she loved me again.

It was beginning to do my head in.

If she wanted my attention, she fucking had it. This shit had to stop.

I put the tickets in my appointment book on my desk and began closing up for the night when my phone rang. It was Mom. She was in Maryland visiting with Chance.

"Hey, everything okay?"

Since Chance's accident, there was always that concern in the back of my mind that she would ring me and tell me the worst news.

"Everything is fine. Chance is awake. They've brought him out of his coma. He's still in and out of consciousness, but I was able to ask him if he'd like to see you and he said he did."

"That's fucking great news, Mom. I'll get the next flight." I opened my schedule again and looked at the following day's bookings. I had two big jobs, but they were regulars and I had a feeling they wouldn't mind rescheduling. "Tell him I'll be there tomorrow or the next day."

"Okay, son." Her voice was husky. She sounded off. And I could only imagine how hard this was on her. "Caleb, you need to be prepared for how he looks. Remember it's the early days. He looks bad but it's still him. It's still your brother."

Mom's words played on my mind as I rode home. No one really knew the extent of Chance's injuries and how badly scarred he would be. From what Mom said, he was covered in bandages to help with the healing process and to protect from infection, but his main injuries were on his back and the back of his legs. Apparently, Chance had been lying on his belly when the bomb went off and ripped apart the building he was in.

When I got home, Honey was in the kitchen attempting to make beef stroganoff without a recipe, which was always going to end badly. Somehow she'd made the sauce turn a weird grey-green color. So after throwing the dinner disaster into the garbage and ordering pizza, we talked about my visit to Maryland to see my brother.

"Will you come with me?" I asked her.

"Do you think it's a good idea? Wouldn't he prefer it if you went by yourself?"

"No. The best thing we can do for him is to keep it as normal as possible. He'll want to know what is happening at home. Plus, I really want you there."

Her eyes softened and she reached for my hand. "Of course."

We flew out the next day and the following evening we arrived at the military hospital where my brother was recuperating from his injuries.

We were escorted by a military nurse called Marc.

"He's heavily sedated but he is out of his coma," he said. "He can hear you, but he probably won't respond. He hasn't said anything yet. His airway was affected in the bomb blast."

Before we went any further, I stopped Marc. "Is he going to be okay?"

"That depends on what you consider okay. If you mean, will he be like he was before the bomb blast, then no. Your brother has second and third-degree burns to a large proportion of his body, as well as internal injuries. He also watched his squad burn before his eyes. The person you knew is not the person he is now. You should be aware of that."

I was grateful to have Honey with me because she calmed my tempest. Hearing those things about my brother cut me to the bone. Pain bit at my insides and rattled my nerves as I took a moment to prepare myself for what I was about to see. Honey slid her hand into mine, her fingers curling around my own as we stood outside my brother's hospital room. But when I opened the door, not even she could prepare me for the sight of my brother lying on that hospital bed. With all those tubes coming out of him and those bandages covering his body. Agony tore through my chest like lightning.

As I approached the bed, Chance's eyes opened behind the holes in the bandages covering his face. Yesterday they had

Biker Baby

started pulling him out of his sedation, but he wasn't showing much response to any kind of prompts. Now recognition lifted the shadows in the blue eyes looking back at me.

"Well, fuck," I said sitting down next to him.

In that moment, the next words out of my mouth seemed really important.

"You're alive and I'm fucking grateful," I said. I chose those words because they were so fucking true. I wasn't going to sugarcoat this by telling him everything was going to be okay. Because it wouldn't be. Not for a long while. "This is just going to take time. Do you understand me, brother?"

He blinked his blue eyes and it took everything I had in me not to let the emotion show on my face.

His eyes shifted to Honey behind me.

"Hey, stop perving at my girlfriend," I joked, a small smile tugging at the corners of my mouth. "Yeah, you heard right, brother, I have a girlfriend. I'm a one-woman man now. This is Honey." She stepped forward and my brother looked up at her through his bandages, his eyes glittering over her. His lips moved, but nothing came out and I wasn't sure if he was trying to say something or not. "And you're going to be an uncle again."

Chances eyes darted back to me and I couldn't help the smile spreading across my lips.

"We're having a baby," I said proudly. "Can you believe it? Another Calley coming into the world, and this one is a girl, so we'd better brace ourselves. Remember how much trouble Chastity gave us when she was born. How she had us all wrapped around her pinky finger." I smiled at the memory. "I really want you to be home when she arrives, okay? She'll need her uncle. Do you understand me?"

His hands fisted at his sides, despite the bandages.

I noticed. So did Honey.

"I'm going to leave you two to catch up," she said. "I'll meet you at the cafeteria when you're ready." Her eyes met Chance's vibrant gaze. "I'm looking forward to hanging out with you when you get home. Caleb reckons you're a pretty good poker player. He told me you're the best he's ever seen, but I grew up in Vegas so I'm going to have to see about that. You can bring your best game, but I'll still kick your ass."

A ghost of a smile tugged at his lips. I was sure of it. But one blink and it was gone.

After Honey left, I sat back in the visitor's chair. It was important to keep it casual. Not show the alarm I felt in my belly.

"She's pretty amazing. Wait til you get to know her. You'll love her. She fits in with the family, hell, Mom likes her, and apart from Indy she's never liked any of the girls we've been with."

Chance looked away. Not just with his eyes but his whole head. And for a brief moment I wondered if bringing Honey and telling him about the baby was the wrong thing to do. I'd thought hard about it before asking Honey to come along. I didn't want to parade my happiness in front of my badly injured brother who may or may not have a chance at a normal life again. But I knew Chance better than anyone else in the world. He would want to see things for how they were. He wouldn't want the sugar-coated reassurances or the cliché optimism. He kept things real.

"Are you okay, brother?" I asked. "Are you in pain?"

He turned his head and looked at me right in the eyes.

"No," he rasped. "I feel fucking nothing."

CHAPTER 40

HONEY

Caleb didn't say much when he met me at the cafeteria. Or during the cab ride back to the hotel. Once we were inside our room, he ran a shower and I left him to his peace and quiet so he could process his visit to his brother. But after he'd been in there a while, I gently tapped on the bathroom door and cautiously walked in. He was standing with his palms flat to the tiles with the water pouring over his broad shoulders, his head bent, his eyes closed. He looked up when I walked in and I knew he needed me. The look on his face. The torment in his eyes. He was in pain.

Our eyes met as I unbuttoned my dress and let it slip to the floor, and they remained firmly on one another as I crossed the marble tiles to the shower cubicle. Opening the door, I stepped in and as he raked his gaze up and down the length of me, lust and desire darkened the vibrant blueness of his tormented eyes.

His big hand reached up and cupped my jaw, pulling me to him and he kissed me with wet, commanding lips.

I dropped to my knees before him, kissing my way down his gloriously muscular body until I found his thick cock. He flinched when I slid my hand along the wide shaft and then trembled as I ran my wet tongue across the smooth, broad head. My name dropped from his lips as I took him into my mouth, my tongue and lips toying with the sensitive area behind the wide crest, his hands dragging through my damp hair as I caressed his balls with the cupped palm of my hand.

I knew what Caleb liked.

Knew what brought him to an orgasm quickly.

Knew what to do with my mouth and tongue to make him quiver.

His fingers gripped at my skull and his knees weakened, his balls tensing in my hand as I fucked him with my mouth, my tongue, and all the techniques I'd mastered with him over the last few months. He started to come, and his groan shook in the air inside the shower cubicle. But I didn't stop, I kept sucking and loving his cock as he weakened against the shower wall and came in pulsating warm bursts across my tongue.

"Angel..." he breathed.

He guided me to my feet and pulled me to him, gently caressing my face, his eyes still molten with heat as they searched my face.

Without a word he kissed me and the kiss was long and slow, his lips gentle but in charge. His body was warm and wet, his fingers tight on my jaw as his mouth moved sensually over mine.

When the fingers of his free hand slid between my thighs and found how aroused I was, he groaned into my mouth, his body shifting to allow him more access. I trembled against his fingers as they flittered over my clit and into the creaminess of my body. I gasped against his lips, my body lighting up with desire as he rubbed and teased the small nub of nerves. My knees grew weak. I wanted to come. But I wanted to come with him inside of me.

"Take me to the bed," I moaned as he kissed his way along my jaw.

He turned off the water, and taking me by the hand stepped out of the shower and led me across the spacious bathroom. He lovingly toweled me off until my skin was only damp, delicately wiping me down until the last sparkle of water was gone. My heart pounded wildly in my chest and my breathing quickened, and I almost came when he brushed the towel over my aching clit.

I watched him with hungry eyes. His body was magnificent. Hard muscle and smooth flesh, his thickening cock growing between his legs.

"I want you so much," I breathed with desperation. And he gave me a look of pure, unadulterated lust as he led me to the bed.

My belly was big now and it was harder to make love in certain positions, but Caleb only saw this as an opportunity to explore new ways to see what worked, what didn't work, and what felt good. He was a gentle lover, reassuring and generous but fiercely commanding and wildly experimental. He had a strong sexual appetite and never failed to let me know how much he desired me. Sometimes he would just come up behind me and nuzzle into my throat and tell me how much I turned him on. Other times we would stand there kissing, and he would do things with his mouth and tongue that made me think I could come just from the way they moved over mine.

But tonight he was motivated by a darkness in him. A torment as black as night. Seeing his brother so injured and broken cut him deeply, evoking his demons from deep inside. He wasn't rough, but he wasn't gentle. And his preoccupation didn't cut our lovemaking short, it only inspired a need in him to take his time. To torture me with all his prowess. To get my body so aroused with only his tongue and mouth, until I was writhing on the bed desperately wanting him to put his cock in me.

This was about me. But it was also about him trying to regain control over something, because in his head, the chaos was spinning wildly in the wind.

My body churned restlessly beneath him wanting to come but he was torturing me in the most delicious way, making me wait, bringing me to the edge but not letting me tumble over into the abyss.

"Please!" I begged, raking my fingers through his hair.

His stubble gently grazed my inner thighs as his tongue pressed against my clit until I was about to explode. And just when I thought I was going to burst, he would pull away and flitter his tongue over a less-sensitive area. I gripped the sheet beneath me and arched my back so my clit found his mouth again, and I gasped with the slight penetration of his tongue into me, mindless with pleasure, wild with need.

"Come for me, angel," he finally moaned against my sensitive flesh. His tongue swirled and licked with the perfect amount of pressure and I unraveled against him. My sex quivered against his mouth as my orgasm possessed me. I breathed out a whimpered moan and dragged my fingers through his hair, lost in the sensation coursing though me.

But he wasn't done with me yet. He spread my thighs wider and nuzzled into me again.

"Caleb... I can't, no more, please. I need you inside me." I was barely down from my cloud when he started at my flesh again and I trembled against his mouth with the beginnings of a new climax. My legs shook. My clit throbbed. And from nowhere, it burst across my body like falling embers. A cry made from raw pleasure tore out of me, and before my body could even adjust to the pleasure consuming it, he ran his big cock through the quaking flesh and thrust deep and hard into my body. The immediate fullness filled me with bliss. Feeling him push into me, feeling him thrusting, feeling him pull away and rub his wide, smooth head against my clit sent goosebumps prickling along my skin. He pulled out and the emptiness was immediate.

"Get up on your knees, baby," he commanded.

I rose onto all fours and backed toward the end of the bed.

"Your ass is beautiful," he moaned, rubbing his hands over my peachy curves.

In this position I felt more exposed to him, more open, all of me on display and begging to be fucked. Standing behind me, he rolled his cock up and down the length of my sex, teasing me, arousing me beyond definition before pushing himself slowly and purposely into me. His groan was saturated with desire and his fingers dug into the flesh of my ass as he began to rock into me.

My body was already ignited by two previous orgasms, but Caleb's slow, controlled thrusts detonated a third, this one coming from somewhere deep inside. I arched my head back and cried out, inspiring Caleb to speed up, to chase his own climax. He grabbed my hips and drove into me, drawing my pleasure out as he pursued his, grinding against me and making me insane until he finally shuddered and rasped my name in pleasure.

He stilled and held me against him, and I could feel his cock pulsing into me as he filled me with cum.

When the gentle throbs stopped and our euphoria receded, he pulled out of me and guided me down onto the bed with him and wrapped his big arms around me. One hand slid down to my round belly, and even though I couldn't see him, I felt him close his eyes and heard him exhale contently.

"Thank you," he whispered into the back of my head.

"For what?" I asked after a pause.

Penny Dee

His voice was thick. "For everything."

We arrived back in Destiny the next day.

It had been a long trip back from Maryland, and by the time we pulled into our apartment complex, it was dark and I was exhausted.

Caleb dragged our suitcase behind him as we made our way across the parking lot and up the stairs. But halfway up the steps I stopped and glanced over my shoulder. Out of the blue I felt... *watched.*

Goosebumps prickled my skin.

"Are you okay?" Caleb asked, placing a hand on the small of my back.

I shivered.

"Yeah, I'm fine," I said, searching the shadows of the parking lot. I couldn't see anything out there, but a cold unease trickled through my veins.

He looked concerned. "You sure?"

I nodded and started walking again. "Yeah, I'm fine."

We continued up the stairs to the front door where there was a parcel sitting on the step.

"Have you been ordering more things online?" he asked.

In the last couple of weeks I'd received a few packages in the mail because buying online was sometimes a lot cheaper than buying in stores.

"Hey, this kid needs stuff," I said, opening the door while he picked up the box.

Inside, I switched on the light and Caleb handed me the package. It didn't weigh much for a box that took two hands to hold. I gave it a little shake trying to remember what I had recently purchased, and whatever was inside, rattled. There was no address label so I had no idea where it was from.

Grabbing the box cutter from a drawer in the kitchen, I sliced open the tape. But as I lifted the cardboard flaps, I gasped and stepped back in horror.

The box was full of decapitated doll heads.

CHAPTER 41

CALEB

Fury ripped through me, unrestrained and ferocious. It was a violent throb in my head. Those doll heads made me want to go medieval on someone's ass.

Honey sat on the couch, her head in her hands.

"We have to call the police." She trembled.

"The police won't be able to do anything."

She raised her head. Through her tears, her eyes were sharp. "We're calling the police."

"This is someone's idea of a sick joke."

"Sick joke? Are you kidding me! It's a threat, Caleb. Directed right at me and the baby."

"We don't know that. The box wasn't addressed to anybody."

"It's my address."

"No, it's *our* address." I sighed and rubbed my head, not sure how to approach the topic. "Listen, there's something I haven't told you."

Her head shot up and her eyes darted to mine. "What?"

Biker Baby

I looked for the words to explain the situation in the least creepiest way.

"I have this . . . I guess you'd call it a secret admirer. I have no idea who she is or what she thinks she's doing." Guilt rolled through me. I should've told her sooner about the gifts. But in the bigger picture, my secret admirer was the least of my priorities. And the gifts she'd sent had never been as sinister as this. "To be honest, I didn't really give her much thought."

"What do you mean?"

"I never though for a moment she would send something here. They always come to the studio."

"You mean you've been sent stuff before?"

"Nothing like this."

"What, a *threat*? Because let's call this for what it is, Caleb." She stood up and crossed the room to the big window overlooking the dark street. She was rattled and rubbed her belly as she stared out into the darkness. "What do they usually send?"

I stood behind her and ran my hands up her bare arms. "It started off innocent. A hip flask. A limited edition *Easy Rider* movie poster. A bottle of Jack Daniel's." I turned her to face me. "Never anything like this. It's why I've never contacted the police. It's some girl who has a crush on me. That's all."

She turned back to the window and folded her arms across her chest. "Yeah, well, your *some girl* has crossed the line. I'm calling the police."

I nodded. As much as I wanted to handle this myself, I knew I couldn't give Honey the peace of mind like involving the police would.

Sherriff Buckman turned up twenty minutes later.

"So take me back to the start. This secret admirer has been sending you stuff for how long?"

"About eight months."

His eyes bounced between Honey and me. "So before you two got together?"

I nodded. "Yes."

"Okay, tell me what was going on around you when you got the first gift."

"What do you mean?"

"With these stalking cases there is usually a trigger. If it started before the two of you got together, then it's not that. So think, what was happening?"

I tried to think of something but there was nothing significant going on when I first received the silver hip flask. It was about two weeks before I met Honey. And as I peeled back those months, I was reminded of how empty my life had been before I met her.

"I can't think of anything."

"And before the box of doll heads, the gifts were tame? You mentioned the hip flask, movie poster, and a bottle of liquor. Anything else?"

I glanced at Honey and then back at Buckman. Avoiding any mention of the worn lacy thong was impossible. I sighed, resigned to it. "A while ago, a pair of women's underwear and a Polaroid arrived at the studio. Not long after that, a box of roses with their heads chopped off turned up on the doorstep of the studio addressed to me."

Honey exhaled deeply. Buckman noticed too and then looked at me.

"What was on the Polaroid?"

It was my turn to exhale deeply. I should've dealt with this earlier. "It was a picture of a naked woman with her legs spread, her pu—*vagina*—exposed."

"A vagina —" Honey stood up with a rush. "Are you fucking kidding me?"

"I didn't tell you because I didn't think anything of it." I stood up, too. "Look, I don't know who is doing this. In all honesty, I thought it was a club girl. Maybe someone like Tiffani. It didn't seem like a big deal until right now when I came home to find someone had left a box of fucking doll heads on my fucking doorstep."

"It could be that your secret admirer's obsession is escalating and she's doing this to get your attention."

Honey moved around the room and nervously rubbed her palms together. "Is it possible this isn't from someone else and not the person sending those gifts to Caleb? Someone who might be pissed about the cannabis fields, maybe?"

"This isn't about the fields," I said.

Because if another MC was going to send a box to my front door, it wouldn't have doll heads inside it.

It would have real heads.

No. This wasn't about the club.

This was personal.

CHAPTER 42

HONEY

I can't lie. The box of doll heads freaked me out.

And hearing about the other gifts Caleb had received from his secret admirer didn't help the situation any.

I had a meltdown.

I mean, what crazy-ass person did that kind of thing?

Caleb assured me that I had nothing to worry about, that he would take care of the situation. Slowly, I started to calm down and believe him, because it was hard to fear anything when he had his strong arms around me and his powerful body pressed hard up against mine. I'd never felt so protected and cared for in my entire life.

I spoke to Autumn about it the next day and she seemed more concerned about some woman coming after my man than she was of some woman doing any harm to us. I couldn't help but share her concern. Because not only did I have to contend with the women who openly pursued him, now it seemed I had to contend with the ones who hid in the shadows.

Biker Baby

When I asked Autumn if she thought I could be in danger, or Caleb, she brushed it off.

"It's not like you're the Godfather and woke up with a horse head in your bed," she said. "Relax. It's some girl with a crush on him trying to freak you out. I really don't think you have anything to worry about."

She was right.

Although, I did get extra locks added to the front door and the windows.

Just to be sure.

By the time I met Indy for lunch two days later, I was feeling less creeped out.

"You're safe," Indy reassured me over Caesar salads at the Lakehouse Restaurant. River was sound asleep in his stroller as we sat out on the deck by the water. "After what happened to me, the Kings have put some pretty hefty security in play. Family is protected."

Caleb had told me about Indy being abducted by an ex-club member but hadn't gone into specifics.

"Caleb didn't tell me the full story..."

Indy looked at her son, then back at me. "The day after I found out I was pregnant, Elias Knight kidnapped me and tied me to a bed in an abandoned house for a day."

"Oh my Lord, Indy! What happened? Did he..."

"Did he rape me? No. He tried, after he had toyed with me for a while. I fought back but it only turned him on." She punched her fork into a piece of chicken in her salad. "Although, he wasn't a fan of the eye gouge or the knee to the balls I gave him. And funny enough, he didn't like the two bullets my husband put in him."

I slumped back in my chair. "That's terrifying."

"It was. But I survived it. And since then, Bull and the entire club have put things in place to ensure family is safe. They have a lot of friends in this town, Honey. A lot of people who look out for them and their family." She pointed toward the inside of the restaurant. "They know we're here. If anything were to happen, it would only be minutes before the club knows."

"You mean, they're watching us?"

I didn't know how I felt about that.

"Watching? No. But aware that we are here? Yes."

I wasn't sure of the difference. But I let it pass.

"Believe me, if Caleb thought you were in any danger, there is no way he would let you out of his sight." Her eyes squinted in the mild sunlight. "You're with him now and that means you're one of the most protected women in this town."

Despite my reservations, that made me feel warm and happy.

"So you're saying I'm reading more into it than there is?" I asked, rubbing my big belly.

"Look, I've seen some women do some seriously bold shit to get a King to notice them."

"Like?"

She thought for a moment. "There was this one girl who had a crush on Hawke. She got a massive tattoo of a hawk on her back as some kind of declaration of love." She pointed her fork at me. "Now that is commitment."

"What happened to her?"

"It got his attention and he married her."

I choked on my water. "So it worked."

She shrugged. "I suppose it did, although they're divorced now. But that was nothing compared to this one girl, God, what was her name? Terry or Kerry, or something like that. Anyway, she pretended it was her birthday and threw a party just so she could invite Griffin. When he accepted the invite, she went all out. Spent a fortune. But he bailed on her at the last minute and never showed up. When she found out he was with another woman, she turned up at his house with thirty pounds of cake and threw it at his front door. Then she committed the cardinal sin and fucked with his bike. Poured sugar in the gas tank. If she wanted his attention, she got it."

"Caleb's ex-girlfriend kicked over his bike."

"Ah, yes, Brandi. That happened not long after I arrived back in town. He was really pissed about that. You don't fuck with their bikes. Just like you don't fuck with their women." She speared lettuce on her fork and took a bite. "But the ones who really get me are the women who flirt with your man right in front of you. Who make offers with their eyes or some kind of lewd body language. They can be blatant. Insistent."

"Like Tiffani."

She nodded. "Yes. Just like Tiffani."

I told her about the encounter with Tiffani at Tully and Heidi's wedding.

"That doesn't surprise me. She's been after him for as long as I can remember. He's never shown her any interest, so she resorts to other things to get his attention."

"I'm not sure if that makes me feel better or not."

Indy put down her fork and folded her arms on the table. "Look, it takes a lot of trust and a lot of patience to be a queen to a King. Especially one with the last name of Calley." She smiled and played with the crown pendant on a chain around her neck. "But you'll learn. It's not easy, but boy it is oh so worth it."

Feeling better, I left Indy with a promise to catch up the following week. When I arrived home, Caleb was in the kitchen starting a pot of coffee. I went to him and put my arms around him, resting my cheek against his shoulder and enjoying the hardness of his body against mine as I ran my hands over his broad chest. His size and strength reminded me that I was with a King and I was safe. And in that moment I couldn't have been more grateful for him. He turned around in my arms and slid a big hand along my jaw. He said nothing. But his eyes glittered into mine as he leaned down and kissed me. I broke off the kiss and took his hand in mine and led him to our bedroom where I spent the rest of the afternoon showing him just how grateful I was.

CHAPTER 43

HONEY

Exactly four weeks before I was due, I was at home alone when there was a knock on the door. Surprise and disgust collided through me when I opened it and saw Charlie staring back at me.

"Hey," he said with a sweet grin.

I raised an eyebrow at him. He seemed to forget the last time we spoke he called me a slut and I slammed the door in his face.

"What do you want, Charlie?"

He dragged his warm brown eyes up and down the length of me. "Wow! You look incredible."

Unfortunately, so did he.

Not that I would ever, *ever*, admit that to him.

Lying, cheating douchebag.

"Can I come in?" he asked.

"No."

"Please?"

I gripped the door tighter. "The last time I saw you, you called me a slut. The time before that, you were getting a blowjob from a girl who wasn't me. So, no, Charlie, you can't come in."

At least he had the decency to look contrite.

"I made a mistake, Honey."

"Yes, you did. The moment you decided to cheat on your girlfriend with me."

"We're done," he said quickly. "Samira and I. We broke up. For good."

I shook my head. "So, what? You come around here expecting me to welcome you back with open arms?"

Surely, he wasn't that much of a narcissist.

"You're having my baby," he said.

"It's not yours, Charlie. I've already explained that to you."

"You're eight months pregnant, right?" When I nodded, his eyes softened and pleaded with me. "We made love eight months ago."

I sighed. "Sorry, to burst your bubble. But I had a period after our last sexual encounter. This isn't your baby."

"What are you talking about? We made love only a couple of days before we broke up."

His overuse of the words *made love* made me want to choke. How had I ever had sex with such a—wait a minute, what was he saying? We didn't have sex that week.

When Mrs. Lawrence, my neighbor in 7B, appeared in the stairwell, Charlie glanced over his shoulder, then back at me. His face took on a pleading expression. "Can I please come in?"

In the interest of not airing my dirty laundry throughout the entire apartment complex, I opened the door wider so he could step in. Closing it behind me, I leaned against it and ensured there was ample distance between us because I had no desire to be anywhere near him.

'We made love the night of the car wreck," he said.

Three nights before we broke up, we were traveling home together from the grocery store when someone T-boned us. Luckily, we all escaped the wreck unscathed, although I was pretty shaken up. When we'd come home, Charlie had given me a couple of pills to calm my nerves.

"Those pills made me sleepy," I said. I couldn't remember much more than that. "I remember taking them and then nothing."

My blood ran cold. The next morning I'd woken up groggy, with no memory of the night before.

"What are you saying?" I asked, goosebumps creeping along my arms. My brain squeezed on itself as I tried to recall the night he was talking about, but there was nothing but a big black hole.

"You wanted me to comfort you. One thing led to another—"

"No . . ." I breathed.

"We made love."

Alarm tingled in the base of my spine.

"This isn't your baby," I insisted.

He reached for my belly and slid his palm over the curve. It was an intimate, affectionate gesture. *Tender*. But Charlie made it feel slimy.

I moved away from him.

I felt sick.

Nauseated by the thought.

This was Caleb's baby. Not his.

"How can you be so sure?" he asked. "You sleep with me on the Tuesday night, and then someone else on Friday night."

The fear creeping up my spine made me defensive, and I thrust my hands onto my hips. "So we're back to calling me a slut. Let's not remember how I caught you getting a blowjob from your girlfriend, you two-timing douchebag!"

He came toward me and put his hands on my shoulders. His voice was smooth and velvety. Too tender to be authentic. Not from him. "That's not what I mean. And I'm sorry that I said that. I was in shock when I called you that. I'd just found out you were pregnant and I didn't know what to think."

Again, I moved away from him, not wanting his hands on me.

"I remember you knowing exactly what you thought about it," I said shakily. "You threw money at me and told me to get an abortion."

He grimaced. He *actually* grimaced.

Well, there you go. I had never seen him do that before. Mr. Cool, Smooth, and Confident was capable of something other than his usual self-righteous arrogance.

He was starting to look like the old Charlie. The one I'd fallen in love with only a few months after we'd met. Before I knew what a douchebag he was.

I opened the door. "You need to leave."

But he didn't move. He just stared at me. The handsome man in the three-piece suit with the chocolate brown eyes and the full set of lips I'd pressed a thousand kisses to. The man who'd pursued me with such vigor I'd finally given in and agreed to date him even though I knew I was probably walking into hell. The man who'd lied to me for two fucking years. The man I no longer loved.

The man who was so completely opposite of Caleb.

"I'll go. But you know it's my baby." He came toward the door and stopped. He looked down at me, his handsome face full of affection. "I think you and I need to try again. For the sake of our baby."

I couldn't believe his audacity.

But then again, he was arrogant enough to think that I would even consider it.

"Get. Out."

He left and I quickly closed the door behind him and slid to the floor. My face crumpled with tears and I let out a strangled sob. Because he was right.

If what he said was true, then there was a very good chance this baby was his.

CHAPTER 44

CALEB

I knew something was wrong the minute I walked in the door.

And by wrong, I didn't mean crazy wrong like we'd experienced over the last few months.

I mean, *fucking* wrong.

Honey had been crying.

She was sitting on the couch, her face tear stained and pinched with emotion. She hugged her DO WHAT YOU LOVE EVERY DAY cushion to her chest. Scrunched up tissues lay scattered across the coffee table.

"What's wrong?" I asked, a tingle of alarm starting in my chest.

Her chin quivered and she wouldn't look me in the eyes.

I sat down next to her, and without a word I pulled her to me, holding her against my chest. I didn't know what was wrong. But as I held her in my arms, she went limp and started to cry.

"Baby . . . speak to me," I said gently.

She pulled away, and the agony on her face shoved my tingle of alarm into a full-blown panic.

She swallowed thickly as she struggled with the words.

"The baby..." she started to talk, but then her chin trembled, and her face broke again. Slowly, she regained her composure and delivered the words that changed my life in a calm and almost alien voice. "There is a good chance it's Charlie's."

It took me a moment.

And then boom!

It hit me like a fucking car bomb.

"What do you mean?" I asked.

She looked at me, her big, beautiful green eyes glittering like the ocean. "Charlie came to see me today."

I bristled at the mention of his name.

"Apparently, we had sex only three days before you and I met."

"Apparently? What, you don't remember?" I didn't mean for my voice to sound so sharp. *But fuck.*

With a shaky voice she explained to me about the night they were in a car accident and about the pills Charlie gave her to calm her nerves. And I swear to God, I saw red when she told me what he did afterwards. Clearly, he had taken advantage of her while she was out of it. My fingers trembled. She couldn't even remember it.

"You and I used a condom. Lots of them," I said, my throat thick. My breathing started to come quicker as my mind buzzed. I hated asking. But I needed to know if the odds were in my favor or his. "Did you use protection with *him*?"

When she didn't answer, I pressed her. "Did you?"

She shook her head. "Not always. We were together two years..."

I stood up. I felt punched in the chest. Heat traveled up my spine and across the back of my neck, and it became harder to breathe. There was a terrifying possibility *my* baby didn't even exist. And that thought fucking killed me.

Biker Baby

I closed my eyes against the thought. My heart squeezed and rattled against my ribs. This was so fucking wrong. We were having a baby together and I was fucking in love with the idea of us being a family. Of holding my daughter in my arms. Of being a good father to her. Of all the milestones. The first steps. The first words. The first loose tooth to the first day of school.

Fuck.

I forced back the pain and opened my eyes. I gave Honey a reassuring but fake smile because *Jesus Christ,* it was hard to make those face muscles work. "We'll work it out."

"It will mean the end for us."

"I'm not with you because you're pregnant—"

"So you've been saying. I guess we'll see..." Her words faded away as she turned her head and sank her teeth into her bottom lip. I wanted to stop those lips from trembling. But damn if I could stop the sudden whirring in my head.

"I'll make an appointment for the doctor—"

She cut me off. "I already have."

"For when?"

"Tomorrow at two pm."

I had a full day booked at the studio, but I would reschedule it.

"I'll pick you up at one thirty," I said, taking her hand and lifting her to her feet. I pulled her to me, as close as I could while there was a big baby bump between us.

Which was fucking ironic.

Her bump was coming between us physically for now.

But was it about to come between us completely?

With two fingers I raised her trembling chin so I could look into her beautiful blue eyes. They were stormy with torment and wet with tears. Without a word, I leaned down and pressed my lips to hers. At first it was chaste, but when it came to Honey I couldn't help myself. Her lips parted and I kissed her hard, my tongue drinking her in, my lips moving passionately over hers. She twisted her fists into my shirt and I felt her agony sweep through me. I pulled away, caressing her face with my thumbs.

"Whatever happens, what we have is real."

Sadness washed over her beautiful face. She nodded but I knew she didn't believe me.

"I'm sorry," she whispered.

"Don't be." I gently brushed her hair from her face as my heart slowly began to break apart in my chest. "We'll see the doctor and take it from there, okay?"

She nodded and I felt her relax a little. But I needed to get out of there. I needed to process what the fuck this all meant.

"Put your feet up. I'll go get us pizza for dinner."

Trying not to look as rocked as I felt, I grabbed my car keys off the coffee table. I bent down and gave her a kiss goodbye and left.

I didn't want her to see the chaos taking place inside me.

My girl might be pregnant to another man and my baby might not exist.

And I was devastated as fuck.

CHAPTER 45

HONEY

"Explain the situation to me," Doctor Perry asked.

Caleb and I sat across the desk from my doctor, the one who'd confirmed my pregnancy only six months ago. I'd just confessed to him that I wasn't sure if Caleb was the father or not.

"I caught my boyfriend of two years with another woman. We broke up and I met Caleb a few days later and we spent the night together." My cheeks began to burn. "We used condoms but I thought one of them might have been faulty because he was the only person I'd had sex with following my period two weeks earlier. Turns out I was wrong."

"How so?" Doctor Perry asked.

"Apparently there'd been an *incident* a few nights earlier with my boyfriend." My face grew even hotter. "And we didn't use a condom. Well, I assume we didn't because we didn't usually. I can't remember because I'd taken a sedative following a minor car accident."

Doctor Perry nodded. "I see."

"So we'd like to do a paternity test," Caleb said. I glanced at him. His body was rigid. His easy-going nature gone. "We're wondering what our options are."

"Of course."

"So what are the chances that this is my baby, Doc?" Caleb asked.

Dr. Perry looked at him over his glasses. "You used a condom. The other guy didn't." His hands parted and then closed together in front of him on the desk. He didn't need to spell it out for us. His silence and the hand gesture spoke volumes. I tried to swallow, but the cold lump in my throat made it impossible.

"So how long will it take?" Caleb asked, his jaw clenching as he shifted in his chair.

"We usually have results back in three weeks."

"Three weeks!" I gasped.

Three weeks.

It was going to be three weeks of hell.

Three weeks of hell to find out it was Charlie's baby.

Because I knew it was.

Even the doctor had suggested that the odds were in his favor.

The look on Caleb's face almost broke me. It was rigid, his eyes hard. I watched his throat work as he swallowed deeply. He was trying to hide his feelings, but I could see this was hurting him.

You've done this to him.

When he caught me looking, he tried to give me a close-lipped smile but failed. Instead, he just looked remorseful. Disappointed. *Hurt.* And guilt crashed through me.

"So, if you're both happy to proceed, we can take some blood from you today," Doctor Perry said looking at me. He turned to Caleb. "And I'll get a cheek swab from you. Then we'll get it sent off this afternoon."

Caleb and I both nodded.

Within minutes a nurse appeared to take my blood and a swab from Caleb. I watched on, stony-faced as she drew blood from my arm and it was then I realized with absolute clarity that this was going to be a complete waste of time.

This was Charlie's baby. And we all knew it.

I felt like crying.

I'd put Caleb through all of this for nothing.

When the nurse took a swab from Caleb's cheek, our eyes met over her shoulder and I could see the hardness in them. I looked away, knowing this was the beginning of the end for us.

During the car ride home, I wrestled with my emotions.

While listening to him try to console me and tell me it didn't matter either way if this was his baby or Charlie's, I knew there was only one way to handle the situation.

Three weeks was a long time.

Finally, while making dinner, I made peace with my decision.

And when I woke up the next morning, I told him I needed some space.

CHAPTER 46

HONEY

"Don't do this," he said, his face stiff.

But I'd made up my mind, and no amount of talking was going to change it. This bullshit stopped now. I wasn't going to put him through a minute more of this craziness. Let alone another three weeks. We needed to put some space between us.

"There is no other way."

"You're breaking up with me because you're scared."

"I'm not breaking up with you. I'm just asking for some space."

He ran a frustrated hand threw his hair. "That's breaking up with me, and you know it."

"Even if I was, I'm pregnant with Charlie's baby, and one day you are going to be pleased I let you off the hook."

"I've never looked at our situation like that." He came toward me and gently placed his hands on my arms. "I want to be with you."

My heart ached.

I want to be with you, too.

But I was done being selfish.

"You were only with me because of the baby."

"How can you say that?"

"Because it's true. All of this is because you thought I was having your baby. How long before the resentment unfurls and you can't stand the sight of me?"

He turned away.

"Please," I begged. "I need you to go."

He turned back to me, and with a terrible achy heart, I realized he had tears in his eyes. He looked up at the ceiling so they wouldn't fall. I'd never seen him cry. Never seen that amount of emotion or raw pain in his eyes. And it was with a heartbreaking realization that it was all because of me.

"I don't want this," he said, his broad chest expanding with the deep breath he took. "I don't want to lose you."

"It has to be this way, Caleb. Because I've seen what this does. It breeds resentment and breaks people apart." It hurt to look at him because he looked so wounded. "I care about you too much to let that happen to you."

"It won't—"

"I need you to go!" I exclaimed. And the emotion behind my words stopped him. He stared at me. Angry. He dragged his teeth across his bottom lip. I took a breath to calm my wildly beating heart. "Please . . . I just need some space to catch a breath."

When he stepped forward his face was set, his jaw hard, his eyes dark. "Fine. I'll give you your space. I'll give you what you want. But only because you're pregnant and I'm not about to make this hurt anymore than what you've already went through. I'll go but it's not because I want to. It's because you're telling me it's what you want because you're afraid I can't love another man's child."

He picked up his cut and threw it on.

"But you're wrong, Honey." His voice was cold. His anger sharp and hard on his face. "So very fucking wrong."

With a slam of the door he was gone, and my heart broke in my chest. I didn't move. Not a muscle. I stood dazed and confused, listening to the rumble of his Harley as he fired it up, and then the roar of it as it took him away from me and disappeared into the afternoon.

I sat on the bed, my world suddenly empty. I burst into tears and cried hard, the heartache spilling out of me with every sob. I was in love with him. But this being Charlie's baby changed everything.

Finally, my body stilled and I slowly relaxed until sleep pulled me into a hazy and unexpected slumber where I dreamed about a baby with bright blue eyes and a head of dark hair. Then my mom was there holding the baby, and its eyes turned dark brown and his sweet features morphed into Charlie. My mom started to laugh. *See, Honey. Doesn't Charlie's daughter look just like him?*

I woke up with a start and sat upright on my bed, struggling to catch my breath. My heart pounded against my chest while my head swirled with the murkiness of sleep. I sighed and rubbed my eyes. As the prickly disorientation of sleep faded away I was able to breathe again. Outside, the sun was working its way toward the horizon, throwing shades of red, pink, and gold across the sky.

I missed Caleb already.

I glanced at the floor and a glint of silver caught my eye. I leaned forward. It was Caleb's St. Christopher necklace.

I picked it up and studied it, the pad of my thumb rubbing over the tarnished, dented metal. The clasp was broken and I wondered if Caleb had noticed. This meant everything to him. He would hate being away from it. There wasn't a lot he held sentimental to his heart, but this was something he did.

Biker Baby

Because family was everything to him.

I started to cry again and held his necklace to my chest.

He hated me.

But it was better this way.

Better to break his heart now instead of dragging it out over the years when he realized that being with me was a mistake.

CHAPTER 47

CALEB

I drank the fifth of bourbon, cranked Led Zeppelin, and lost myself in my art.

When the music stopped, I looked up to see Pandora standing in the doorway. She looked incredible. Red lips. Blonde hair. Thigh-high boots. And if I thought her dresses were tight in the past, this one was damn well painted on.

"What are you doing here?" I asked.

I was slurring like fuck.

"I saw the light on. Saw your bike parked outside. Are you okay?"

It was hard to focus on her. "Sure."

Her gaze dropped to the empty bottle tipped over on its side on my desk. "You want to talk about it?"

"No." I looked down at my sketchpad and was taken back by what I saw. Honey looked back at me from the paper. Without realizing it, I'd drawn her with precise detail. "There's nothing to talk about," I said, not lifting my eyes from the beautiful face on the sketchpad.

Biker Baby

Pandora moved to stand next to me and put her hand on my shoulder as she looked at the drawing.

"She doesn't love you, you know," she said.

"What are you talking about?" I asked broodily. My head was murky with too much liquor.

"I've been watching this disaster unfold for months. Watching how she tortures you. Watching how she raises you to crazy heights only to kick you behind the knees and drop you to the floor with her craziness."

"She's not crazy. The situation is."

Pandora's hand slid from my shoulder to the back of my neck. Then the other one joined in and she started to massage both my shoulders.

"She doesn't get this lifestyle. I've seen the look on her face. She's as out of place as a salmon at a grizzly bear tea party." Her fingers swept up and down my shoulders and across the nape of my neck. And even though I was hammered, I realized what she was doing was more like a caress than a massage.

I stood up to put some distance between us, but I was more drunk than I thought and dropped down onto the chair in front of my computer.

"Whoa," I moaned as the world spun and my vision blurred.

Before I could stop her, Pandora hoisted up her already short dress and climbed onto my lap.

"What are you doing?" I mumbled.

She straddled my hips and blanketed her body against me as she leaned forward. "Let me be with you," she whispered against my lips. "Let *me* love you."

When she tried to kiss me, I turned my head away from her mouth but she gripped my chin with vise-like strength and sharply turned my head back to face her. She kissed me hard, her lips devouring mine, her tongue thrusting into my mouth with ferocious desire.

I pulled away. "I don't want to do this," I slurred. Christ, when I opened my eyes there were two of her. But when I closed them I felt a wave of vertigo pull me backwards.

"We can be together," she said, gasping as she rubbed her pussy against the front of my jeans. She pressed down with all her weight and started to get off on the hard bulge of my zipper. But despite all the rubbing, my cock wasn't interested.

I tried to push her off me, but another wave of vertigo washed over me and my arms fell limp at my side and my head fell back. Pandora lifted my head so she could brush her lips over mine again. "She doesn't want you. But I do."

She grabbed my hand and forced it between her legs. She wasn't wearing any panties, and the moment my fingers felt her slick pussy, she lit up like an atomic bomb. She cried out and furiously rubbed herself against my hand. With a yank I pulled it free.

"Get off me," I demanded. Despite my extreme inebriation and total lack of coordination I successfully pushed her off me. "What the fuck are you doing? You're about to get married."

"Don't you get it? I'm in love with you, Caleb. I have been for years. And Roger asking me to marry him made me realize I needed to either face up to it or move on." She slid back onto me and wrapped her slender arms around my neck. "But I can't move on from you, Caleb. Can't you see that? I'm so in love with you it hurts. But you've never paid me any attention. Why do you think I send you all that stuff?"

My head swirled. I was either going to puke or pass out.

Wait. What?

"What stuff?" I asked, confused.

"It's me," she breathed against my lips. "I'm your secret admirer."

I heard her words, but they didn't make sense. *She* was my stalker? The owner of the worn panties and Polaroid? She was the psycho who sent a box of decapitated doll heads to my home?

I went to protest but she mashed her red lips to mine and moaned as her tongue swept into my mouth. Shifting on my lap, she started grinding against me again.

"It's not your baby," she whispered into my ear. "But I will give you one."

Even in the murkiness of too much liquor, her words stung. They reminded me of just how fucking pitiful I was because my heart ached like I was in a fucking country music song.

"How do you know about that?" I asked, confused as fuck by everything unfolding.

"I heard you on the phone to her before I left." She moaned as she rubbed herself harder against my zipper. "She doesn't want you now that she knows it's not your baby."

"We don't know that—"

"Shhhhhhh," she breathed against my lips. "Let me take care of you. I promise I will be real good to you. I will give you everything."

Honey had given me everything.

And then she'd taken it from me.

Now she wanted me to move on.

But I didn't want that.

"I said get off me," I said sharply.

But Pandora didn't listen. It wasn't until she heard the voice from the doorway that she stopped.

"You heard him," it said. "He said get the fuck off him."

We both turned and looked, and there was Honey standing in the doorway.

CHAPTER 48

HONEY

I stood in the darkness of the studio. I'd taken a chance that this was where he'd go after leaving our apartment and I was right. When I walked in, I overheard Pandora confessing her love to him. Heard her admit to being his secret admirer. Heard what she said about me. Heard what she was offering him.

I'd heard about enough.

I made my way to Caleb's office and pushed open the door.

Seeing Pandora straddling him made me crazy.

When I told her to get the fuck off him, both of them turned to look in my direction. At first, Pandora didn't move, but then she slowly slid off Caleb's lap. Standing up straight, she pushed her hem down and adjusted it.

"You're making a mistake," she said to Caleb as she walked away from him. When she reached me she paused. "Do him a favor and let him fucking loose. Let him be with someone who actually wants him."

Anger ripped out of me. "Stay the fuck out of my business."

She went to move away but stopped. Her eyes flashed across at me. "It's not even his baby."

I gritted my teeth. "Get. Out."

She scoffed at me while I murdered her a thousand times over with my eyes.

With a huff, she left and I went to Caleb and knelt in front of him. He was almost passed out.

"I can't leave you alone for five minutes without you getting into trouble," I joked, trying to help him to his feet. But being drunk, he was a dead weight and we fumbled.

"I don't want her," he mumbled.

"I know."

"I want you."

I ignored his comment. Because I wasn't here to go over the same argument with him. I was here to bring him his St. Christopher.

Well, that's what I told myself anyway.

Truth was, it was the self-sabotaging part of me that I wanted to see him. You know, the crazy part that just couldn't let him go without seeing him one last time because somehow it was going to make things easier than if she didn't.

She was quite demanding. She also wanted to make sure he didn't do anything stupid while he was drunk.

Like Tiffani.

She also knew she had no right to be there. But now that she was, she couldn't leave him like this.

"Come on, you should lie down," I said, guiding him to his feet and leading him over to the couch in the corner of the room. The plan was to get him into the recovery position so he could sleep off his intoxication safely. But as we neared the couch, Caleb became all feet and we stumbled onto the couch. I landed softly onto the cushions, but he fell hard onto his knees in front of me.

"Baby..." he moaned drunkenly. "Are you okay?"

I nodded. I was fine. He was between my legs with his hands on my thighs. The air crackled between us. His hands drifted up to my big belly and I saw the torment in his face as he looked at it. His fingers slid over the roundness and he stared as if he was mesmerized by it.

"It's my baby," he whispered. He lifted his eyes and they focused on mine. "And you're my girl."

In that moment, I wished that were true. More than anything in the world.

But the simple truth was, he was wrong.

CHAPTER 49

CALEB

I woke up in a world of pain.

Jesus Christ.

I sat up and squinted. I was in the studio, on the couch, a painful pulse rocketing through my skull. Across the room, an empty bottle of bourbon lay on its side on my desk. I couldn't remember fuck all about the night before, and I had a fair suspicion that empty bottle had something to do with it. I stood up but had to pause and wait for the wave of nausea to pass before heading out of my office and down the hall to the bathroom. Standing in front of the mirror, I splashed water on my face, rinsed the stale taste of the night before out of my mouth, and took a moment for the dust to settle in my head. I looked at the mess looking back at me from the mirror. Bloodshot, tired eyes. Stubble. Messy hair. I was a wreck.

Last night was a mystery. But as I stood there, bits and pieces began to shift and move into place. *Led Zeppelin on the stereo. A bottle of bourbon in my hand. The portrait of Honey in my sketchbook. Pandora turning up and telling me—*

My head shot up.

—she was in love with me. Her straddling my lap and rubbing herself against me. Her grabbing my hand and shoving it into her wet, shaven pussy.

I straightened, feeling unsettled by the memory. All this time Pandora was the one sending me those gifts and carrying on like a psycho. The decapitated doll heads. Breaking into Honey's apartment.

It didn't make sense.

I looked at my watch. It was ten past eight. She would be arriving to work any minute and I needed to confront her and put an end to this behavior straight away.

As if on cue, I heard the key in the lock and the front door open. I splashed more water on my face and ran a wet hand through my hair, desperate to waken up and control the thumping pulse in my head before facing my secret admirer.

Pandora was at her desk when I walked in, her dress tight, her hair perfect, her makeup immaculate. She looked like the perfectly put-together ice queen she'd always been, except her shoulders were slightly slumped, and her expression was sad as she put items from her desk into the box on her chair. When she heard me walk in, I saw her skin flush and her eyes fill with tears. I wasn't used to seeing her look so contrite, so… *humiliated*, and the empathy I felt for her caught me off guard.

We stood across the room from one another. An awkwardness hung in the space between us as I looked at her and she pretended not to notice I was there.

"We need to talk about last night," I said hoarsely.

She looked up and dragged her white teeth over her bottom lip. "I don't know what to say. I'm so embarrassed. I suppose you want me gone straight away."

I felt sorry for her. I was prepared to be angry. Prepared to fire her on the spot for what she'd done—not for hitting on me, but for sending Honey the doll heads and for breaking into our apartment. But seeing her standing there looking nothing like the confident, outgoing woman I knew her to be, it tugged at my heartstrings and I couldn't help but feel sorry for her. She would have to go. But I wasn't going to throw her out on her ass. Years of loyalty demanded a kinder tactic.

"What happened, Pandora? I thought you were in love with Roger?"

"I am." Her chin quivered and she couldn't look me in the eye. "I just love you more."

"You don't mean that."

"That's the thing, Caleb. I do."

I didn't know what to say. I'd known Pandora for years. She was always the tough-talking ball breaker, the one who could handle a room full of foul-mouthed, uncouth bikers with one look.

She was only ever a friend.

And despite her love of the unusual, I never picked her to be a psychopath.

I sighed and dropped the anger as I approached her. "I could live for a million years and I would never have seen this coming. You know I care about you—"

"Please, spare me the *I care about you* speech."

"But I do, Pandora. I do care about you. You're my friend and if I ever did anything to make you think—"

"You didn't." She turned away and started putting her things into the box again. She picked up the stapler. "It's like you never even noticed me. But I noticed you. Every damn day. And every day I'd tell myself not to love you. Not to want you. Not to notice how special you are. But my stupid little heart wouldn't listen."

She threw the stapler into the box.

"I'm sorry you feel that way. Fuck, the last thing I want is to hurt you. But, Pandora, this shit, it crosses the line."

"I know. I crashed and burned." Her tape dispenser joined the stapler in the box. Followed by the stationery caddy, pens, pencils, and a sugar skull coffee mug. "I'm sorry about last night. I made a fool of myself."

"Last night I can swallow. We've all done things we've regretted. It's the other shit that we need to talk about. The fucked-up shit."

With a dramatic turn of her head, she looked at me.

"I sent you a couple of gifts. A hip flask. A picture. Tickets to Bob Seger—"

"And what about the worn panties?"

She pulled a face.

"What worn panties?" Her perfectly arched eyebrows drew in. "What the hell are you taking about? Do I look like I'd send worn panties to someone?"

I didn't reply because I was confused.

And because she absolutely *did* look like she would send a pair of worn panties to someone.

But her embarrassment was running deep through her, so I didn't press the point any further.

"What about the black flowers? The decapitated doll heads?"

"Decapitated doll heads? What the hell?"

"You also broke into Honey's apartment. Stole her necklace. Pandora, that's psycho shit."

"Break in?" She thrust her hands on her hips "What the fuck are you talking about?"

I had to give it to her, she did look genuinely confused.

"Don't try to deny it. You admitted to it last night. You're the girl who was doing all this crazy stuff."

"Sure, I sent you a couple of gifts. But breaking into your apartment and stealing jewelry?" She looked mortified. "Fuck you, Caleb, I may be a little crazy for you, but I'm not a fucking psycho."

"You're denying it?"

"Hell yes, I'm denying it. You're right, that *is* crazy shit." Her hands fell to her sides as she took a step toward me. "You might take my breath away, but you haven't completely voided me of my sanity."

A slow tingle began its ascent up my spine.

"You really didn't send me that crazy shit?"

She cocked an eyebrow at me. "Worn panties? Decapitated doll heads? Fuck, Caleb. You need to ask yourself, who the fuck did you drive crazy?"

Her words burst like a confetti ball across my brain.

You know you always drove me crazy.

My breath left me as alarm ripped through me, and it was all I could do to rasp out her name when I realized what was happening.

"Honey…"

CHAPTER 50

CALEB

I pushed my Harley to its limits as I roared back to Honey's apartment, my mind crazed with worry.

All this time she had been watching me.

Watching Honey.

Waiting for the right moment.

And if I was right, last night Honey and I had given it to her.

Brandi.

She wasn't back in Los Angeles.

She was right here. Getting ready to pounce.

Pulling up out front, I bounded up the stairs two at a time, and when I reached the top, a flare of panic shot off inside of me. The front door was slightly ajar, and through the crack I could see Honey and Brandi sitting at the table. Honey was sitting very still while Brandi was animated as she ranted, using her hands and her arms to drive her points across.

I pushed the door open and walked in. Brandi looked up and stopped talking, her face breaking into a big smile.

Biker Baby

"Baby! Finally, you're home," she said, her eyes wide and bright with madness. "We've been waiting."

My eyes shifted to the gun sitting in the middle of the table, and then to Honey. She looked terrified.

"Brandi, what are you doing?" I asked in a low, calm voice.

My ex-girlfriend looked at me with crazed eyes.

"Well, now that you ask, I'm here to tell this stupid bitch to back the fuck off from my man." She stood up and came toward me. She looked like hell. Normally well put together with an air of confidence, her once luscious hair was in a wild tangle and her usually beautiful eyes were bright with a craziness that exceeded a bad mood. She was having a psychotic breakdown. She was maniacal.

She was dangerous.

I needed to get her out of there and away from Honey.

"Honey hasn't done anything wrong. You're angry. But you're angry at me, no one else."

"Oh, I disagree." Her eyes were dark, her face hard and rough. She looked at Honey like she wanted to end her. "She's done nothing but keep you from me."

"That's not true. This isn't her fault. It's between you and me. Let's keep it that way. You need to let Honey go so you and I can talk."

"And let her call the police so they can take me away? Because that's what she wants, don't you see that, Caleb? She wants me out of the picture so she can keep you all to herself."

I looked at the gun on the table. "Why is there a gun?"

"Why?" She scoffed, like she was genuinely surprised by my question. "Because I'm sick and tired of being ignored, Caleb. And people tend to listen to you when you have a gun in your hand."

"You don't need a gun for me to listen. I'm here; I'm ready to hear whatever it is you want to say. Just give me the gun first."

"I don't think so. If I do that you'll end this and go running back to her."

"She's pregnant," I said. "Don't put her through this."

"Do you think I give a fuck? No, she needs to hear this. The bitch needs to know that you're my man and not hers!"

I put my hands out to calm her. "Okay, I get that, but I need you to think about her condition."

I decided to play to her reason. But it was a mistake because Brandi was so far gone she no longer had any reason left.

"You're supposed to be having a baby with me!" she yelled angrily. "But now you're having a baby with her."

"No, he's not," Honey said quickly. "He isn't having a baby with me. I got the paternity test back. I paid more and they put a rush on it." Her eyes found mine and a prickly fear took up in the base of my skull as her mouth formed the words I'd dreaded to hear. "This isn't his baby."

I tried not to let it show, but her words hit me like a fucking truck.

This isn't his baby.

"You're lying," Brandi said.

"Caleb and I had one night together. We used protection. Charlie and I didn't. By the time I met Caleb, I was already pregnant."

Even in this unfolding nightmare, her words shook me right through to my bones and my world—the one I'd fallen in love with— crumbled away.

So it was true. It was Charlie's baby.

I felt furious.

Bitter.

Gutted.

Hell, I felt like crying because that wound cut fucking deep.

But I had to hide my true emotions from Brandi.

"Are you sure?" I asked, unable to hide the sharpness in my voice.

Honey nodded, and I could tell by the way her chin quivered that she was telling the truth.

My baby had never even existed.

"But you love her," Brandi said, turning her attention to me.

I looked at Brandi, and then to Honey. "No, I don't love her."

Brandi relaxed next to me. While my words seared through Honey. I watched in agony as she closed her eyes slowly and processed what I'd said. But when she opened them again, she smiled. A big, sunny, *fake* smile.

"See," she said brightly. "There is a future for the both of you. I'm not even in the picture anymore."

Brandi's eyes bounced between Honey and me. "Is it true, Caleb? Do we have a chance?"

I eyed the gun again.

"We should go somewhere and talk about it," I said. "What about Cavalry Hill?"

"Where you and I used to go when we were dating?"

"It was always our special spot," I said.

Brandi sighed. "I would like that."

I stood up, with the intention of getting her out of the apartment. "Let's go."

"Is that a good idea?" Honey asked with a tight, strained voice. She looked worried, her brow furrowed, and her eyes pleaded with me not to go with my crazy ex-girlfriend.

Unfortunately, it set Brandi off. She frowned and picked up the gun from the table. I saw Honey stiffen and I felt a surge of panic rip through me.

"Stop. Interfering. You. Stupid. Fucking. Bitch!" She snapped. Her eyes had glazed over again, and I didn't like the way she was spiraling even further out of control. It was like she could lose her mind any second and do something to harm Honey.

"Come on, let's get out of here," I said, stepping forward.

Brandi looked at me, and then jerked her head toward Honey. "And her?"

"Forget about her. She and I are done."

Honey looked down, her face stiff with emotion. My words hurt her. But Brandi needed to hear them. I needed her to stop seeing Honey as a threat.

Brandi looked at me, and a small smile broke on her lips. "We're going to be so happy, Caleb."

I looked at the gun in her hand.

"I think you need to leave that behind," I said.

But she just smiled and held onto it. "I don't think so. You never know when I might need it."

Before we walked out the door, my eyes met Honey's. She was fighting back tears, her throat working hard as she swallowed deeply. Her eyes begged me not to leave and I wished more than anything that I didn't have to, that I could stay. I wanted to tell her it was going to be all right. But I had a feeling Brandi would lose her shit if I showed Honey any kind of concern.

Plus, I wasn't sure it was true.

Brandi had a gun. She was in the middle of a psychological meltdown. And she was desperate. All perfect ingredients for this shit to end badly.

I could take her. Take the gun.

But there was a slight chance it could go wrong and I wasn't going to risk it when we were still at the apartment.

So we took her car. Brandi drove. After all, she was the one with the gun. It rested on her lap and I kept my eye on it, waiting for the opportunity to grab it.

"You need to slow down," I said when she raced through the streets towards Cavalry Hill. But she didn't hear me. She was too busy ranting about how happy we were going to be. How miserable she'd been without me. How crazy in love she was.

Biker Baby

"Listen, we just need to take things a bit slow," I said. "Starting with the driving."

"What do you mean take things slow?" She glanced at me and frowned. "I love you. We can be together now. Isn't that what you want?"

When I felt the car skid, but then right itself, I grabbed onto the seat.

There was a real chance we were going to have a wreck, and it just seemed so unfair, so fucked up for it to go down this way.

Feeling a surge of anger, I looked at my deranged ex-girlfriend. "Why are you doing this?"

Her eyebrows crashed together. "Really, Caleb? You really have to ask me that?"

A pendant of silver glinted on her neck. It was the tree of life symbol in a circle of diamonds.

Honey's necklace.

"It was you who broke into Honey's apartment, wasn't it?"

She laughed maniacally and it sent shivers through me.

"You think you could just move on with her? You think you could cast me aside and move on with another woman?"

"But why break into her apartment?"

She hastily wiped her eyes with her arm. "You have no idea how hard it was to watch you with her. Watch you kiss her. Date her. Watch you arrive on her doorstep and twirl her around in your arms. I was there, you know. That day. I saw you ride off and then come back not long later. When she opened the door, you took her in your arms and you kissed her so passionately. And it was such a promising kiss. Just like you used to kiss me, do you remember, Caleb? How you would kiss me with so much promise?"

I was ashamed to admit it, but I'd only ever kissed her with lust and a primal need to fuck her.

"So I had to see for myself. See what kind of *whore* had gotten her claws into you."

"So you broke in and stole her necklace."

She looked at me darkly. Which made me nervous for two very good reasons. One, the look was pure psychotic. And two, she wasn't paying any attention to the fucking road.

"She took something of mine, so it was only right I took something of hers."

She reached up and touched the necklace. Which was fucking great because now she only had one hand on the steering wheel.

"It was you who sent me the lace underwear and the black roses," I said flatly.

She glanced at me, darkly. "Don't forget the doll heads."

I shook my head. "Why?"

"I've been watching you for months. I came back to be with you, but you had already moved on," she scoffed. "After telling me you didn't want a commitment, you went right ahead and took on the biggest commitment of all with another woman. A woman you didn't even know for very long." Tears rolled down her cheeks. "You were supposed to have a baby with me!"

"I wasn't expecting to meet Honey, or to be a father so soon." Despite the disaster unfolding around me, I couldn't help but feel an ache in my heart about the baby not being mine. "It was never a plan. I didn't break up with you because I wanted someone else."

Outside, rain started to fall.

Inside the car, Brandi started to cry.

"I love you so much, but you simply cast me aside." Her chin crumpled, but then she sucked in a deep breath through her teeth and a weird calm settled across her face. Her voice was low. Dangerous. "Tell me you love me." When I didn't say anything, she screamed it. "Tell me!"

She had a gun. And she was in charge of the vehicle. So of course I *fucking* loved her. I would do or say anything she wanted.

"Yes, I do. I do love you. Now will you please slow the fuck down."

For the briefest moment, her face softened and her eyes glanced at me pleadingly. But then her madness returned and they turned sharp and wild. "No, you're just saying that!"

I felt the tires slip beneath us with the increase in speed. I needed to reassure her.

"Baby, please . . . I love you."

"Then why are you with her?" she cried, almost veering us off the road.

I grabbed onto the seat again. "Because I thought she was pregnant with my baby."

"And because you love her and not me."

"No, that's not true. If the time away from you has shown me one thing, it's how much I . . . miss you."

She scoffed. My words had lost their affect on her because she had spiraled too far down the rabbit hole of craziness. I had to act. I had to end this now before she killed the both of us.

I lunged for the gun on her lap. But she slammed on the brakes and the car spun wildly off the road, tires screeching, our world spinning in circles, around and around. When we came to a stop, we both sat stunned and breathless. Brandi slowly looked at me and I saw the light go out of her eyes and the madness shimmer across her face. With a wild, psychotic scream she slammed her foot down on the accelerator, and with a squeal of tires, drove us straight off the road and into a tree.

CHAPTER 51

HONEY

As soon as they left, I called the police.

And then I rang Cade.

After hanging up with him I wanted to run to my car and speed off in the direction of Cavalry Hill. But the police insisted I stay where I was and wait for the deputy who was on his way. I paced the floor waiting for him, chewing my thumbnail down to the nail bed as I panicked, my head wild with thoughts of a crazed Brandi behind the wheel. When the deputy turned up five minutes later, I grew frustrated by the minutes we lost as I explained to him what'd happened. How Brandi had knocked on my door and insisted she needed to show me something. How that *something* ended up being a gun. How we'd sat at the table at her insistence and she'd demanded I stop seeing Caleb. That he loved her. That they belonged together. That I should be ashamed of myself for trapping him with a baby.

"They're heading to Cavalry Hill. Please, you have to stop them. She's crazy."

Biker Baby

"It's okay, ma'am. The sheriff and another deputy are on their way. We'll find them."

Panic was a violent wave crashing through me. Brandi was so unhinged it could already be too late.

I rubbed my big belly. My daughter was restless and kept moving. This morning when I'd woken up, she seemed to have dropped lower and my belly appeared to be even bigger than it had been when I'd gone to bed the night before. After leaving Caleb in the studio, I'd come home and crawled into bed, absolutely exhausted from breaking up with the man I was in love with, and cried myself to sleep. The longing to be in Caleb's big, strong arms was crushing, and now the idea of him being hurt by his psychopathic ex-girlfriend was too much to bear.

I stopped pacing and sat down at the table, my heart thumping wildly in my chest.

"Are you okay?" the deputy asked when I started to rub my lower back.

Before I could answer him, his radio crackled and I recognized Sheriff Buckman's voice as he requested assistance. "We've found them. But we're going to need an ambulance."

Alarm shot up my spine.

I tried to swallow, but my throat wouldn't work.

Seeing my panic, the deputy requested further information. "Can you confirm you have the suspect?"

Again the radio crackled. "Both suspect and passenger are in need of medical assistance following a single vehicle accident."

I stood up so quick I saw stars. "Is he alive?"

The deputy excused himself and stepped outside to speak to the sheriff while I tried desperately to control my madly beating heart. I took up pacing the floor again, chewing my poor thumbnail and rubbing my belly. When the deputy walked back in, he looked at me gravely.

"There's been an accident," he said, and I watched his throat work as he swallowed with the hesitation of telling someone bad news. "Both passengers have been transported to the hospital."

"Please tell me he's alive."

Again, another deep swallow. "I can't tell you that. I'm sorry, miss, but that information isn't clear."

I drove to the hospital with shaking hands, terrified. *Panicked.* I don't even remember the drive. I was on autopilot.

What had Brandi done?

Was Caleb alive?

By the time I got there, he was already in the ER. I wasn't able to see him straight away. After being assessed, he was transferred from the ER to surgery.

It was hell waiting for news. I paced the crowded waiting room where Caleb's family and half of the MC also waited. No one seemed to know anything. No one knew the extent of his injuries or if he was conscious, and it was torture.

"Maybe you should sit down," Cade suggested, adjusting his baby son in his arms. We were standing with his mom and Bull, while seven of his club brothers filled the noisy plastic chairs that wheezed every time they moved their massive bodies in them.

Thankfully, Indy was able to find out what was going on.

"He's going to be okay," she said calmly, walking back into the room from visiting the ER. This was her world. Where she worked. "He has been X-rayed and has a couple of breaks in his ankle. He's being prepped for surgery."

"Is he in any danger?" Ronnie asked, looking understandably rattled. Her youngest son had been driven into a tree by a crazed ex-girlfriend.

"There is always danger with surgery. But as far as his injuries are concerned, no, he's not in any danger."

A relief settled across the room.

Indy walked over to us and took her son from her husband.

"I was able to speak with him," she said to me. "He's groggy and in a lot of pain. But he asked for you. He wanted to know you were alright."

Affection and longing flared in my chest.

"Can I see him?" I asked.

Indy shook her head. "He's already in surgery."

"He's going to be okay," Cade reassured me.

"Maybe you should go home, get some rest," Indy suggested, rocking her son in her arms. "I'm heading home to put this one to bed. I'll give you a ride."

"No. I want to stay here. I want to be here when he comes out of surgery."

I felt my baby move and shift, and I rubbed my belly. She had been very active all morning, and in my fatigue she felt heavier, my pelvis fuller.

"Is my grandbaby awake?" Ronnie asked, her tired eyes momentarily brightening.

My heart dropped. It was going to disappoint Ronnie to the bone when she found out this wasn't her grandbaby. And these people. What would they think when they found out?

The truth was, I still didn't have the paternity results back from Dr. Perry's office. I'd told Brandi I did because I was terrified she was going to hurt someone. I lied to her, and I was so convincing even Caleb believed me. I'd seen the hurt on his face. Seen the disappointment momentarily replace his concern for the high-tense scene unfolding before us. And in that moment I knew, just knew, I'd done the right thing by breaking up with him. Because the look on his face and the emotion in his eyes told me just how gutted he was, and how he would always struggle with it. Over the years it would eat him up.

I rubbed my lower back as a tightening spread through my abdomen. I let out a deep breath.

"Are you okay, sweetheart?" Ronnie asked.

I nodded, sliding my hand beneath my round belly. Everything felt... *tight*. "I'm fine."

But Ronnie looked concerned. She looked at Indy. "Maybe Honey should see a doctor."

Indy's big brown eyes studied me. "Are you having some tightening in the abdomen? Contractions?"

"No. Well, tightening, yes, but contractions, no."

Indy put her hands on my big belly as a minor cramp tightened through me. "I think maybe we should get you into a room. It will be safer to get you checked out."

"I'm fine, honestly," I replied. But one look from Ronnie and I knew I would be going to an ER room.

Ten minutes later, I lay on a hospital bed with a doctor checking me out. After hooking me up to different monitors and doing a thorough check, he sat down on the chair next to me, flicking through a chart. He looked up and smiled kindly at me.

"Braxton Hicks," he said. "You're not in labor."

"I'm not?" Relief spread through me.

"No. You're not." He smiled reassuringly. "And everything looks good. I'm releasing you."

I nodded, relieved. The last thing I needed was to go into labor three weeks early. And definitely not when Caleb was in surgery following his ex-girlfriend's death wish into a tree.

"Is Caleb okay?" I asked the doctor. He was friends with Indy and knew exactly what was going on.

He nodded. "He'll be in a bit of pain, but he'll be fine once they've set his ankle."

"And the girl he was with when the accident occurred?'

He paused, unsure if he should share the information with me or not. Thankfully, he relaxed and took pity on me. "She came out of it rather unscathed. But she's been admitted to psych. I'm not sure she was right in the head."

CHAPTER 52

HONEY

Four days later, Autumn drove me out to her family's lake house. Caleb was recovering from two surgeries to his ankle and was in and out of consciousness. I'd spent hours at the hospital but I was only allowed to see him briefly, and even then he was so high on pain medication he didn't even know I was there.

I needed some time out. And the lake house was just what the doctor ordered.

Literally.

Yesterday, when I was visiting Caleb, my doctor ran into me in the corridor and told me to get some rest away from the hospital.

When Autumn and I arrived at the lake, I knew he was right. The time out would do me a world of good. I needed to catch my breath. I needed to sit out on the magnificent veranda and watch the boats on the water. I needed to still my mind and suck in the heady scent of the trees fringing the waterline, and the smells of fall like smoke from chimneys and the crispness in the air.

Biker Baby

Winter was almost here, and the trees dotting the shore were a collage of red, gold, sienna, and burnt umber. In a few weeks, Christmas would be on our doorstep, and then a new year.

A new year and a new start.

"For someone only staying one night, this thing weighs a ton," Autumn said, placing my suitcase on the double bed in the main bedroom of her parents' large vacation home. Open planned and with sprawling timber floors and a high-pitched roof, it was the perfect place to take some time out and catch my breath.

I followed her back out to the spacious living room.

"I brought a couple of books with me. This kid is going to be here in less than a month and I have no idea what to do with her. Best I start learning."

With a yank, she parted the curtains and the vastness of the lake came into view. In the distance, storm clouds gathered over the bay.

"Looks like there is a storm brewing." She swung around and gave me a gentle look. "I must be crazy letting you stay out here by yourself. Not when you're about to pop."

"My due date isn't for another three weeks. And you know how much I need some time out."

She did. But she gave me a pointed look.

"You have tonight to chill out and then I'll be back tomorrow morning." She pulled a Tupperware container from her oversized bag and gave it to me. "Here, Mom made your favorite. Spicy chicken tomato soup."

I grinned. "Thanks, Mom."

"I told her not to put too much cayenne pepper in because I didn't want you going into labor early."

When I went to mention my due date again, she held up her hand and waved them around. "I know, I know, you're not due for a while yet."

She dug into her bag.

"And here, this is from Maverick." She handed me a can with some kind of air horn on the end.

"Maverick knows I'm here?" I asked, momentarily distracted from the weird object I was now holding.

Autumn shrugged. "He was kind of inside me when you called."

As usual, TMI from my best friend. Although, it was nice hearing she was giving him a chance and seeing him again.

"That's waaaaay too much information," I said, looking at the can in my hand. "What is it?"

"It's a bear horn."

I raised an eyebrow at my friend. "Maverick thinks I need protection from a grizzly bear at the lake?"

"The noise . . . it'll scare off potential threats. Animal or human."

I couldn't help but smile at the gesture.

"Please thank him for me. He is very sweet." I put the air horn on the table. "Oh, but let him know that if he tells Caleb where I am, I *will* cut him."

Autumn rolled her eyes at my lame threat, and then paused in the doorway. "Are you sure you don't want me to stay?"

I loved Autumn. She was the best friend every girl should have. Since day one she'd always had my back. But for right now, I just needed to be alone.

"I'm sure. Now go. Don't keep that Jason Momoa lookalike of yours waiting."

Autumn grinned and her eyes glazed over. "He's such a beast."

She sighed dreamily and I had to shoo her out the door to actually get her to leave. After watching her pull away, I closed the door behind me and crossed the room to the big bay windows overlooking the lake.

Finally, I was alone.

Finally, I could breathe.

Finally, I could work out what the fuck I was going to do from this moment on.

I pulled a crumpled envelope from my pocket. It had arrived earlier that morning and contained the results of the paternity test. I wasn't lying when I said I'd paid extra to put a rush on it.

I looked out over the lake. This was it. After days of uncertainty I was about to find out the truth.

With trembling fingers I ripped open the envelope, unfolded the letter, and began to read. And as the truth began to settle through me, I began to cry.

CHAPTER 53

CALEB

"What the fuck are you doing?" Came the voice from the doorway.

I looked up to see Cade walking into the room.

"Trying to get the fuck out of bed! What the hell does it look like I'm doing?"

One thing about breaking your ankle in two places, it was hell getting out of bed. Especially if that bed was a hospital bed so high up off the ground you were practically sitting in the ozone layer.

Everything hurt. It had since the day of the accident. But that wasn't going to stop me. After one operation and four days spent lying in the hospital, I was done. I knew what I needed to do, and no hellfire or brimstone was going to get in my way.

Or two broken bones.

"I have to get out of here," I said to Cade who continued to watch me struggle. I glared at him. "Are you just going to stand there, or are you going to help me?"

"Are the doctors releasing you?"

Biker Baby

"Fuck the doctors," I said, trying to get my goddamn ankle off the bed since my asshole brother refused to help. A ball-searing pain shot up my leg as my booted foot hit the floor. "Fuuuuck!"

"Why the fuck are you trying to leave?" Cade asked, taking pity on me and handing me my crutches.

"Because I have a girl out there who thinks I don't love her."

Sweat poured down my temples and I struggled to talk, because goddamn it, I was in so much fucking pain it was torture.

"You're putting yourself through this to go tell Honey you love her? Have you not heard of a phone?"

"You're so fucking funny, asshole." Frustrated, I held up my cell phone. "It's dead."

I tried to stand up, but the pain was almost unbearable.

"Why the fuck are you in so much pain? I thought they put you on kick-ass medication."

"Yeah, well, I didn't take them earlier."

Cade looked at me like I was crazy. And maybe I was. But I'd spent the last four days high on pain medication, hell, I was still a little high, and I didn't want anything more in case it knocked me out. I had to find Honey and somehow get to her. And I didn't want to be as high as a junkie when I asked her to marry me.

"You're fucking crazy, brother." Cade helped me get stable with my crutches. My brother was a mountain of a human being, which was good, because I appeared to have no control over my legs.

"I love her, man. I don't care that the baby isn't mine. I will be a good father to her."

"You know for sure it's not yours?"

"She got the results back the other day. Told me it wasn't mine."

A familiar ache punched its way through my medicated haze.

"And you're okay with that?"

My jaw clenched. At first I hadn't been. I was gutted. My biological daughter was gone. Replaced by a child fathered by another man.

But when my psychopathic ex-girlfriend drove us into a tree and almost killed us, it kind of put things into perspective.

Well, that, and four days lying on my goddamn back with nothing to do but think while high on drugs and in excruciating pain.

I was in love with Honey.

And I wanted to be with her.

"I will love that kid with everything I've got," I said. "It doesn't matter that it's not mine."

"It's a big commitment, brother."

"I don't care. I want to marry her and be a family."

"Marry her?" Cade's eyebrows shot up. "Are you still fucking high?"

Despite the pain, I smiled.

Hell, I grinned like a motherfucker.

Because I had never been so sure of anything in my entire life.

"I'm going to find her, and I'm going to make her my queen."

CHAPTER 54

HONEY

I sat out on the veranda watching the boats come in off the bay. It was only lunchtime, but it was getting dark because of the approaching storm. Across the water, dark clouds rumbled with thunder. The weather channel said it was going to be a short but ferocious storm, with winds up to forty miles per hour and a lot of rain.

I sat curled up on one of the outdoor deck chairs, a blanket over my lap and a cup of ginger tea in my hands.

I'd already checked to make sure there were enough candles to ride out the stormy night if we lost power, and my cell phone was fully charged.

Wind blew in off the water and tangled in my hair. I sucked in a deep breath to still my chaotic mind and was rewarded with the simple calmness I was looking for. I was happy here. It was the perfect place to process the letter from Dr. Perry's office.

I leaned forward and rubbed my lower back. As I got closer to my due date I was getting more and more uncomfortable. Parts of me were grumpy. This morning I'd woken up with a persistent lower back pain, which finally went away after I'd been walking around for a while. Last week, the soles of my feet started to complain every time I went barefooted. A few days earlier it was my fingers.

But it was all totally worth it.

All of it.

Because it didn't matter whose baby this was, I loved her with all of my heart and every morsel of my soul.

I rubbed my big belly and felt consumed with love. Every time I felt her move, I was reminded of the joy I was about to welcome into my life.

And I was grateful for those feelings because it kept things in perspective for me. And also because they pushed back the heartache and longing I felt whenever I thought of Caleb and everything that had happened.

After reading the results from Dr. Perry's office, I had tried calling him, but he never answered. I wanted to let him know once and for all who the father was, now that there was no doubt.

I picked up my phone and looked at the screen. There were two messages from Charlie wanting to talk. After calling Caleb, I'd called him. And just like I knew he would, he took the news with his usual smugness and condescension.

A sudden rush of wind blew in off the bay and danced with the towering pines that lined the property.

Inside, a door slammed.

I sent Caleb a text.

Me: *Call me, please.*

Thunder rolled in the storm clouds as they moved across the bay. It was time to go inside and shut the house up for the evening. Light some candles. Heat some soup. Get a fire started.

Biker Baby

There were still a couple of hours of light left, but I was ready to close the curtains and settle in for the night. Maybe have a bath. Maybe put on my pajamas and curl up with one of the books I'd brought with me.

And try Caleb's phone again.

I didn't know if his phone was dead or if he was deliberately avoiding my calls.

But I was going to keep ringing until I got ahold of him.

And if that meant calling Cade or Indy, then I would do that, too.

CHAPTER 55

CALEB

Oh, Christ. They were the biggest set of steps in the world.

I looked out the windshield as Caleb pulled up to the lake house. It was a sprawling, two-story home with a large set of stairs leading up to the wraparound porch. As I climbed out of the car, the relentless throb in my lower leg reminded me that this was going to suck.

Outside, thunder crashed through the clouds and wind whipped around the swaying branches of the cypress and pine trees. A light scatter of rain danced across the leaves on the ground and then stopped.

"Let's get you inside before it starts to fucking rain," Cade said, coming around to my side of the car and looking up at the stairs leading up to the porch. "I think this might take a while."

Using crutches, I hobbled over to the steps where Cade threw my arm over his shoulder and helped me take my first step. Pain like an absolute motherfucker tore up my leg and shot into the very core of me. I gripped the railing and gritted my teeth.

"You okay?" my brother asked.

Biker Baby

I nodded, my jaw set, sweat trailing down my temples. Another scattering of rain hit us as I took my second step, growling as the pain rolled through me.

"My wife is going to have my balls if she finds out I'm helping you destroy your ankle like this."

"I'm not destroying my ankle. I'm coming after the girl I'm in love with. You know, a grand gesture of love and all that."

"Yeah, well, I hope it's fucking worth it. Indy will have your balls, too. We're both going to have to face her after this."

Again, thunder rattled in the sky above us, and I took a moment to catch my breath.

"She'll appreciate the gesture. Girls love this shit."

"Since when has Indy been sucked in by grand gestures?"

I winced with more pain. "She married your sorry ass, didn't she?"

Cade helped me up another two steps and said, "If I don't get laid because of your grand gesture, then I'm going to knee you in your balls."

I glanced at him. "Because clearly I'm not in enough pain as it is."

Cade hoisted me over the last step and up to the front door.

"Fucking thank Christ!" he said. "You're an insane motherfucker, you know that?"

He handed me my crutches and I straightened.

"Insane and crazy in love with the girl behind this door," I said.

"Well, you look like shit. Like you're about to pass out. You sure you don't want me to take you back to hospital?"

"You're fucking kidding me, right? I didn't climb those stairs for nothing."

I sucked in a deep breath, right into the depths of my lungs in an attempt to force back my pain. I was out of breath and a mess, but I was ready to claim back what was mine.

"Are you ready?" Cade asked.

I nodded. "I was born ready, brother."

He knocked just as another roll of thunder rumbled in the clouds overhead.

When Honey opened the door, a fierce need to take her in my arms and mash my lips to hers overwhelmed me because it was the first time I'd seen her in days, and my longing for her had me all tied up in knots. Seeing her was a relief. A total fucking relief. I wanted to kiss her more than anything in the entire fucking world.

"Caleb!" She breathed my name as if she was absolutely fucking relieved to see me, too. "You're here."

"Can we come in?" I asked, swallowing back the agony in my ankle.

She opened the door wider and I hobbled in, followed by Cade.

"They released you from the hospital?" she asked, closing the door behind her.

"No, I released myself."

"Are you insane? That's crazy—"

"Listen," I took a step toward her. "I think I've only got a couple of minutes left in me before I pass out, because sweet baby Jesus, I'm in the seventh realm of hell with this ankle. But I couldn't wait another moment, Honey. I had to see you. I had to tell you." I huffed out a breath. "I'm in love with you. Do you understand me? I'm so crazy in love with you that being with you is all that matters to me. I know you think I can't love this baby, but I can. And I will. It doesn't matter that she isn't mine. I've been here from the start. I've loved her from the moment I knew she existed. *Me.* Not *him.* That's got to count for something."

"Caleb—"

"I'll be the best damn father to her, baby. I promise. And if you'll have me, I'll be the best damn husband to you. Just give me a chance."

"Caleb—" She went to protest, but the look of shock registered on her face instead. "Wait, you're asking me to marry you?"

"Baby, I'd marry you today if I didn't think I was going to pass out from this fucking pain." I moved closer to her, and leaning all my weight onto one of the crutches, awkwardly took one of her hands in mine. "Let me be the man you deserve. You and Bump."

Tears sprung to her eyes. "You really want to marry me?"

I nodded. "More than anything."

She started to cry so I wiped them away with the pad of my thumb. "Please don't cry, Angel."

"I love you," she cried, overwhelmed with the emotion. "I love you so much."

She pressed her lips to mine and emotion spiraled through me.

This woman.

She was everything.

She pulled away and looked up at me, her eyes sparkling with tears. "I've been trying to call you."

"My phone is dead."

"I lied to you," she said, her face crumpled. "When I said I had the paternity results back. I lied because I didn't want Brandi to hurt you. I didn't have them back then, but I have them now."

I followed her gaze to the open letter on the dining table. Cade moved across the room and picked it up, bringing it over to me. I could barely swallow over the lump in my throat as I read it.

The words danced before my eyes.

And I huffed out a deep, relieved breath.

"I'm the father?" I raised my eyes and looked at her in wonder. "Bump is *my* baby?"

She started to cry as she nodded. "Yes. She is."

I re-read the words on the letter, confirming my paternity of the pregnancy, and a love as fierce as a wild fire burned through me. I wrapped my free arm around Honey and pulled her to my chest where my heart beat wildly.

My baby.

She was my baby.

Not Charlie's.

"I love you so much," I breathed into her hair, happiness and relief momentarily easing the torment in my ankle and every other cell in my body.

"I love you, too. I'm so sorry. I made so many foolish decisions."

"Don't be sorry. Just say you'll marry me."

I felt her nod against me. "Yes, I will marry you."

I pulled away, but my smile suddenly faded because I really was about to pass out. "Whoa."

"Are you okay?" Honey looked alarmed.

"I think I need to sit down."

I felt clammy and sick.

"That's it, Romeo, I'm taking you back to the hospital," Cade said.

"I just need to sit down."

Cade put my arm around his shoulders and guided me over to the dining table, easing me down onto a chair.

"Should I call an ambulance?" Honey asked.

"I'm sure they'll come out here real quick when they find out he checked himself out of the hospital less than an hour ago."

"I just need a minute and I'll be fine," I insisted.

"You're going back. You need bed rest and drugs." Cade was adamant and I was starting to feel like he might be right. Being in this much pain was exhausting. His phone buzzed and he pulled it out of his cut. "It's Indy. She's probably found out about you. Hope you're ready for an ass kicking."

Sure enough, she had. And she had a very strong opinion about it.

After listening to his wife for a minute, Cade handed me the phone.

"Are you insane, Caleb Calley?" she exclaimed into my ear.

"You're like the third person to ask me that in the last hour. So, I don't know, maybe?"

"You know you're doing all kinds of damage to yourself right now. You need to get your ass back to the hospital immediately. Don't make me come out there and drag your sorry ass back myself."

"Okay, boss. I'm on my way."

"Don't say that and not mean it. You've got an hour to get back here before I call your mom!"

I handed the phone back to Cade. "She pulled out the big guns. She's threatening to involve Mom."

I watched as he put his phone to his ear. "Yeah, baby, we'll call an ambulance. He's turned kind of pale. Actually, more of a grey color. That's what I said. Serves him right, I know. Yeah, he is a dumbass."

I showed him my middle finger just as he turned away to talk to his wife.

Honey sat down next to me.

"You didn't need to put yourself through this," she said gently.

I took her hand in mine. "I couldn't go a moment longer without letting you know how I felt. I'm sorry I never told you sooner. I've loved you for so long and it just seemed so wrong to let another moment tick by without telling you."

Cade hung up from Indy and walked toward us.

"Indy said there's been a four-car wreck just out of town, so there's a delay with the ambulance. It'll be quicker if I drive."

Honey was already locking up the house and turning off the lights.

"You don't need to come to the hospital. Stay here and wait out the storm," I said.

"You checked yourself out of the hospital, drove out here in a world of pain—not to mention, braved eighteen steps wearing a boot—all so you could ask me to marry you." She gave me a wink and closed the front door behind her. "You really are insane if you think I'm spending one more moment without you."

CHAPTER 56

HONEY

As we left the lake house behind us and started the long trip toward Destiny, the heavens really opened up and it started hammering us with rain. Up ahead, lightning danced across the darkening sky.

"How you holding out there, buddy?" Cade asked his brother over the sound of the rain.

"Don't you worry about me, brother. I've got everything I need." He glanced over his shoulder at me and winked. My heart squeezed with love. This man. This crazy-ass man wanted me to be his wife.

"So your girl said yes. What now?" Cade asked.

"Well, now I'm going to get some kickass drugs into me that'll hopefully knock me out for the next couple of days. Then, when I wake up I'll be hoping this wasn't all a dream and Honey really did agree to marry me."

"You can't get rid of me that easily, Caleb Calley," I said from the backseat. "You're stuck with us now."

I was rubbing my belly and thinking about marrying the man of my dreams when it happened. The pickup came out of nowhere. One minute we were driving along, and then boom, the black Ford came out of the misty rain and plowed straight into us. All of a sudden it was like being inside a washing machine, the world started spinning and I was bounced about in the backseat. Glass shattered and metal buckled as the pickup crumpled our rear passenger door and sent us whirling off the road.

When we finally came to a halt, I heard Cade let out a string of expletives and I raised my head. Looking out the shattered window, I saw the dust settle and the full extent of what had happened. We were off the side of the road, perched on a small embankment. Across the debris-scattered road from us, steam spewed from the crumpled engine of the Ford pickup.

I moved and realized I was covered in shattered glass.

"Honey!" Caleb exclaimed. He struggled to get the door open but it was too buckled and he growled with frustration.

"I'm okay," I breathed, slightly dazed.

Cade was able to climb out and rip open the back passenger door to check on me. "Are you sure you're okay?"

I brushed the glass off me. "Yes. Go get your brother out."

By the time I was able to climb out of the car, Caleb was out and hobbling frantically toward me.

"Baby, are you okay?" He held my face in his big hands and flooded my face with kisses. "Are you hurt? The baby?"

"I'm okay, I'm okay." It was a relief to be standing in the cool wind. The rain had dampened and a light, fairy rain fell from the grey sky like gentle, comforting kisses against my skin. It was soothing. Cooling. In the distance, lightning slashed through the clouds again.

"I'll go check on the other driver," Cade said, disappearing into the dewy rain.

Caleb put his hand on my belly. "Are you sure you're all right?"

He still looked pale, but I imagined his adrenaline had kicked in and was overriding his ankle pain.

I nodded because my mouth was dry. "Yeah, it was just a shock but I'm—"

I froze.

Startled.

I stayed very still and waited.

Then it happened again.

Motherfucker.

The pain that hit me was like nothing I'd ever felt. It tore into me, biting at my insides and overwhelming me. Goosebumps spread across my skin and my knees went weak.

I keeled over.

"Fuck, baby. What's happening?" Caleb asked alarmed.

I bit down on my bottom lip.

That was a contraction.

"Braxton Hicks be damned," I moaned. My hand chewed into his shirt as I looked up at him. "I'm in fucking labor."

His eyes widened. "Are you sure?"

In response, I doubled over with pain. "You need to call an EMT. And you need to call them now!"

Cade came running over. "The other driver is fine, but I think he has whiplash and a broken wrist. I've told him to wait in the car. Whoa, what's happening here?"

"She's in labor," Caleb replied.

I let out a long moan of pain as another contraction squeezed at my insides. "We need an ambulance now."

While Cade tried to get a signal on his phone, Caleb tried mine.

But we were in the notorious black spot between the lake and Destiny where there was no cell coverage for a few miles.

"Fuuuuuck!" Caleb moved my phone around in front of himself like a water diviner to see if he could get a signal. He hobbled with his booted foot. "I've got no signal."

Cade looked at his screen. "Me neither. Looks like we're going to have to deal with this one ourselves."

"What do you mean?" I asked, panicked.

"It means you're in good hands," Caleb said soothingly.

I was expecting the EMTs to arrive and I would give birth surrounded by all the medical equipment and comfort of an ambulance. But looking at Caleb's ashen face, I knew my reality was going to be vastly different.

My face crumpled. "Are you telling me I'm going to have my baby on the side of the road?" When Cade and Caleb's expressions confirmed it, my eyes widened. "Oh, no. No, this isn't happening."

Caleb gripped my hand so I'd look at him. "Listen to me, whatever happens, I've got you. Okay? I'm not going to let anything happen to you or our baby."

His voice was calming, and the way he was looking at me made me believe him. I swallowed back my pain and nodded. Instead of freaking out, I focused on my breathing.

When a set of headlights approached us through the bad weather, relief spread through me. "Oh, thank God."

A car pulled up and a window rolled down.

"Everyone okay?" The elderly driver asked.

"We have one injured in the pickup and a lady in labor," Cade explained.

"We need to get Honey to a hospital," Caleb added. "There's no cell service so we can't call for an ambulance."

"This spot is notorious for no phone coverage. Climb in, I can take her and anyone else who needs to go. I should be able to make a call few miles down the road. Send some help."

"You and Honey go with him, I'll stay here with the other driver and this mess," Cade said.

"No!" I cried out. Liquid trickled down my thighs. My water had broken. This baby was coming, and it wasn't waiting around for an ambulance, and she sure as hell wasn't going to wait until we got to the hospital. "We won't make it to the hospital in time."

"Take the other driver," Caleb said. "And call for the ambulance as soon as you can."

The elderly gentleman nodded. Cade helped the driver of the pickup into the car, and within minutes the car drove off.

"See, baby, helps is on the way," Caleb said, stroking my cheek.

His face was calm, his blue eyes full of confidence and comfort. He sat me down on the back seat, but just as he did, my labor pains started all over again and I leaned forward and let out a loud groan.

"That one was the worst," I moaned. But just as the pain began to wane, it suddenly flared up again and I cried out. I looked at Caleb. "Oh God, I need to push."

His bright blue eyes glittered over my face and they were full of confidence. "I've got this. If I have to deliver our daughter on the side of the road—"

"Now!" I cried. This baby was coming. "Oh, God, she's impatient."

Caleb nodded and sucked in a deep breath.

"You okay to do this?" Cade asked him.

"No, not him," I cried. "I've heard what happens when a man sees his woman's hoo-ha giving birth."

Both men looked at me like I was crazy.

"Angel, lots of men deliver their babies—"

"Please," I sobbed.

When I started crying they both nodded and a silent agreement passed between the two brothers.

"All right, let's do this!" Cade said.

Caleb sat behind me doing his best to soothe me, rubbing his big hands over my lower back. I kept my head down and focused on my breathing, praying to God that an ambulance was going to arrive soon.

Another contraction hit me and I cried out in pain. I had a very sudden urge to push and I couldn't fight it. My body clenched and started pushing, overriding the very specific command from my brain to not push. "Oh, God, she's coming."

Cade disappeared to the back of the car and I heard him rummaging around in the trunk. He reappeared holding a towel and a picnic blanket.

"Here, put this under you," he said, unfolding the towel and laying it across the backseat. It was a reminder that things were about to get messy and I felt an overwhelming need to cry.

I turned to Caleb. "I don't want to do this."

His face softened. His thumbs gently caressed my hands. He leaned in and kissed my tears away. "By the looks of it, our girl takes after her mama. Once she's made up her mind, there's no stopping her."

Cade kneeled into the back seat of the Acura. "Hey, I've got this."

"You've delivered a baby?" I asked between the rapid onset of contractions. There was no space between them. They were right on top of each other.

"Not exactly. But I was in the room when Indy gave birth to River." He winked at me. "Practically makes me a pro."

"Are you fucking kidding me?" I yelled. My eyes shot to Caleb. "Is he fucking kidding me right now?"

"Baby, you need to breathe. There's not a lot Cade can't do." Caleb tried to sound soothing, but I could see he was just as concerned about his brother delivering our baby as I was.

Another spasm gripped my uterus and shook it about like a dog with an old shoe. I cried out. Never having given birth before, I didn't know what was going on down there, but it pretty much felt like a bowling ball was attempting to crawl out of my vagina.

"Okay, now I need you to try and relax a little for me." Cade positioned himself at my feet. "I need to see what's going on down there."

When he tried to pry open my knees, they wouldn't budge.

"Okay, Honey. You need to open these," he said.

"Are you kidding me, that's how I got in trouble in the first place!" I sobbed, overwhelmed by it all.

Cade grinned. "You're safe with me, sweetheart. I promise. I'm a well and truly-married man."

I wanted to burst into tears. I wanted to open my legs up and expose my crowning vagina to Cade about as much as I wanted a lobotomy with a hacksaw. But as another spasm tore at my body, I realized I didn't have any other options.

I threw my hands over my face and spread my knees, showing Cade everything.

"Wow," he said. He looked at me, his face set. "I'm no doctor, but I'm pretty sure that this is what they call crowning. And if I'm not mistaken, I think your baby is almost here."

Another spasm hit me. Followed by a need to push.

"I have to push," I breathed. I gripped the edge of the seat. "I'm not kidding, I need to push *now*!"

"Okay, good." Cade seemed to study my vagina, but I was in too much pain to give a goddamn anymore. "Now I need you to breathe, Honey. Take a deep breath."

"Breathe, baby," Caleb echoed, squeezing my hand to the point of pain.

I wanted to push so bad.

I turned to look at the tough biker crouching down beside me.

"I'm scared," I sobbed to Caleb.

He wiped a lock of sticky hair from my forehead.

"I know, baby, but I'm right here, okay." He kissed my temple. "You can do this, do you understand? You've got this."

I looked up into his beautiful face, and the way he was looking at me gave me strength. I squeezed his hand as another contraction squeezed my uterus and screamed until I couldn't push any more. Feeling spent, I collapsed against the back seat.

"I told you I can't do this," I panted.

"Yes, you can," Caleb said. "You're the strongest woman I know."

I shook my head. "No, I'm not. I'm a pussy. And I'm scared."

He leaned his face close to mine. "Don't be scared, baby. I love you. And I know that if anyone can do this, it's my woman. And that's you, Honey. You're my queen."

"You're only saying that because I am squeezing a goddamn watermelon out of a hole the size of a nickel. A watermelon *you* put in me," I sobbed.

He smiled, and then his face softened as he wiped my sweaty hair out of my eyes. "I'm sorry I haven't told you before today. But I love you so much, baby. And I can't wait to be a family with you and Bump. I don't want to lose you. I know I should have told you all of this sooner. But I didn't because I am an idiot, and I didn't want to crowd you. Christ, Honey. I'm so in love with you. I can't imagine doing any of this with anyone but you."

"Really?"

The look of affection on his face left me with no doubt.

"Really," he assured me.

Another spasm flared in my uterus and I felt our baby stretching me. I winced and gritted my teeth, and with one more push, I felt our baby's head enter the world.

Biker Baby

"We have a head!" Cade cried. "Holy shit!" He looked at me. "Alright, Honey. You're going to need to push, okay. One big, almighty push and your baby will be here."

I looked at Caleb and gripped his hand. And summoning up what little strength I had left, I pushed and I pushed, and I screamed and then I pushed some more. And just when I didn't think I could push anymore, I felt our baby leave my body and slide into Cade's waiting hands.

Within seconds, our baby's cry echoed through the car.

"Congratulations, mama. You have a baby girl," Cade said, wrapping our daughter in a towel and holding her up for Caleb and me to see. He gently placed her on my chest and my arms instantly went around her. Love overcame me then, and all the pain and discomfort was forgotten. The fact that I was lying there in the back seat of an Acura with my legs spread and vagina exposed to the VP of the Kings of Mayhem MC was forgotten.

There was only love.

I looked at Caleb and his face was stiff as he fought his emotions. His eyes welled up. "She's beautiful," he whispered and pressed a kiss to my temple. "I love you so much." And then he leaned down and pressed his lips to his daughter's forehead. "And I love you, too, my little princess."

Cade laid the picnic blanket over me so I felt a lot less exposed. "Thank you," I choked through my tears.

He winked. "My pleasure, sweetheart."

Caleb gave him a nod. "Thanks, brother."

Our daughter squirmed against my chest and I realized that I had no idea what to do next.

Thankfully, the ambulance arrived not long after, thanks to the elderly driver calling for help as soon as he could.

Half an hour later, I was in the back of an ambulance with my newborn daughter in my arms. The EMTs cleaned her up and wrapped her in a warm blanket with a soft cotton cap on her little head.

Caleb rode with us. The EMTs took one look at him and quickly gave him some pain relief.

"I have a daughter," Caleb murmured with disbelief, his eyes fixed firmly on his baby.

His baby.

"Yeah, you have a daughter." I looked up at him. "How do you feel about that?"

He smiled and nodded. "Think I'll buy a shotgun."

EPILOGUE

CALEB
Twelve Months Later

I didn't think life could be this way. Well, that's not exactly true. I knew it could be as blissful as this because of Cade and Indy. They were so in love, and so damn happy, they could convert the biggest cynic.

But me?

Until Honey, I didn't think I would ever find that girl who could me wake up every day feeling like I had won the fucking lottery, but I had. Every single day I woke up surrounded in the warmth of my beautiful woman, and I would wrap my arms around her and hold her against me, absorbing her into me, losing myself in the scent of her. Some mornings we would just lie there, entwined and wrapped in one another, and I would think how amazing life was with her in it and how magical every moment with her really was.

Other mornings I would be hard as fuck and consumed with a need for her, I would slowly make love to her, savoring her body, relishing in her passionate kisses as I moved in her. There would never be another woman for me. She was it. My goddess. She had given me my daughter, and I couldn't wait to make her pregnant again. I didn't care if it was a boy or girl, hell, our girl Ruby was the most beautiful little lady that ever existed. But I'd be lying if I said I didn't want a son, and every time I made love to her, I prayed we would be making him.

This morning Honey stirred beneath my touch. Still asleep, her lips parted in a moan as my hand made its way across her flat stomach and slipped between her thighs. With tender fingers I slid into her, slowly working her up, gently rubbing that little nub of nerves that drove her into euphoria whenever I paid it special attention. She shifted slightly, moaning and licking her lips, and I felt her body respond. It was more than I could take. With a growl, I rolled onto her, nestling myself between her strong thighs, dropping my mouth to hers and kissing her. She began to kiss me back, strong, hard, passionately, and she shifted beneath me, her body seeking my cock as I pressed my hips into hers. Unable to hold back any longer, I plunged into her with one long, hard thrust and she opened her eyes with a cry. Internal muscles clenched around me, pulsating around the intrusion, and I swear to God, I was so ready to come I had to do some serious mathematical equations in my head to stop myself from blowing my load.

Without words, we moved together, our hips meeting in perfect rhythm, our bodies moving in perfect time as we both worked toward our own ecstasies. Honey reached hers first. She cried out and pulsated around me, her thighs gripping me tightly, her nails trailing down my back as she came on my cock. I couldn't hold back any longer. I dropped my face to her shoulder and moaned as I came hard.

Lost in her, I exhaled into the warmth of her neck and then rolled off her and onto my back, my heart pounding against my ribcage. Curling one arm around her, I pulled her to my chest and held her against me. I loved these moments the most. That time when my body was satiated from our lovemaking and my arms were full of the woman I was obsessed with.

Just then, Ruby started to cry in her crib down the hallway, and I felt Honey grin against my shoulder. "At least she waited until we were finished this time."

"That's Daddy's girl," I replied. "She's the best wingman in the world."

Honey giggled as she sat up. "I'll go get her."

I sat up. "No, you stay, I'll go get her."

Honey put her hand against my chest and pushed me down. "Stay there, Caleb Calley. I've got a present for you."

"You do?"

She grinned mischievously. "I wanted to give it to you last night, but you got in so late."

"I know, baby, that security detail we're doing has got us working some crazy hours."

Since expanding the weed fields to cope with increasing demands, Bull had us all doing extra work to cover shifts, which meant crazy hours until we could get more Kings of Mayhem patched in. A few members from the Dakota and Carolina chapters were patching over, and once they were in, things would get back to normal.

My gorgeous queen leaned forward and pressed her lips to mine. "It's okay. You wait here."

She climbed out of bed and I watched her with a head full of lascivious thoughts as she covered her gloriously naked body in one of my flannel shirts. She disappeared down the hall and I heard her talking with our daughter as she picked her up out of her crib. I tucked my arm behind my head on the pillow, listening to my girls.

Christ, I was a lucky man.

Honey and I had been married nine months now. We'd gotten married when Ruby was three months old, and Honey could bear to spend a night away from her. Since then, we'd settled happily into domesticated bliss with our adorable daughter. Honey's cupcake business was thriving and she was able to hire more staff so she didn't have to work as many hours.

Chance was back home. For the first few months he'd been required to stay in Maryland and receive ongoing treatment for his injuries. Now he alternated between home and the local hospital. It was a long road to recovery, but he was as strong as he was determined. When he put his mind to it, he could move mountains.

He didn't talk about what happened the day he was injured, other than he was with his unit when a bomb ripped through the building they were in, but I got the feeling there was a lot to talk about eventually. Because my brother didn't only look at me like a man who'd been to war, he looked at me like a man who'd lost his heart. Something had happened over there and one day he would tell me.

When he was ready.

It made me realize just how lucky I was and to not take a moment of it for granted.

I smiled as I listened to my queen chatting to our princess in the next room.

A few minutes later my beautiful woman appeared with her very own mini-me at the end of our bed. Dressed in a white onesie with bumblebees all over it, my daughter looked too adorable for words. Her sweet little face broke into a smile when she saw me, and she stretched her arms out for me.

Yeah, she was Daddy's girl, alright. And I loved it.

I cradled her in my arms as Honey sat on the edge of the bed. That was when I noticed the piece of paper in her hand.

I gestured to it with a nod. "What is it?"

Biker Baby

Honey grinned. "Caleb Calley..." She handed me the picture. "... meet your son."

I looked down at the black and white image between my fingers, then looked back up at Honey. "This is a sonogram."

"Yes, it is. A sonogram of your son."

It took a few seconds to register.

Honey was pregnant?

"Since when?"

She settled herself onto the bed and tucked her legs under her. "Since I went to the doctor yesterday. I had my suspicions. I mean, my boobs have been tender and I suddenly can't stand the thought of tomatoes."

I studied the black and white image of our baby, and a tide of emotion welled up inside of me. Ruby cooed in my arms, and I looked down at her. Was it possible one man could have so much luck?

"We're having a son?"

"In approximately six months and two weeks. Yes, we are."

She grinned, and in my chest a wave of happiness crashed against my heart.

"A son," I breathed out.

But one look at my beautiful queen and I knew that wasn't the only thing she had to tell me.

"What are you up to?" I eyed her suspiciously.

With a mischievous grin, she leaned in and pointed to the sonogram.

"See this?" she asked.

What I saw was a faint smudge amongst a blur of grey and black tones.

"That's your second son," she said with a big smile.

Wait.

"Twins?" I asked.

"Yep. Seems you knocked me up with two babies. A bit lazy, if you ask me." She gave me a wink and I fell in love with her all over again.

Twins.

"So what do you think about that?" she asked, curling up beside me and playing with the crown pendant around her neck.

"Twin *Calley* boys?" I huffed out a happy breath. "Our ride just got a hell of a lot wilder."

THE END

Next in the Series
Hell on Wheels: Kings of Mayhem MC Series Book 4

Want to know what's next for the Kings of Mayhem? Turn the page for a sneak peek at what you can expect from book four, Hell on Wheels (Chance's book).

Biker Baby

HELL ON WHEELS
Kings of Mayhem Book Four

Before

I woke up to her blanket of dark hair moving slowly across my chest. Her breasts, ample and full, were pressed up against my chest, her long legs entangled in mine as she stirred against me, her hand sliding down from my shoulder, over my chest and across the dips and grooves of my stomach, moving lower and lower. My body responded in all the usual ways when a beautiful woman curls her fingers around your morning wood.

My lips parted. My breathing picked up speed. My eyes fluttered and slowly opened as she gently began to rub me, her palm gliding up the length of me, her fingers paying special attention to the wide, smooth head of my cock. I breathed out a moan feeling the pleasure stir in my balls. I reached for her, my brain slowly waking up, my body already minutes ahead and wanting more. I pulled her down to me and kissed her hard, enjoying her whimpered moan of pleasure into my mouth.

She rose up, her warm body blanketing me, her nipples hardening against my chest as she shifted herself onto me. Her kisses were sweet and hot, her tongue filling my mouth as her body came alive against mine.

She sank down on my cock and I was lost to her as she rode me slowly, her slim hips rocking against me, her firm thighs straddling me, her wet pussy milking me. But it was more than that. These physical feelings, the ones that had been so hard to deny at first, now took second place to what was growing between us, what had *already* grown between us. I could love this woman. Give her my all. Take her back to my home in the US. To my life before here. To my family.

"Oh, Chance," she whimpered my name as she started to come. Her head dropped back, her long, dark hair swirling over her dark, polished shoulders as she lost herself to the orgasm she was taking from my cock.

I followed quickly. Exploding inside her. Pulsing. Filling her. And when the pleasure receded and the euphoric haze fell on us, she collapsed against me, blanketing me in her gloriously smooth body.

I closed my eyes, my heart slowing, my breathing evening out as my post-orgasmic bliss settled into me.

"It's almost dawn," she finally said, her sexy voice hoarse and sleepy. "I need to go before someone sees me."

I hated that she had to leave before anyone knew she was here. Hated that we had to move around in the shadows because of who she was and who I was. Two people divided by war. She was a villager. I was a soldier on a classified mission. We'd tried to deny our feelings. Tried to ignore the attraction that pulled us closer and closer together every time I walked past her family's little restaurant on the far side of the village. At first we'd met in the darkness in the alley. Stolen moments of whispered conversations and kisses full of longing.

"Wait," I said. I didn't know what I wanted to say. Only that I wasn't ready for her to leave. When she turned back and smiled down at me, I reached up and cupped her beautiful, sweet face. I could love this girl. See a future with her. Make her mine.

Every goodbye was getting harder to do.

"Will I see you tonight?"

Her dark eyes gleamed with the mystery I'd come to love about her. "I will try."

It was her standard response. What I'd come to expect her to say every morning when we said our goodbyes in the cool, pre-dawn light. Sometimes she would turn up and we would spend the night in one another's arms, drinking wine and making love with wild abandonment. Other nights I'd spend alone in my small, one-bedroom dwelling just off the dusty main street of the little village, missing home, missing my family, missing the familiar sights and sounds of a life half-a-world away.

I ran the back of my fingers down her arm. It was smooth, golden tanned and perfect. She glanced back at me again.

"I want to meet your friends," she said.

"You've met my friends. When we come for dinner."

Her father owned the small restaurant my unit and I frequented. He loved Americans, he said. And he would fuss over us with enthusiastic delight whenever we visited his establishment for a meal and a night where we could forget we were in the throes of war.

"But I want to meet them as your girl." She raised her chin slightly. "I don't want to sneak around anymore."

"I don't like it either. But we need to wait until my unit and I are reassigned somewhere else. And then we'll tell your father." I sat up and pulled her hand into mine. "Then we can be together."

Until then I couldn't afford for anyone to know about us.

It was too risky. While this village was considered safe, there were eyes and ears everywhere. She could easily become a target for people who didn't want us here, and I couldn't risk her getting hurt. This was war.

She frowned, her mood darkening. "It's always wait, wait, wait. Wait until I get reassigned. Wait until it's safe."

I moved behind her and pressed a kiss to her shoulder. This wasn't the first time she'd cried about not being with me and my friends. She wanted to be a part of my life, she said. Wholly and openly. She wanted to walk through the streets holding hands. She wanted to kiss me and touch me, and not worry if anyone saw us. She wanted to come with me when my unit went to dinner or had drinks at the nearby bar we frequented.

"And we will. I promise. My unit will move on soon and I will be free to stay for a while as a civilian." I tangled my fingers in hers. "Then I'll walk the streets holding your hand. Kissing you. Hell, I'll even dip you in my arms and kiss you senseless for the whole world to see!"

Her eyes shone brightly but her jaw was jutted. My lighthearted promise was lost on her. "It has to be now."

She rose to her feet and moved away from the bed, the sheet slipping away from her body. Naked, she was perfect. And confident. She moved across the room and stood at the window. Outside, the pale streaks of dawn lightened the sky and I admired her curves silhouetted in the dim light.

"Tomorrow night, you and your unit are celebrating something. What is it?" she asked, not turning around.

The mood had changed. She wasn't appeased by my promises any more. And maybe if I'd been paying more attention I would've realized that I'd never once mentioned anything about celebrating Sergeant Healy's birthday the following night. I never told her anything about my unit or the men in it.

Instead, I sighed and rubbed my eyes with the heel of my palm. "It's someone's birthday."

"And you're going to a bar?"

"I'm not sure."

She turned back to me. "You take me with you. Or we're done."

I was a little taken aback. There had never been an ultimatum before.

But before I could reply, she quickly crossed the room and climbed onto the bed, pushing me back onto the pillows with a sudden frenzied energy, and straddled me. She kissed me hard, *pleadingly*, her pussy rubbing against me as she tried to convince me to take her with me the following night. Her hand reached between us, grabbing my cock and rubbing it through the damp folds of her pussy. She nudged the head inside, surrounding my crown with creaminess and sending a flare of pleasure through me.

But this craziness had to stop.

I pushed her hands off me and rolled away from her.

"What are you doing?" I breathed.

"I want to be a part of your life now. No more waiting." Her eyes were dark fire, her hair a wild mess as it tumbled over her shoulders. "It starts now. Or it stops now."

"You know I can't—"

"Then we are done!" She climbed off the bed and snatched up her clothes.

"Don't do this," I said.

But she said nothing. She shoved on her clothes and stormed to the door where she paused and turned around. "You should have let me come."

And with that, she disappeared out the door, letting it slam behind her.

I hadn't seen her in over a week. I'd visited her father's restaurant but it seemed her frostiness extended to him as well. It was a good idea, he said, if we didn't go there anymore. I couldn't lie, it hurt. And it confused me. How could she cut me off like that and disappear? And where was she? She wasn't in town. She wasn't in my bed. She wasn't anywhere.

My job kept me busy. Kept her from my mind. We were due to leave in less than a week and our final mission had come through.

The cell we'd been slowly annihilating across several villages along the countryside had arrived into the village just as our intelligence anticipated. Months of waiting for this to happen was now paying off. Our mission as an elite team of SEALs was to take out the cell hierarchy. A woman known as *the dark one*, and two men who were thought to be her brothers.

I leaned down and pressed my eye to my scope. And then she appeared. My target. The person responsible for participating in the catastrophic attacks on several American Marine units resulting in high casualties. I pulled back, my brows slamming together. No. It couldn't be. Blood whirled in my ears as my pulse quickened. I peered into the scope again and watched my target moving through the street, walking with two men known for orchestrating attacks on American and Allied soldiers. And there was a fleeting moment where I wondered if she was somehow being held against her will. That perhaps she was not involved in any of this as a willing accomplice. But her body language wasn't that of someone who was in fear for her life. She walked with purpose. Confidence. The beautiful body I'd spent hours making love to was relaxed. Those long legs, the ones she'd wrapped around me as she rose to meet the thrust of my cock, strode confidently alongside her companions. The mouth she had kissed me with a thousand times spoke fast and with confidence. And those eyes . . . the ones that had looked at me with so much lust and affection, and at times with what I was sure was growing love . . . were now hard, sharp, *deadly*.

My finger twitched on the trigger. My jaw tightened. In my ear, my commander instructed me to take the shot. I had a clear line of vision, my weapon was accurate. *Take the shot.* If I squeezed the trigger, a .338 caliber bullet would roar through several hundred yards of air and thrust into her, devastating every tissue fiber in its way as it carved a deadly path through her body.

Slowly, everything came into focus and started to make sense.

How she had pursued me.

Encouraged me.

Used my loneliness against me.

How she had come to my room at night and warmed me with her body.

Take the shot.

All this time she had been lying.

Working against me.

Using me.

Take the shot.

The reason she wanted to meet my friends?

She wanted to kill them.

And me.

Take the shot.

Bitterness tore through me.

My finger grazed the trigger.

Take the shot.

As I squeezed, an almighty eruption lifted me up from the ground and cartwheeled me across the room of the abandoned building. I heard the startled cries of my unit as the explosion ripped apart our surroundings, turning our world inside out and upside down. I hit the floor, my face smashing against something hard and rough. Heat and fire flashed across the room, searing the uniform from my body and sending a sharp, burning pain deep into my skin.

Confusion smothered my brain, suffocating me, disorienting me.

Who was I? Where was I?

And then it slowly came back to me as the pain searing into my body pulled me back from my bewilderment.

Penny Dee

I was a sniper in a land far, far away.
And I had taken the shot.

CONNECT WITH ME ONLINE

Check these links for more books from Author Penny Dee.

READER GROUP
For more mayhem follow:
Kings of Mayhem MC Facebook page.
http://www.facebook.com/TheKingsofMayhemMC/

NEWSLETTER
Sign up for my newsletter
http://eepurl.com/giFDxb

GOODREADS
Add my books to your TBR list on my Goodreads profile.
https://www.goodreads.com/author/show/8526535.Penny_Dee

AMAZON
Click to buy my books from my Amazon profile.
https://www.amazon.com/Penny-Dee/e/B00O2OKT5G/ref=dp_byline_cont_ebooks_1

Penny Dee

WEBSITE
http://www.pennydeebooks.com/

INSTAGRAM
@authorpennydee

EMAIL
authorpennydee@hotmail.com

FACEBOOK
http://www.facebook.com/pennydeebooks/

ABOUT THE AUTHOR

Penny Dee writes contemporary romance about rockstars, bikers, hockey players and everyone in-between. She believes true love never runs smoothly, and her characters realize this too, with a boatload of drama and a whole lot of steam.

She found her happily ever after in Australia where she lives with her husband, daughter and a dog named Bindi.

Printed in Great Britain
by Amazon